Into the Sunset

Books by Mary Connealy

THE KINCAID BRIDES

Out of Control
In Too Deep
Over the Edge

TROUBLE IN TEXAS

Swept Away
Fired Up
Stuck Together

WILD AT HEART

Tried and True
Now and Forever
Fire and Ice

THE CIMARRON LEGACY

No Way Up
Long Time Gone
Too Far Down

HIGH SIERRA SWEETHEARTS

The Accidental Guardian
The Reluctant Warrior
The Unexpected Champion

BRIDES OF HOPE MOUNTAIN

Aiming for Love
Woman of Sunlight
Her Secret Song

BROTHERS IN ARMS

Braced for Love
A Man with a Past
Love on the Range

THE LUMBER BARON'S DAUGHTERS

The Element of Love
Inventions of the Heart
A Model of Devotion

WYOMING SUNRISE

Forged in Love
The Laws of Attraction
Marshaling Her Heart

A WESTERN LIGHT

Chasing the Horizon
Toward the Dawn
Into the Sunset

The Boden Birthright: A CIMARRON LEGACY *Novella* (All for Love *Collection*)

Meeting Her Match: A MATCH MADE IN TEXAS *Novella*

Runaway Bride: A KINCAID BRIDES *and* TROUBLE IN TEXAS *Novella* (With This Ring? *Collection*)

The Tangled Ties That Bind: A KINCAID BRIDES *Novella* (Hearts Entwined *Collection*)

A Western Light • 3

Into the Sunset

Mary Connealy

Bethany House
a division of Baker Publishing Group
Minneapolis, Minnesota

Published by Bethany House Publishers
Minneapolis, Minnesota
BethanyHouse.com

Bethany House Publishers is a division of
Baker Publishing Group, Grand Rapids, Michigan

Printed in the United States of America

Library of Congress Cataloging-in-Publication Data
Names: Connealy, Mary, author.
Title: Into the sunset / Mary Connealy.
Description: Minneapolis, Minnesota : Bethany House Publishers, a division of Baker Publishing Group, 2024. | Series: A western light ; 3
Identifiers: LCCN 2023056647 | ISBN 9780764242670 (paperback) | ISBN 9780764243998 (casebound) | ISBN 9781493448098 (ebook)
Subjects: LCGFT: Christian fiction. | Western fiction. | Romance fiction. | Novels.
Classification: LCC PS3603.O544 I57 2024 | DDC 813/.6—dc23/eng/20231228
LC record available at https://lccn.loc.gov/2023056647

Scripture quotations are from the King James Version of the Bible.

Cover design by Dan Thornberg

Baker Publishing Group publications use paper produced from sustainable forestry practices and postconsumer waste whenever possible.

24 25 26 27 28 29 30 7 6 5 4 3 2 1

This book is dedicated to:

Elle, Isaac, Luke, Katherine, Lauren,
Adrian, and Quinn.
My grandbabies who make life so sweet.

1

August 10, 1873

A bullet smashed into a boulder, ricocheted off, and burned Dakota Harlan's cheek. He threw himself backward, landed hard, flipped over, and was crawling on his elbows, shoving forward on his belly as another shot fired, then fired again. He moved without thinking.

A Winchester 73. Dakota recognized the rifle's loud peal because he had one of his own. He gripped his Winchester now, always keeping it close to hand, and he'd been relentless about that since the day he survived an earlier attack.

Judging by where the shooter was located, and Dakota knew his land well, he crawled farther, keeping himself low. He slithered more like, not wanting to give the shooter anything to aim at.

At last he reached a row of sheltering stones, each of them half the height of a man. These boulders hadn't found their way here by accident. He'd ringed the edge of the pasture with them. It was months of brutally hard work in the hot sun. In fact, two years of Dakota's life had been spent getting the boulders dragged around into this shelter. He had many such shelters all through his valley.

He'd analyzed the entrances to this meadow, the lookouts where a sneaking gunman might set up, the likely places and a couple less likely where a man was likely to open up on him from cover. He'd hoped to never need them, but right now he was grateful for every hard hour he'd spent, every blister he'd earned.

The rifle stopped firing. That fool out there had emptied his weapon, even one that held as many bullets as the Winchester 73. He was probably reloading now. Dakota had counted the shots. Thirteen rounds, the number of bullets in a fully loaded Winchester, one with the longest barrel and the smallest caliber.

Dakota crawled on, angling, keeping in mind his assailant's position. He wondered if the fool would decide to move. Probably not. Most likely he thought he had Dakota pinned down. But Dakota knew exactly where the would-be killer was hiding.

His breathing slowed as he circled the meadow, closing the distance between them. He needed to leave the meadow, get to higher ground. He headed toward a fall of rocks that were perfectly placed, also there by the sweat of his brow. He'd use the rocks to conceal himself while he climbed into position.

His pulse slowed. His mind focused on something so sharp, so vivid, it was nearly painful. Dakota drew from all his years of accumulated knowledge, from his time spent on the wagon train, the miserable year homesteading, the wandering he'd done. And finally the decision to find a quiet, safe place near a good friend where he'd start a ranch.

The rifle picked up firing again. The shots shattered rock and ricocheted all over with ugly pings, but they were one hundred feet behind him and fifty feet below. It was a harsh reminder that he hadn't managed the quiet, and he sure as all get-out hadn't managed the safe.

For this wasn't the first killer to come calling.

Inching along with his Winchester, he made it to the rocks that would shelter him as he moved upward while that fool unloaded his gun again into the place where Dakota had vanished.

The man must dearly love the sound of gunfire. Or maybe he loved buying bullets because he was wasting a lot of lead.

Shielded by the massive stones, Dakota went up and up until he knew he'd gotten high enough. Surely the gunman wouldn't unload his rifle again, would he? Maybe he figured he'd winged Dakota with one of his shots.

A trickle on his chin had him swiping his face with his shirtsleeve. Sure enough, his hand came away red. The sidewinder *had* grazed him! He thought of the bullet earlier that struck the boulder near him and ricocheted. Thankfully it hadn't done much damage.

A few moments later, Dakota reached the spot he was aiming for and stopped. Lying on his back, his rifle clutched in both hands across his chest, Dakota listened, waited, and then, sure as the sunrise, the shooter opened up again. He'd be focused on those same rocks, now far away from Dakota.

Dakota could have climbed higher and come up behind

the varmint blasting away, but he wasn't about to shoot anyone in the back. Instead, he leaned forward to a perfectly located crack between two rocks. From there he saw the reckless, bullet-wasting gunman emptying his rifle again. He'd climbed out of a decent hiding place and was now in plain sight.

Slowly, Dakota closed the space between them until he was only about twenty feet away. He'd circled a good portion of the meadow, closed in on his assailant, and could finally get a good look at him. He didn't want this. He didn't want a life of always being on edge.

A life of fight or die.

The gunfire ceased when the Winchester was empty once again. Gathering himself, Dakota sprang to his feet and leveled his rifle on the man. "Drop your gun! Get your hands in the air now." Dakota's eyes stayed locked on the man. Something about him hit a nerve, but Dakota didn't allow himself to be distracted by whatever was buzzing around in his head.

The man lowered his rifle, taking his time with dropping it. Rage glinted in the varmint's eyes, and it seemed like more than just fury that Dakota had gotten the drop on him. The rage was personal. Yet Dakota didn't know this man with the silver-gray hair and black eyes. He had a weathered face and a strange hawklike nose. Something about him, though, niggled Dakota's memory.

The rifle clattered when it struck the stony ledge the man stood on. Dakota had him under his control now. He'd tie him up, then haul him to the sheriff nearly a full day's ride away.

After the man let go of the rifle, his right hand swept up

lightning fast. In the hand was a pistol he'd pulled from a holster under his coat.

"No!" Dakota howled, then pulled the trigger of his Winchester.

Bright red bloomed on the man's chest.

The pistol fired into the ground over and over, the gunfire echoing off the walls of Dakota's canyon.

His eyes met those black ones. "Why? You had no chance. Why would you want me dead?"

Then the eyes and the beak nose clicked in his memory. Two memories, in fact. Dakota had faced off with two men very much like this one. It could just be chance, but with a sinking stomach Dakota knew it wasn't.

The man pitched forward and fell. He'd been high up on the rocky ledge, and now he plunged forward.

With a cold feeling in his gut, Dakota noticed he hadn't fallen far from another grave. Sickened, he realized he had his own cemetery now. Or he would once this man was buried.

The smell of gunpowder faded. The breeze wafted with the scent of pine. A cow mooed down on the grasslands of his meadow. This beautiful place Dakota had found. Heavily wooded in spots, a rich piece of land full of belly-high grass. A stream nearby ran with cold water teeming with trout. Mountains stood all around, arranged in such a way that they cut the wind even in the bitter-cold Idaho winters.

It was the perfect place to make a home. But not if killers came calling.

Sighing, Dakota went over and stared down at the dead man, a grizzled old-timer. He wished he'd been given a chance to reason with him.

The ice he felt in his chest was hard enough, and cold enough, he wasn't sure how his heart went on beating. The way this man had shot at him from cover was too much like the other one. And he held a strong resemblance to the man who'd attacked before.

Dakota knelt beside the man, wondering if he could find anything on him to learn who he was. Who were *they*? He searched the body and came up with a letter, folded and still inside its envelope.

Slumping to the ground to sit, Dakota opened the letter and read the name Darnell. Closing his eyes, he didn't read on. Not yet.

The Darnell name told him enough. The bank robber he'd run afoul of during his year of wandering was called Vic Darnell. And he'd been a dark-haired man with a hawkish nose and black eyes.

And this letter was a call to kinfolk. A blood feud. With Dakota's name in it and precious little else. Which might explain why it had taken this man so long to find him.

Of course, Dakota hadn't known where he was headed when he and a few others had stopped Vic Darnell from a wild killing spree when Vic had been cornered after a murderous bank robbery.

Dakota had been wandering. Who would have known to find him here? It'd taken a lot of work and some skill to track Dakota to this meadow. He hadn't even bought it yet, though he intended to. He'd found the spot, knew it was near his friend Jake, and had moved in and set up ranching.

He looked down at the letter again. Crude handwriting, full of misspelled words, from a man who barely knew how to write.

Mort,

Yer boy Vic's bin kilt by a man name'a Dakota Harlan. I'm writin' t'others and coming west to put this right. No one kills my grandson, yer son, and lives. See if you can pick up the scent. It hapend in Oregone, but the vermin what kilt our kin is runnin' skeered, or he had oughta be. A blood feud. I'm callin' fer it.

If'n you find him first, it's yer right to settle this on yer own. If'n you don't find him, help's a-comin'.

Pa

Dakota flipped the envelope over and saw *Ezra Darnell* scrawled in one corner and the letter addressed to Mort Darnell. How many of these letters had been sent? And how many more Darnells were out there searching for him?

He'd have to live his life on a razor's edge from now to the end of his days to survive, because judging by the two who'd come here, these weren't face-to-face kind of men. They didn't stand before you and challenge you. They were back-shooting coyotes. And that kind wasn't much on talking.

Dakota was a man of faith. He hadn't wanted a life that was surrounded by the need to kill. He had no idea how to end this feud. It seemed he was trapped in a cycle of danger and death. He had no hope he could convince one of these Darnells to reconsider the back-shooting and live a peaceable kind of life.

He went and got a shovel and half an hour later had

a hole dug. Dakota dropped the man into the hole and buried him. He left a heap of dirt on the grave. The other grave had nearly disappeared back to meadow grass.

By the time he was done, the day had worn down. The sun slanted steeply in the west over the jagged tops of the mountains that guarded that side of his ranch.

Those mountaintops reached for him like claws, sent to Dakota by God to grab ahold of him and crush him before he could hurt anyone else.

His chest ached as he stood and let himself be cast in shadow, just as his whole life had been cast in shadows. He stood staring at the pair of graves, unmarked because it seemed blasphemous to put a cross on the graves, and unwise to risk drawing attention by posting the Darnell name on them.

He stood there alone. And because he was alone, because he would always be alone, he thought of a pretty redheaded Irish girl who might have joined her life to his at one time in the past.

Before her father had died and before Dakota had treated her wrong. Before he'd told her the unhappy truth that they had to roll on and leave her father far behind on the lonely prairie. His grave by now was as vanished from the world as these would soon be.

He'd had no choice, and yet she hadn't seen it that way.

And all the anger that so often followed death got landed straight on Dakota. His shoulders were strong enough to take it, but that didn't mean he wasn't sorry he had to do it. And that was before Dakota's life had become something he could never dare let anyone share.

She'd seen him as a heartless brute.

He wondered if maybe she was right. If Maeve O'Toole could see this crude little graveyard of his, she'd know she was right and would set her heart even more against him.

Dakota sat down hard on the ground and studied the final resting place of the ones who'd come with intent to kill. His cold heart thawed a bit, and he felt the pain. His throat hurt. His soul ached with loneliness and the utter belief that God couldn't want Dakota to kill like this.

But he had no notion of how to stop it.

"You are what?" Maeve O'Toole stared at her mother. Her question echoed loud in her head but came out in a shocked whisper.

Fiona's eyes narrowed as they tended to do when she was displeased.

"Bruce and I are courting. Sure, and you won't be taking that tone with me, Maeve."

Bruce stood beside her, his hat in his hands.

Ma with her hands on her plump hips, her tightly curling red hair escaping from its no-nonsense bun as always, blue eyes sharp with disapproval of Maeve's reaction.

In all ways, Ma was a match for Maeve, for the whole family. A bunch of Irish redheads come west to settle in the fertile Snake Valley in Idaho.

Maeve's hips might not be so plump, but other than that, they were alike and that included their attitude. The red hair covered a fiery temper. They loved each other and worked well together, but that was with the deep understanding they would both keep a tight clamp on that inner fire. Except sometimes they couldn't quite . . . Maeve bit down hard on the words she wanted to say. Words that weren't fair. But it hit hard to think of her da, and he was all she could think of right now.

Bruce was smart and hardworking and quiet. He had dark hair and light blue eyes. Very much a match for his two brothers, Oscar and Joseph, who lived in Hidden Canyon with Ginny Rutledge and her daughter, Beth.

They'd all traveled west together on a wagon train. Instead of going all the way to Oregon, they'd turned off and settled in Idaho as more and more folks were doing. The area was filling in fast since they'd first arrived in the late summer of 1869.

Bruce had helped out the O'Tooles when they'd homesteaded here. While he'd planned to live with his two brothers in the canyon, Maeve and Fiona and the family had needed help for a fact, and he'd made a huge difference in how fast they'd tamed the land. And it had always seemed as if he'd done it for no other reason than because the O'Tooles, with Da dying on the trip west, had needed help more than the others he'd been traveling with.

Had that been true? Had he notions about Ma from the first? Had he stayed here working for four years because he had his sights on Ma?

It had been only a couple of months after Da had died that they arrived, and it made her stomach sink to imagine Bruce already with his eye on a widow.

But why else would he have stayed on? At the time she'd just thought he did it out of the goodness of his heart. Now she had to wonder.

Then this morning they'd sprung their courting news on her. And once she'd been told and reacted badly, Bruce, in his own kind, quiet way, had looked at Maeve as if he were disappointed in her. A fatherly kind of look that only deepened memories of her own da and the stubborn knowledge in her head that no man had a right to treat her as a daughter except her own beloved da.

Bruce said he planned to stay through the first winter and help them get settled in their cabins. And then he'd never left. He'd lived here with them, or at least with Donal in one cabin on the land he'd homesteaded, while the rest of the family—Ma, Maeve, her little brother, Conor, and little sister, Bridget—lived right across a meandering stream from them.

Maeve had never seen any sign of affection between Ma and Bruce Collins. Never a hint, never a whisper to warn her of this.

"You want to get married?" Maeve knew she was overreacting, but this came as a complete surprise.

"Maybe we need to wait longer, Fee. I talked to Donal, and he seemed all right with it."

Ma said, "It's not that we're getting wed today. Of course, we'll give you time to get used to the idea, Maeve."

Maeve's eyes darted to Donal, who was working in the field. Between Ma, Donal, and Maeve, they'd claimed three homesteads and owned four hundred and eighty acres. All fertile land that grew good crops in a place they called the Snake River Valley. Bruce had bought a plow and trained a team to pull it. Most of their crops were up already—corn and hay, a field of oats, another of wheat. Bruce had known how to do all of it. The O'Tooles weren't a family of farmers, though Da had grown up on a farm and knew the way of it.

When he'd drowned in an accident on their way west, they'd been in trouble, aiming to be landowners with no clear idea of how to go about it. Yet Bruce had made working the land simple for them. Now Donal ran Bruce's plow through a field where they'd already harvested oats. They would plant beans and get a crop out of them before winter came down on their heads.

She heard a hawk scream overhead, and it drew her eyes upward. The land was vast, the future bright.

Or it had been until now.

"You'll have some time to get used to it. But, Maeve?" Bruce added with a wrinkled brow. He had the nerve to look confused, even hurt. "How could you not have known? Surely you've noticed how I admire your ma and have for a long time."

How could she not have noticed? What had there been to see? *Was* there something and she was just that naive? That childish? She was a woman nearing twenty-two years old. Not some little girl who needed to be in leading strings.

Now here she stood so churned up, she couldn't stand to admit what a fool she'd been. She wanted to get away from both of them with their eyes that saw too much because they knew her so well.

They were on Ma and Maeve's side of the stream. Ma and Maeve shared a cabin built on the property line of their homesteads. They'd built among a stand of trees that cast cooling shade in the summer and slowed the howling wind in the winter. Did that mean Bruce would move into that cabin with her and Ma? He'd have to. Ma had to live there for another full year and a month in order to prove up on her homestead. Maeve had to do it, too. No one had much choice of getting any distance between them.

Maeve could see they wanted to talk this through with her, let her ask questions. Let her, as they'd said, get used to the idea. Well, she wouldn't stand for all that calm, reasonable talk. She wasn't about to listen to her mother and Bruce discuss a romance as if Ma had never had a real husband.

Maeve just never imagined anyone replacing her beloved da. Maeve didn't think about Da every day anymore. He was a sturdy, good-humored man with hair as red as the rest of the family. He liked to tell stories, and he and Ma used to reminisce about their early days, their courtship and marriage, the tiny cabin they'd lived in back in the "old country" as Ma still called it, before they'd sailed the Atlantic Ocean to reach a new land.

Now Ma loved another man. She'd put some other man in Da's place as if he meant nothing to her. How could Ma do this?

"I can't discuss this now." She turned toward the creek.

"Maeve, you come back here." Ma had that stern tone in her voice that Maeve never disobeyed.

Maeve stopped, drew in a deep breath, and turned back even as Ma walked up to her.

Maeve rested a hand on Ma's arm. Their eyes met, Ma's looking stern and yet laced with sadness.

"Ma, please. Can I have some time? Bruce is a good man. I know that. It's just brought memories of Da back to me. That's not fair to you or Bruce. Don't be angry with me. Of course, your courtship is, that is . . . I don't . . . I can't." Maeve bit off her ragged speech. "Let me settle down for a bit, please? Say a prayer for me, and I'll do the same, for me and for all of us. But just for now, I need a wee bit of time."

Ma nodded and gave her a tight hug, the kind that had made Maeve feel safe all her life. "You have your bit of time, girl. Go on now. We'll talk more later."

Maeve nodded. "Tell Bruce I'm sorry for the way I acted. I'll apologize properly later." She crossed the stream on rocks Bruce had dragged into place using their draft horses, so that walking to each other's homes would be easier.

She walked past the garden, full of ripening vegetables that Bruce had taught them how to plant and tend.

"But, Maeve, how could you not have known?"

She twisted around in her head trying to think of an admiring look, a quiet smile. She hadn't known.

She walked on past the corral with their two dozen head of black cattle, driven here by Oscar from the herd he had growing in Hidden Canyon.

"Surely you've noticed how I admire your ma and have for a long time."

Had they ever touched, even a pat on the shoulder or a hand resting on an arm? No, she hadn't noticed. Bruce had never homesteaded. He'd never built his own cabin. To her mind, he'd always intended to move into the canyon where his brothers lived.

She hadn't known. Now she felt like a fool, and the long-accepted pain of losing her da flared like a fire. She needed time to think, to calmly accept. It'd been four years, but she still needed just a wee bit more time.

2

"It's time, Beth. This year I'm going."

Beth, quietly rocking baby Lydia, froze the rocker in place and looked up at her mama with a sharp jerk of her head.

Silence stretched between her and mama as their gazes held. Mama was an older version of herself, and she saw grim determination in those matching blue eyes. Fighting down the need to shout *No*, she looked at Mama. She'd known the time would come.

They had to do this sometime. It just always seemed like later was better.

Trying to cover her panic, Beth said, "I should have gotten pregnant again."

Ginny Rutledge, ready to go face being Eugenia Rutledge and fight for her freedom, smiled. "That stopped me last summer, and I suppose it would have stopped me again."

"How's the canyon entrance? I've noticed you walking that way a few times."

"It's good enough. Better than it was when Kat and Sebastian got out. We can get through. It's August for heaven's sake. How could there still be snow in August?"

"Mountains help. Northern Idaho helps."

A snort from the back room turned both their heads. Before Ginny could rush after one of the twins, Jake came out carrying his daughter. Jake had taken to sitting in the twins' bedroom during naps, reading and waiting and hoping to pounce on one toddler before the crying woke the other. He had Marie, who was rubbing her eyes and looking around through heavy lids, safe in her papa's arms.

Marie was a match for Beth and Mama, too. Dark curls and fair skin. Thick lashes around her blue eyes. Jake's hair was straighter, his eyes a brighter blue, like Jacob Jr.

Beth thought of her own father, Thaddeus Rutledge. Had he ever once held her? Certainly not that she remembered, but maybe when she was really young. Maybe for a few moments on the day she was born.

Beth shied her thoughts away from what was an old pain, one she'd accepted long ago.

"Mama is ready to go out, Jake."

Jake, grinning down at his daughter, looked up, the smile gone now. He focused on Mama. "You're sure, Ginny? No reason we can't wait another year. Another five years. Maybe you can outlive your old coot of a husband. We're happy here."

"We are. We're cut off from the whole world except when your friend Dakota brings us a newspaper, or the occasional O'Tooles' visit with mail from Kat and Sebastian. And Joseph has made a few runs into town."

Joseph was the one who was the least likely to be recognized, so if they had a serious need, he was the one to go. But they were more likely to go to the O'Tooles and give them a list and the money to cover purchases. Of course, they didn't need much.

They were right to be wary. Father still had men out there hunting Ginny. Dakota and the O'Tooles had been questioned more than once.

"Oscar's not gonna like it." Jake bounced little Marie, then lowered her to the floor to play.

Mama gave her kindhearted smile. She loved Beth, her only child, without reservation. Jake was the son she'd never had, and she respected him and was thrilled to have him in the family. She'd said often enough that her grandchildren were gifts straight from a loving God.

But Oscar was her best friend. He was their hero. His intelligence, skill, hard work, and loyalty had saved Mama. Oscar had led them to this place they called Hidden Canyon.

He'd supported Beth in her planning to get Ginny to freedom. He'd known about this canyon, recruited his two brothers, Joseph and Bruce. The three of them traveled here and worked hard to make it a comfortable sanctuary. His skill and cunning, plotting things out with Beth, saved Ginny from being caught and returned to the asylum, where her husband had locked her away when she wouldn't hand over the inheritance she'd received from her parents.

Even more, Beth hadn't known this, but Father had demanded Mama hand over Beth's inheritance, too. But Ginny had been willing to pay any price to defy him, to protect her daughter.

Beth had gotten her out, and her friend Kat as well. Kat was another asylum resident who had come with Mama. Beth brought the three of them to Independence, Missouri, where a wagon train was heading west. Oscar had wagons outfitted and ready when they arrived. He'd led them across the country on the wagon train.

They'd come to this hiding place late in the summer of 1869, and now in 1873 they were still here. And in that time period, Mama hadn't stepped one foot outside of the well-hidden canyon.

Without drastic action, Ginny would still be under lock and key in the Horecroft Insane Asylum back in Chicago. After four years, they'd decided they were safe here. Mama was profoundly angry at the injustice that was done to her and was being done to many other women. It was time to come out of hiding, to face down the laws of the land that made it dangerous for a married woman to be under the power of a tyrannical husband.

Oscar came to the door, Joseph just behind him. They often came in for an afternoon coffee break about the time the babies were up from their naps.

Though Oscar didn't make a sound, somehow Jacob Jr. sensed that it was time to get up and play. A shout of "Mama" came from the back room.

The cabin had three bedrooms now. The baby, Lydia, slept with Jake and Beth. Mama slept in the second room. The twins had the third bedroom to themselves.

Oscar's eyes went straight to Mama. His frown was fierce, but they'd had this talk many times, and he must've known this was coming. "I saw you out at the canyon entrance this morning. It's time then?"

"You know I have to go."

"Like I said before, you do *not* have to go. We're safe here. We're happy, aren't we? We can stay in this canyon for as long as your fool of a husband lives. He's an old man. Maybe he'll get himself planted in the dirt soon."

Joseph stepped into the cabin. His one arm didn't work right because it had been broken when he threw himself in front of stampeding wild mustangs to save Yvette, the last member of their little family of recluses. Since they lived too far from a doctor, they'd taken him to the O'Tooles and then ran for a doctor and hauled him back. It'd been over a day later before the doc arrived. The man had done his best after getting there far too late.

Living so far out came with risks, and Joseph's permanently crooked arm was one of the prices they paid for Mama's safety.

Behind Joseph, at a distance, stood Yvette. She came closer these days, but still never entered the house. She hadn't had a violent outburst in years, but they all treated her very carefully, so it was hard to be sure she wouldn't have one still if the wrong thing happened. She'd come a long way from the dangerous, badly abused, mentally traumatized woman she'd once been after being set free from Horecroft by Father because she had clues as to Mama's whereabouts.

"What are we going to tell Yvette? She'll think we all abandoned her."

Joseph said, "I'll talk to her." He had talked once, briefly, about losing a baby girl long ago. He treated Yvette like his own long-lost child. But he was still careful in how he went about it.

Yvette would strike out wildly when anyone touched her. But they'd learned if they gave her a lot of time, she would sometimes touch them. She'd rest a hand on someone's arm or tickle one of the toddlers under their chin.

She was a beautiful woman with haunted, lonely eyes. She lived in a cave away from the rest of them, with a hot spring that kept one room warm in winter. They'd built a bedstead to make it comfortable.

Mama and Beth had learned to sew well enough to make Yvette any clothes she needed. But she was still a distant kind of creature, timid and shy as a deer.

Mama had said that the asylum had many women in it that were fully sane and had no reason to be there. They'd been locked away on account of abusive relatives, who had them committed to the asylum against their will more because they were inconvenient than for any reasons to do with madness.

But the Horecroft Insane Asylum wasn't a terrible place just for unjustly diagnosed sane people. It was also the worst possible place for those people who were in fact insane. The treatment there was cruel and harsh, the medical attention nonexistent, the rooms cold and deliberately made to be miserable.

Mama wanted to free herself from the tyranny of her husband, but she also wanted to free all those poor souls who still lived in the Horecroft Asylum. She wanted humane treatment for the folks with illnesses of the mind.

Her first step was to get a ruling on her own sanity. She and Beth had been writing to their friends Kat and Sebastian Jones to get advice on how best to do that, and they had a plan in place.

Ginny would take the next step, assuming she won, and try to free the others who shouldn't be there and find better treatment for those who needed help.

"I'm going, Oscar." Mama leaned near to Beth and took the now-awake Lydia into her arms.

A long silence settled on the room, broken by Lydia's babbling, Jacob's hollering as he ran into the room, and Marie's sweet laughter at her brother's antics. But even with all that, a long silence.

Finally, with a firm jerk of his chin and a scowl on his face, Oscar said, "Let's talk about the details."

Oscar was a man who liked to plan.

Jake went to get a pot of coffee brewing.

Beth resumed her seat in the rocking chair. "We've written back and forth with Kat. I'll tell you what I know and where we might find the best help." She began going over points they all already knew.

Mama chimed in now and then, but Beth thought she looked strung tight as a clothesline. One little extra bit of weight and she might snap.

Oscar paced, his hands behind his back, as he reminded them of all that could go wrong.

"You're going back to the asylum, Ginny?" Yvette rarely spoke.

Every head in the house came around hard at the sound of a delicate, musical whisper, but one laced with terror.

Yvette stood in the doorway. Her hair, so white-blond that it was nearly colorless, was nicely styled in a way most women would need a lady's maid to arrange. Her large blue eyes looked as if soaked in fear, and she was slender to the point of being almost breakable. She was an unusually pretty women, fragile as spun sugar. Her hands clutched together, tucked tight to cover her heart. She stared at Ginny, her eyes filled with tears.

Then Yvette stepped just one pace inside the door. She'd never come inside before.

After a few moments of stunned silence—even Lydia seemed fascinated—Mama said, "No. I am not going back to that horrible place, Yvette. I will never go back, and I would never let anyone take you back. But I am leaving the canyon. I'm going to talk to a judge and demand he rule that no one has the right to lock me away like that without some proof I am truly insane. I hope we can find a judge who will hear my case and rule fairly, and a jury who will declare me sane and refuse to allow me to be locked up."

"If they listened to me"—a single tear escaped Yvette's left eye; typically she was more inclined to run and hide and possibly scream than to cry—"they would rule against me. Then they'd lock me back in that asylum. I deserve to be there."

"No one on this earth, no matter how troubled they might be, deserves to be locked in that wretched asylum." Ginny took a step toward Yvette, an arm outstretched to comfort the woman.

Yvette cringed and moved away. Fallen tears now streaked her face.

Joseph said, "Let her be, Ginny."

Frowning, Ginny stepped back.

Joseph produced a handkerchief from his pocket and extended his hand slowly to offer it to her. He waited, they all waited, as Yvette, her hand trembling, reached out and took the white kerchief. Her hand never touched Joseph's.

"Th-thank you." She pressed the cloth to her eyes in such a way that her whole face was covered with it. Her shoulders trembled but no sobs escaped. Her misery was all the more heart-wrenching for its silence.

Beth had never heard what had happened to Yvette to send her to the asylum. The woman was obviously troubled, yet she cared for herself well here. Did she have a husband who had deemed her insane and forced her behind those heavy doors of the asylum? And why did she hate to be touched?

Beth couldn't help but believe that someone had treated Yvette terribly to cause her to have such a reaction to human touch.

They all held their breath and wondered what she'd say. Instead, she stepped to the side of the doorway, then leaned against the wall right inside the door.

Her tears finally ended, and she lowered the now-drenched handkerchief to just below her chin. "How long will you be gone?"

"I don't know, Yvette."

Joseph, who'd become a father of sorts to Yvette, said quietly, "I'm staying here. I'll see to it no harm comes to you. You go on living in your cave and come here as you like, for meals and such. We'll wait in safety in the canyon until they return, be it a week or a month."

Or forever, Beth thought, being careful not to say that out loud.

She hated leaving. The canyon walls and the oddly hard-to-find entrance had acted like a fortress, protecting them for years now. But no more living behind these walls. Mama needed to start a fight that would change her life and maybe, just maybe, with God's help, change the world.

It made Beth's stomach twist with fear. Because if they failed and somehow Father found and dragged Mama away, Beth might never see her again.

3

There was a letter from Beth in the mail today." Kat Jones had gone to town this morning for supplies. She'd arrived home in time for the noon meal, cooked it, then waited for Sebastian to come in so she could share the excitement of a letter from their Idaho friends.

Seb was a hard worker and a creative inventor with several patents, and she was very proud of him. And even more proud that he was living up to his promise to make his faith in God and his love for his wife the top priorities in his life. He no longer had the obsession for working in his laboratory that he'd brought into the marriage.

Kat had waited until he got inside since the letter was to them both, but now she smiled at him, tore the letter open, and read quickly. "There's a lot here, but the main thing I see is they're leaving the canyon, Ginny included."

"Ginny's coming then?" Seb drew the cup of coffee close. Even in the heat of late August, the man loved his hot coffee.

Their eyes met. They knew it was a serious business. She

studied her husband. He had blond hair a shade darker than hers and blue eyes that shone with intelligence, curiosity, and his deeply inventive way of thinking.

"Yes, and it sounds like most everyone is coming with her. Beth and Jake and the children. Oscar is coming, and the wagon master from our days on the wagon train, Dakota Harlan, may come as well. He ranches in that area. Jake talked to him and asked him to join them to help protect Ginny. Joseph will stay back and take care of things in Hidden Canyon."

Kat exchanged a somber look with Seb. They both knew Joseph hadn't fully healed from his broken arm and likely never would.

And Yvette would stay put in the canyon.

Kat, with her stunning inheritance from her deceased husband's family, had done investigating in any direction she chose, and they'd tracked down Yvette's family and found enough tragedy and abuse in her past to drive anyone mad. But Kat was working on an idea to help the poor woman.

"We haven't even met the baby." Seb's expression brightened. "A girl, right? Lydia?" They'd gone back to visit their Hidden Canyon friends last summer. Riding the Transcontinental Railroad was a long journey, but rumors abounded of a train spur going to Boise that would take them much closer to their friends. They'd talked about going again this summer, but now their friends would come visit them here.

"Yes, she's nine or ten months old. She must be getting close to the age babies walk. And the twins are three now. I wonder if they're still such little balls of endless energy."

Kat pushed a plate of fried chicken across the table. Since Uncle Patrick had died and she'd sold her holdings tied to the Wadsworth fortune, she was a wealthy woman. Of course, they didn't need much money, not here on their homestead near Cheyenne, Wyoming.

They'd added on to their home in anticipation of a growing family and brought in some modern conveniences like a boiler to heat water, pipes to bring it inside, and an indoor water closet and shower bath. All luxuries, but when the Wyoming winter winds howled, they were grateful for them. They had a nice, very modern cookstove and a potbellied stove to heat their bedroom. They'd built a much larger barn and expanded their homestead by buying a tract of land in the steep hills to the west. No farmable acres, but there was lots of good grazing. They'd purchased a herd of cattle and hired cowhands to tend them, which led to their having to put up a bunkhouse and a foreman's house. More horses were bought as well to keep everything running smoothly.

No children had arrived yet. All the lavish preparations for a comfortable home were fairly well wasted on Kat and Seb. Kat mostly preferred her time in the kitchen, and she'd gotten involved in projects in Cheyenne, the territorial capital, and interesting things were always happening there. Seb had his laboratory and all the odds and ends he needed for his experiments and inventions.

"I knew Oscar wouldn't let Ginny come without him." Seb helped himself to a leg of fried chicken. Kat knew he always went for that first, and she loved how well she'd come to know the husband she'd married rather recklessly.

"Everyone's coming except Joseph. He'll stay home and tend the ranch; long travel can be painful for him."

"You said Dakota Harlan is coming? I haven't seen him since we turned off the Oregon Trail and the rest of the wagon train went on west. He's a tough man and will be good to have around if there's a fight."

Kat sincerely hoped and prayed it wouldn't come to that. She read the letter again, slowly this time, then handed it over to Seb before turning back to her meal. "I need to contact Mr. Etherton. He said he'd represent Ginny at trial. He's talked with me a lot about the asylum, the conditions there, Ginny's temperament, and how she'll handle this whole ordeal. He's also been looking into Rutledge and his situation back in Chicago. The man has lost most of his wealth."

"He's still hiring investigators, we know that." Seb read the letter while he tore a chunk of chicken off the bone with his teeth. They'd had one of the investigators at their home already this summer. They weren't Pinkertons anymore. Kat had put a stop to that by traveling to Chicago, finding Allan Pinkerton, and demanding he face the truth that he was being manipulated, which had resulted in the abuse of a fine woman.

The investigators these days were of a much rougher sort.

"How can he afford to pay the men who are hunting for Ginny when he's supposedly financially ruined?"

"Rich men have a different set of rules than the rest of us. I'm sure his definition of *ruined* is very different from a regular person." Kat would like to take Rutledge's no doubt weighty money bags and beat the man over the head with them.

"What else do we need to do to get ready?"

"I'm going to ask Mr. Etherton just that."

"Let's ride to town this afternoon."

"Really, right now? You'd leave your work?"

"Getting away from it helps, I've learned that. Moving, breathing clean air, riding a horse, and pulling away from my thoughts of the experiments often gives me new ideas. I was a fool to work such long hours before. Being a better husband has made me a better inventor."

"Then let's go. Mr. Etherton needs to see what's in this letter." Cheyenne was about a fifteen-minute ride away on horseback. They could go into town anytime they wanted if the weather was good, and on this late August day it was beautiful.

Thinking of the short ride in the warm sunshine didn't stop a chill of dread from running up Kat's spine. "Just thinking about Ginny going to trial for something so stupid as to prove she's sane makes me sick. It's ridiculous. It's unfair. It's guilty until proven innocent."

Seb got up from his chair and rounded the table to pull her close. "Don't let it upset you, honey. You know, however the trial comes out, it's not like it's some *law* that she has to be locked up. The only reason to do this is so she can defy her husband if she ever comes face-to-face with him. She can wave the court document in his face as proof of her sanity, and he won't be able to do anything about it. He'll be forced to leave her alone."

"Someone will still have to always be close to her side to guard her. What she needs to do is divorce that horrid man. That way he wouldn't be able to touch her ever again."

Seb lifted her gently to her feet and just held her for a moment.

Divorce was a scandalous thing. To turn your back on vows made before God was an awful sin. But when a husband betrayed and abused his wife as profoundly as Thaddeus Rutledge had betrayed and abused Ginny, well, God would understand, wouldn't He?

"The way I understand divorce law is that both husband and wife have to agree to it. There can be no divorce unless both parties sign the papers saying it's what they want. And I doubt Rutledge would ever agree to it."

"Surely that's not true in such a modern territory as Wyoming." Then Kat's eyes narrowed. "Why would you know so much about divorce law?"

Sebastian looked at her, grinned, then laughed out loud. "You could never get me to sign such a paper, my pretty wife. You are stuck with me as surely as if we'd been soldered together with fire and iron."

"That sounds rather painful."

He laughed again and hugged her tighter, swinging her back and forth. After Sebastian released her, he said, "It's not even a law in this territory that a husband can lock his wife away without a judge declaring her insane. That's only true in some states, and Wyoming is not one of them." He pressed a kiss into her hair and spoke in a voice that soothed her. "I know this brings it all back for you. Being in that asylum, having your freedom and all your rights taken from you. You feel it more deeply than the rest of us."

"Ginny was in there for three years. I was only there for one. I don't know how much longer before that asylum drove me truly mad. It's no place for anyone, sane or not. It's the worst possible way to treat someone who isn't in their right mind. And being married to you protects me from anyone declaring me insane. Since only a husband has that right. But to even imagine going back—" her breath caught, and she had to swallow hard to go on—"is unbearable. And yet there are women still locked away there. They need to be saved. The sane ones need to be set free. The insane ones need better care. I know just how Ginny must be feeling right now."

"At least here and now we can hope to have a quiet little trial and get everything in order without Rutledge finding out."

Hope was a wonderful thing, but Kat also believed in facing up to reality, and she knew Rutledge would be listening closely for any word of his wife. He needed her because poverty didn't suit him. He wanted her because he wasn't a man who accepted failure.

It would suit Kat to never hear from the man again.

Thaddeus Rutledge slammed the sheaf of papers down on his desk. He stood. Too fast, for his right leg buckled. He was about to catch himself on the desk when his left arm failed him.

Thaddeus fell face-first onto the top of his desk and was glad no one was in his office to see such humiliating clumsiness.

It was all Eugenia's fault. His right leg had been injured

when Yvette, a madwoman, stabbed and slashed him and nearly killed him after he'd caught up with his daughter in Idaho. Elizabeth was married now. Her new husband had her money.

He'd broken his arm when he'd been thrown off a train by Sebastian Jones, yet another husband married to a woman he wanted to get his hands on. Another madwoman who had escaped the asylum and run off with Eugenia. Katherine Wadsworth Jones, Eugenia's partner in the escape, had information he wanted, and he'd almost died in his attempt to get it.

He'd almost gone to jail, too. It had taken a good deal of his money, very generously and discreetly spread among judges and juries and lawmen, as well as politicians both state and local, to make the kidnapping charges go away. He hadn't been charged with a crime. He hadn't gotten any information either.

And now Katherine Jones had full possession of the Wadsworth fortune. She'd sold every bit of it and now lived in a hovel in Wyoming. She must have squandered that huge fortune. No one seemed to believe she still had it. Thaddeus had traced her generous donations to churches from Independence, Missouri, to Omaha, Nebraska, and all the way along the Union Pacific Railroad line to Cheyenne, Wyoming, where reports came back to him that she'd settled, had added on modestly to her hovel, bought a good-sized chunk of hilly land and a herd of cattle.

Thaddeus's investigators had done their best to find out what Katherine knew about Eugenia's whereabouts, but they'd failed to unearth anything. He knew she'd traveled to Idaho on a wagon train, and then she left the train and rode north. He'd tracked her as far as the O'Tooles' place, but after that it was as if she'd vanished. No one could find any sign of Eugenia moving on from there. But Thaddeus had seen Elizabeth at the O'Tooles just before Yvette had stabbed him. Eugenia had to be in the surrounding area.

Yet Idaho was a vast territory. And the O'Tooles had claimed ignorance regarding Eugenia's whereabouts. All he had to do was look at that Irish trash to believe they were indeed ignorant of most everything.

He glanced at the sheaf of papers again. Now this.

Everything hurt. Thaddeus fumbled in a drawer for his bottle of laudanum, took two quick gulps to take the edge off, and straightened. He shoved down the pain. Then, worse than physical pain, he shoved down the fear.

It wasn't something he was used to feeling. But what he'd just read frightened him.

It had finally happened. The creditors were through waiting, and he could no longer rob Peter to pay Paul. Peter and Paul were both destitute. As was Thaddeus—except for what he had hidden.

Now he had no choice but to flee, and flee fast.

He gathered himself, adjusted his suit coat, and rang the bell he kept on his desk. Hard.

Sykes came in fast. Hand on his gun that was tucked into a shoulder holster. The man could read the message in the way Thaddeus had rung the bell. Good to know.

"We need to move." Thaddeus turned to the wall behind his desk. A tidy line of bookshelves. Thaddeus had read them all. Books about great men like Vanderbilt and

Carnegie, Astor and Jay Cooke. Thaddeus had learned from those great men.

Now he'd need to apply everything he'd learned. Except none of those men had ever run up against as much trouble as he had.

He suspected they all had instilled a great deal more fear in their wives.

Bracing himself for what lay ahead, he did something he'd never done in front of a witness before. He tugged on the book closest to the left on the center shelf. It tilted, then clicked, and a whole section of the wall opened.

It'd always been a secret, and he'd chosen the man who built it for him carefully. But the time for secrets was over.

Thaddeus dragged out a large bag and tossed it behind him. Sykes caught it. Thaddeus drew out two others, both medium-sized satchels. The bags had been packed months ago with everything he needed and a bit for Sykes.

He reached in and extracted the fourth satchel. Smaller than the others but heavier, more carefully packed so that nothing clinked. Taking it in his right hand because his left couldn't bear it up, Thaddeus turned.

He locked eyes with Sykes, and what he saw there reminded him of himself. Cold and cruel. Sykes was a stout man who had built up his strength for the work Thaddeus had him do. Which was to collect rents from the scum who lived in his tenements and the crudely built little shops he charged so dearly for.

Those rents had fattened Thaddeus's pockets for a long time. Still, he'd had to take on mortgages to buy them and so had spread his money thin, letting the banks shoulder the risks rather than him. It had worked for years.

He'd thought his whole life was going up in smoke when the Great Chicago Fire had swept through the town only two years ago. And there was no denying that Thaddeus had taken a brutal hit. But he still owned valuable property under the smoldering rubble, and he'd extended himself even more recklessly to rebuild.

Eugenia's father had always counseled against taking on debt. The old fool was dead now, and that money should have been Thaddeus's. But the old miser had written his will very carefully so Thaddeus couldn't touch any of the man's money.

Even so, development in Chicago was explosive, and Thaddeus had taken advantage of the bankers and the gleeful race to rebuild the city. He'd tightened his belt and spent very little on himself as he tried to get ahead. He'd gone on expanding his empire. Then the day came when the bankers decided they didn't like the looks of the Rutledge empire. They began dunning him to reduce his rate of borrowing. He'd put them off, over and over again.

And today his main bank had said no more. They were calling in the loans. Thaddeus had no choice now but to leave town, away from his creditors' reach.

There was enough money in his smallest satchel to push back this day, but he wasn't parting with any of it. He'd leave. He'd intensify his search for Eugenia, and he'd come back to Chicago in triumph.

And there stood Sykes, very likely deducing exactly what was in the bag Thaddeus held on to. It occurred to Thaddeus that the man might be a danger to him because this fourth, heaviest bag was worth a fortune. All Sykes would have to do was grab it and run.

But if Sykes's intent was to steal, he wouldn't do it right now. He'd need to do his own running, and he knew Thaddeus was a man who would hunt him down, never giving up.

Sykes would bide his time.

As for Thaddeus, he had his own gun—smaller, better hidden, and just as deadly. He closed the hidden compartment and walked to the back door to his office. The one he always kept locked. The one to which only he had the key.

He unlocked it and snapped, "Follow me." He stepped into a small room, waited for Sykes to enter, then closed and relocked the door. "Emergency trip." Thaddeus led the way to the elevator he'd had installed in secret after his leg injury.

He and Sykes rode the elevator down to the ground floor of his heavily mortgaged building, where the two of them exited into an alley.

The alley was narrow and filthy, and it disgusted Thaddeus to have to set foot there. Today it seemed he was making an exception to every rule. "Hail us a cab," he told Sykes.

There were always carriages to rent. Thaddeus had his own, but the whole point of this was not to leave a trail.

He was soon riding in a shabby old carriage, heading toward the railroad station.

Once there, he had Sykes buy two tickets, and they were training westward within the hour. It wasn't his own private railway car. He didn't have a cook or a maid along. He hadn't even paid for a sleeper berth. All very rustic.

He had to wonder if Sykes had figured out yet that they weren't going back.

Pounding hooves from the north had Maeve whirling around to see who was coming.

"It's Oscar come to visit. I wondered if we'd see him this summer."

Bruce sounded happy. Maybe he was just excited to spread the news about his courtship.

Maeve squelched her unworthy thoughts. She realized a whole crowd was coming. She saw Beth riding with a small child in front of her, with Jake beside her, a matching small child riding in front of him. They had three-year-old twins. But hadn't there been a new baby? Beth was expecting one when Maeve had visited her last summer. There was no sign of the little one.

Then Maeve gasped at the sight of—

"Ginny's come to visit." Ma announced it like the queen herself were riding in. "I'll go put coffee on. Bring them all in as soon as you can."

"No. Wait and say hello to her, Fiona. She's finally left that canyon." Bruce sounded like the voice of doom. "I can hardly believe it. She must've decided it was time to face the past."

Ginny Rutledge had ridden into Hidden Canyon in the fall of 1869 and was just now emerging. And she'd vowed she never would because the outside world, as it was run by her horrid husband, was dangerous for her.

Maeve had heard the story of Ginny, the nicest, calmest,

most sensible woman Maeve had ever met, being locked into an insane asylum by her tyrant of a husband when she wouldn't hand over the money she'd inherited from her parents. Furthermore, she refused to hand over their daughter Beth's money.

Maeve studied the group. Oscar rode along with Beth, Jake, Ginny, and . . . "Where's Joseph?"

Bruce said, "They look like they're planning a long stay out of the canyon. Reckon someone had to stay back and do the chores."

More hoofbeats thundered, this time coming from the west. Lots of hoofbeats. She knew who she'd see before she looked in that direction because only one man had that many horses, and he came by with them regularly.

Dakota Harlan, a reckless, foolish, hard-riding, rude man who'd led them all west as the master of their wagon train. And when the O'Tooles and the Collinses had turned aside, Dakota had gone on to get the rest of the pioneers to Oregon. He'd tried homesteading there in Oregon in a spot with a cabin already on it, built a year earlier by Jake, but Dakota found it didn't suit him. He returned a year later and settled in the nearby mountains, though Maeve wasn't sure where exactly.

Dakota caught wild mustangs that roamed the Sawtooth Mountain Range, broke them, and took them around the country, selling the horses. He was a dab-hand at gentling the animals, and everyone knew he sold them for a fair price. The horses sold so fast he rarely got to town. He always said he was on his way to Fort Bridger, but his horses were always long gone before he got that far.

In fact, the O'Toole family could use another horse. Maeve's little brother and sister had been riding double with Bruce and Maeve's brother Donal, but they were getting too big for that. The family needed two horses now, so it was perfect timing for Dakota to arrive.

4

Dakota saw her, a vivid, redheaded, freckle-faced beauty. A woman too innocent and too fine to want any part of Dakota's attention.

He tore his eyes away from that pretty woman and saw Jake.

"Dakota!" Fiona waved a hand high. "Welcome! You're just in time for coffee."

Fiona O'Toole, welcoming him. The sweetest sound he knew.

Dakota's throat ached. Fiona reminded him of his own ma. His ma wasn't Irish, of course, and she'd had hair as dark as his, her eyes blue like his. But Fiona had a way about her. A loving, gentle, and sometimes fierce way that sure enough reminded Dakota of his ma.

Fiona always welcomed him with the utmost kindness. She'd fill just a little bit of that lonely cavern in his soul. He gave her a wide wave back and smiled. Then his eyes settled again on Maeve, and he saw something that shrunk his smile. He wasn't sure how exactly he thought he could tell, but something was wrong. Maeve needed his help.

What had happened?

Dakota swung off his horse in a patch of tall grass, with the string of well-trained mustangs stopping as his own mount did. The horses all went to cropping grass without any fuss. And it was all Dakota could do not to run to Maeve's side. Ask her if she was hurt, sad, sick. Ask her if he could chase away a mouse or smash a spider, slay a dragon if need be.

Much as he wanted to, he didn't walk straight toward her.

Jake, Beth, and Ginny were reaching the O'Tooles just as Dakota did. Oscar was busy getting the horses settled in the same grass Dakota had picked out. Bruce helped him with the horses.

Donal shouted a greeting from the field right across the little stream that divided Donal's property from his ma and sister's place.

Dakota had his own horse all leathered up, while the rest had halters only, so switching things so his critters could graze took seconds.

Jake reached out a hand to Dakota, who shook it firmly and with a lot of sincere pleasure to see his friend. And that was when he noticed a baby peeking over Jake's shoulder. Dakota saw the little blue-eyed tyke with curly brown hair like her mama's and laughed. "I saw the two little ones. I didn't see you'd strapped one on your back like a papoose."

"We've been toting the baby around like this all the time, even when at home. She seems content back there. So you're bringing horses out to sell?"

"Yep, this is my third batch this year. Usually I can get

ten trained at a time, then get to work selling them. Of course, I don't have to wait until September to get off my ranch."

Dakota gave Jake a clap on the shoulder. "It looks like you're headed east for a fight. I'll keep on moving and get my horses sold, then meet you in town. If I don't get them all sold, I'll load them on the train and sell them wherever we happen to stop."

As the womenfolk traded babies and began gabbing, Maeve approached Dakota with purpose in her gaze. "We need two horses."

"You're finally ready to get horses for your little brother and sister?"

Maeve nodded. "Bridget and Conor are too old to ride double with an adult. We had a couple of nice colts last spring and two more this spring. We're gentling them and should be able to ride the older two soon, but not soon enough. Maybe we'll have horses to sell before long."

For some reason, though her words were light, there was a weight to Maeve's expression.

"They've really sprouted," Jake said as the younger O'Toole children followed their ma inside. "Conor is near your Donal's height, and Bridget looks nearly your twin." Every one of the children was a redhead. A matched set with their ma and pa.

"She's thirteen. And don't think such a thing." Maeve gave Jake a good-natured backhand to the belly, no force behind it and an amused look of scolding on her face.

"Conor's near Pa's height, just as Donal is. Bridget will be as tall as Ma soon and will pass me up at the rate she's going. So yes, they need horses. Donal is set to marry soon—I wonder if we need a third horse for Suzie."

Mentioning the youngsters growing up reminded Dakota that they'd be doing it without a father. Thinking of their pa hurt, so he turned his thoughts to Maeve and whatever was bothering her.

Dakota watched her closely, wondering if she'd speak of what had upset her. But he didn't push. "I know Suzie's family, and her pa will send a horse along with her when they get married. She's got a favorite, and her pa sees it as her own. So you'll only need two horses, and I'll give you the pick of the herd since I'm talking to you first. The black mare is a favorite of mine."

Dakota pointed her out. The horse was young and took well to being gentled. "If you want breeding stock, take the red stallion. He's not a mustang, but he was unbranded and running with the herd, wild as the deer. I'd guess he's been running wild a long time, probably most of his life. I thought about keeping him, but I don't want to build a herd of horses, that's not my goal. Instead, I aim to catch the wild ones and gentle them to sell. I've seen a passel of them, so I can keep busy for years. I've seen your OT brand. I'll tell Bruce and Donal to brand the red with your own iron."

"Sounds fine." Maeve reached out a hand, and, after an awkward moment, Dakota shook it. A slender hand, with skin like silk. There were freckles on the back of her hand just like across her nose.

The deal was done on a handshake. Hard feelings or not, the two trusted each other. Such things as written contracts and bills of sale weren't necessary.

"I'll leave 'em behind then. They're well trained, but a stallion is always gonna be a handful."

"I think Donal will take him and give his bay mare to Conor. The boyo learned to ride on her and has a fondness for her. Bridget can take the black mare."

Bruce, Oscar, Jake, and Donal headed for the house, talking earnestly. Maeve watched the men a bit too closely.

Dakota found himself alone with Maeve. "What's the matter?"

She turned from watching the men, and her eyes met Dakota's. She studied his face for a moment, right where that bullet had grazed him. The wound had healed, but he knew the mark was still there. He had an excuse all ready, but she didn't ask. Instead, there was a stretch of silence that lasted too long. Then her eyes slid to Bruce, and her lips curved into a frown. Quietly, she said, "Bruce is courting my ma."

Fiona was inside. Dakota watched the men go in. "Really? You sound as if it came as a surprise. Couldn't you tell they were interested in each other?"

"No!" Maeve shouted the word, then slapped a hand over her mouth. Lowering her hand, she took two deep breaths. "No, I couldn't tell," she said much more quietly. "It came out of the blue. I'm a bit shocked, I am. Pure gobsmacked. Ma talks of Da a lot."

She crossed her arms tight and took a few seconds as if to regain control of herself before continuing.

"She loves to share memories of him and talks about how they met as children. Talks of their wedding day and their first home and how they lived on fresh air and love for a while because they were so poor. She's full of funny stories of Da. I . . ." Maeve's eyes swung back to Dakota. "I'm so sad about this. I know it's not fair of me, but I can't seem to be happy for them." Maeve's jaw tightened until Dakota thought she might crack her teeth.

Dakota said, "My ma died when I was about ten. I had four little brothers, so there was five of us in all."

"No sisters?" Maeve sounded horrified, and that almost made Dakota smile.

"Nary a one. She died birthing the fifth son. Pa had no idea what to do with a little baby. My pa's folks lived nearby, and Grandma came over and helped at first. She even found a neighbor lady who'd recently had a baby and arranged for the baby to be fed by her. But before long, my little brother was old enough to be weaned, and right about then my grandma died, and it all landed on me."

"Landed on you? Really? You were handed the raising of four little brothers when you were ten?"

"I was near twelve when Grandma died, so I took over then. I managed them as best I could, and Pa had no more notion of how to handle them than I did. I did the cooking, washed their clothes, gave them baths when I could wrangle them into a tub. My little brothers were a big help, though. We mostly worked together, except for the two-year-old, Mikey. I spent a lot of my time trying to keep him from casting himself into the fire."

Dakota shook his head as he remembered that rambunctious little brother of his. He'd helped a lot while Grandma was alive because she was ailing more all the time, her joints hurting.

"My pa never remarried, and I was glad of it. 'Course, I grew up in Dakota Territory, and we didn't have what you'd call an overly large supply of womenfolk." Dakota shrugged. "Maybe it's just that your ma and Bruce are here together and want to be with someone. Maybe you shouldn't look at it like she doesn't love your pa. Maybe Bruce is just close to hand."

Maeve slapped him across the face.

Stunned, Dakota stepped back out of reach in case she took another swing at him. He locked eyes with her. Her face was red as a robin's belly. Fire flashed in her eyes. What had he said? She'd knocked it out of his mind, but it must've been a knuckleheaded thing to say.

She clapped both hands over her mouth. Then, speaking between her fingers, she said, "I'm sorry."

That fire still flashed at him, though, and he didn't come closer.

"Idaho is filling up a bit, but it's got mostly the same problem North Dakota had—very few women, and most of them youngsters or married. So Bruce is just marrying my ma because she's close to hand?"

"Now, Maeve, I didn't mean it that way. I'm sure they care for each other."

Her eyes seemed to almost catch fire. She was sure burning him with them.

"If he cares for her and she for him, that's even worse." Maeve threw her arms wide. It wasn't like she was intending to slap him, but he was glad he'd stayed well back. "You can see that I'm in no way happy about this."

"You're of an age to get married. You should rustle up a husband and get out of here."

"I have to live here one more full year to prove up on my land. I can't just go haring off."

Dakota knew the rules about homesteading. "You have to live here six months of the year. You should go get yourself snowed in at Hidden Canyon for the winter. You could do that and still manage your six months, since you've already got them in for this year."

"So now I'm getting kicked out of my own home?"

Dakota clamped his mouth shut. Everything he said only seemed to make things worse.

She spun around and stomped toward the house.

Dakota lingered, then turned to settling the horses the O'Tooles were buying into the corral with the other horses and making sure everyone in there was going to get along. He was giving himself time so he wouldn't go inside with a red handprint on his face.

5

Maeve didn't believe in hitting people.

Not that she'd ever made a rule about it. But it wasn't something she ever did or figured it to be how she was. She was a nice woman. Gentle. Not violent.

And then Dakota Harlan had started talking, and she'd just exploded. Well, one slap. But it sure came as a surprise to her. Dakota, too, no doubt.

Why that sidewinder Dakota brought such a thing out of her, she had no idea. Yet she was sure it was all his fault. At least she'd slapped him on the cheek that wasn't marked from an injury, so she gave herself some credit for restraint. Not much, but some.

She entered her very crowded cabin, glad no one asked why she had a violent expression on her face. She was sure trying not to have one. Heading straight for the coffeepot, she kept her face averted from the others.

The house buzzed with chatter. Ten people were packed inside the place. It was a good-sized house, but ten people nearly overflowed it. Everyone who could fit sat at the kitchen table. Bruce and Oscar, along with Jake, leaned against the wall with their coffee cups and cobbler. They managed by setting the dessert down on whatever was close by, then switching for a sip of coffee. They'd saved a chair at the table for Maeve. She appreciated that.

They'd all been served before Maeve came in. Bridget got up and began refilling cups.

They were discussing plans. Ginny was going to court to have herself declared sane. Maeve thought that ought to be easy since anyone with one working eyeball could look at Ginny for about three seconds and make that declaration.

It must be a little chancy, though, since Ginny had been hiding, putting off taking this bold step, for years.

Maeve sipped her coffee and listened closely to figure out just what was involved in all of this, but nothing prepared her for the question Ginny asked.

"Maeve, I . . . that is, *we* wondered if you'd ride along with us?" Ginny, already pale and a little shaky, looked at her. Something gleamed in her bright blue eyes. Maeve wasn't sure what it was. Not fear exactly. Not anger or excitement. Sure as certain not violence.

Maeve set her fork down on her plate with a sharp click. She was going to be able to get away from here, and she no longer tried to read anything in Ginny's eyes. "I'd love to come." Maeve had heard the whole story, about Ginny hiding in the canyon with plans to never emerge as long as her husband was alive.

A man held great power over his wife, which Maeve didn't quite understand. But Ginny had said it was so.

Maeve's ma and da had run things together, both of them working hard to keep their large family fed and clean and safe. There'd been no notion of Pa wielding a lot of power, and no time for such things. Pa had always worked so hard he didn't have the energy for much besides sitting down for the evening meal.

Ginny looked at Ma. "Would you be able to get along without her?"

That struck Maeve all wrong. She was a twenty-two-year-old woman. Most women her age were married. She shouldn't have to ask her ma for permission to do anything.

Ginny's hands clutched together under her chin. "I'm sure Maeve is a tremendous help to you. But having her along, with the three children and a long trip ahead of us and no idea if I'll be . . ." Ginny's voice broke. Her lips trembled. Her hands moved up to cover her mouth.

No idea if I'll be . . . what? Maeve's eyes sharpened as she saw tears pooling in Ginny's eyes. She knew then that she hadn't been able to tell what she was seeing in Ginny's eyes because there had been so much.

"Mama, you're coming back." Beth stood from her chair, thrust the baby she was cradling at Maeve, and rushed to her mama's side to hug her.

Maeve looked down at little Lydia. If she was going to help with the youngsters, she might as well start now. Though truth be told she loved all the little ones and didn't have a single qualm about caring for them.

"If I lose this legal fight, I could end up locked in an asylum again." Ginny shuddered, and her clutched hands rose higher to cover her eyes. "But I don't want to live locked away in a canyon anymore either. I love that canyon and plan to go back and live there, but I want to be able to leave it when I want, visit neighbors, ride into town. I don't want to live in fear of the world outside that canyon anymore."

Maeve had heard Oscar demanding she stay in hiding.

She'd heard Jake say he'd get Ginny away from her husband if need be, no matter what a judge ruled.

She could hear the worry in Beth's voice.

But here she was. Emerging. Finally ready to fight. Clearly, thoroughly terrified.

Maeve's heart warmed . . . no, heated . . . no, burned. Her heart burned with rage that someone as sweet and obviously sane as Ginny Rutledge could be locked up on the say-so of a husband who stood to gain financially if he could be cruel enough to his wife. Of course, Maeve only knew Ginny's side, but she didn't need to hear the other side when someone as good and kind and sensible as Ginny sat right in front of her.

Maeve looked at Ma. She very carefully didn't look at Bruce. She wanted to go on this trip because she could help—not because she needed to get away. Getting away would be a nice extra benefit. Getting away, well, the very thought had her heart hammering and her ears almost buzzing with hope.

"You know Donal is sparking a young woman, and they've talked of marriage." Ma looked at her son, whose cheeks turned a bit pink, but he nodded.

"We've talked of marriage before the snow flies, within the month possibly." Donal smiled as he spoke of his upcoming marriage.

Maeve knew Suzie well and was happy about the union. A stab of worry made her wonder if Bruce was marrying Ma because he knew he needed to move out of Donal's cabin to give the newlyweds their own home. That reason for marrying made Maeve almost as upset as Dakota suggesting they were simply marrying because there weren't that many women in Idaho.

And here was Ma close to hand.

"We'll have Suzie to help us soon. And Bridget and Conor surely aren't youngsters anymore. There's no concern about caring for them like there is caring for your little ones."

Bridget was at the countertop, dishing up bowls of cherry cobbler. Cherries from their own trees. Bridget flashed a smile over her shoulder. No, she most certainly didn't need much looking after.

Conor was sitting at the table by Donal and drinking coffee. He was near to being an adult man.

Ma nodded. "Yes, Maeve can go if you believe you'll need the help."

The burn in her heart changed to excitement.

"We're riding on right now. We want to get to Alton by nightfall. And we hope to catch a train soon. We hope to be gone a very short time. Of course, we have to wait for the train, and who knows when it'll pass through. We could find ourselves staying in the hotel in Alton for a week or more."

A train? Maeve's heart sped up. She'd never been on a train. And a hotel? She'd slept on the ground all the way west on the wagon train. No hotel had ever brushed near her life.

Maeve looked down at the little girl in her arms. Newborn last fall. Ten months old probably. She was a sturdy, happy little thing who probably slept through the night and came very close to feeding herself, maybe even walking. She'd be a pleasure to care for. And the twins, what they mostly needed was someone quick enough to keep up with them. Helping out with them would be fun.

"We'll see to Maeve's fare," Jake said. "And see to her meals and a room when we reach our destination. She can share a room in the hotel with Ginny, so it will be completely proper. And it's only right that she earn a salary if she travels with us and helps with the babies."

"Oh, that's not necessary," Maeve said.

Jake smiled. "Tell me that again when you've got a fussy toddler on your lap on a ninety-degree day, for hours on end. I know for a fact you'll earn every penny, Maeve."

Maeve asked, "Where are we going?"

Jake's eyes met Beth's as if they'd discussed what they wanted to tell the others. "We know you're as trustworthy as the sunrise." Jake looked back at Maeve, then turned to Ma. His eyes scanned Bruce, Donal, Bridget, and Conor. "But we don't want it to be known as to where we're heading. We've done some studying on it, and we've written a lot of letters because Ginny has been pushing for this for two full years. We hope we've found a judge who'll be honorable with Ginny. That's all we ask. Simple fairness. Still, we aren't going to tell anyone where we're going. We know Ginny's husband is still searching for her."

"He's had men come here several times. He saw Beth here that first summer, so he knows you're probably in the area."

Dakota came to the door. "I've talked to men three times, different ones each time, and I've torn down posters saying Ginny is a wanted outlaw. It's best not to mention where you're headed. Word could get out."

The O'Toole family nodded.

Maeve, the one who'd find out first, almost bounced with her eagerness to know where she was going. Even so, she nodded along with everyone else.

"We've been in contact with Kat and Sebastian Jones, and they've been bothered several times by investigators wanting to know where Ginny is. If you don't know where we are, you can't reveal it. Not knowing is safer for you as well as for us. Is that all right, Fiona? If it's not, I'll understand. But in that case, Maeve had better not go along."

Suddenly Maeve couldn't breathe. It was as if her whole life hinged on this moment.

Ma didn't hesitate. "It's fine for her to go. I know she'll be in good hands with you folks."

Air gasped out of Maeve's lungs, and her excitement returned.

"I'll want to speak with you privately before you leave, lass." Ma had a determined glint in her eyes. "Let's go pack a few things so you can be on your way."

Eager to be gone, Maeve nodded and said to Ginny, "I'll be quick."

"We've got our coffee to finish." Ginny gestured with her cup. "And your ma's good cobbler to eat. No need to hurry."

Maeve started heading for the room she shared with Bridget.

"Maeve, wait!" Jake's voice stopped her in her tracks.

She turned around, wide-eyed, wondering what she'd done or said that would ruin this chance she had to get away.

"Leave the baby." Jake came up to her, smiling. He plucked the little one out of her hands and tucked her against his side. "Now you can have both hands for packing."

Maeve felt her face heating up in one of her horrid blushes. It was something that seemed to go with her red hair and freckles, and she despised the bright red that often plagued her cheeks. She whirled away and hurried to her room, glad of an excuse to leave.

Once she was in the room, Ma came behind her and shut the door with a bit too much firmness.

"You're going, my lass, and I'll not deny you a chance to travel a bit with good companions. But when you come back, I suspect you'll find your brother married."

"Suzie is a good friend, Ma. I'm looking forward to having her join the family."

Maeve found a satchel under her bed and dragged it out. It had been shoved under there years ago and not touched since. Their family went to town once or twice a year, yet not long enough that it was necessary to pack a bag.

"Mind me now, Maeve. I'm wanting your full attention."

It took a force of willpower to turn and look Ma in the eye. Maeve knew good and well why Ma had followed her to her room. It didn't take two women to pack Maeve's one extra dress and a nightgown, her hairbrush and a rack of hairpins.

"You will come back to find me married, too. There's no place in Donal's house for Bruce once Donal is married.

But there is a place in this house for him." Ma's eyes turned sad. "I'll not have you thinking I've forgotten my own precious Shay. He was the love of my girlhood, and he gave me the loves of my life in you children. But Bruce is a fine man. I'm ready to add a fine man to my life. We'll build another room onto the house so we're not quite so crowded in here. Suzie may not want to take all her meals here as Donal does. She may want to run her own home and keep her own kitchen. We'll have to see."

They'd built this cabin on the property line of Ma's and Maeve's homestead claims, and they were four years into the proving out. They had one year left to go. Would Ma want her own cabin once she was married? Would Maeve end up living here alone?

"It's hard for me to see another man in Da's place. But, Ma, I know you've found a good man. I'm sorry I've been unkind, and I'm trying to do better. I think this time away will do me some good."

Maeve knew it was past time to find a husband of her own, but her life had been full and happy, and yes, a man or two had come courting. Still, she'd never considered taking that very grown-up step. Now she wondered why.

She thought of some of the young men around, and none of them had appealed to her. Maybe it was time to get on with growing up.

"Can I at least have a hug from my girl before you go off with such sadness in your eyes?" Ma opened her arms, and Maeve walked into them. She hugged Ma back fiercely because her love was strong and true. Then they quickly packed her things and left the room, both of them heading for something new.

Thaddeus looked out the first-floor window at the people who dwelled in the neighborhood. With contempt he heard foreign languages. German, he thought, though he certainly didn't speak it.

He'd rented a house in Omaha that was a hovel compared to his mansion in Chicago. Of course, his mansion was mortgaged to the hilt, as were the rest of his buildings.

The house was close to the river. While there were richer neighborhoods with bigger houses, in his opinion, Omaha was a backwater. Yet the Transcontinental Railroad running through here from east to west had made it a boomtown.

He studied the street outside his window, feeling frustrated and edgy because he had nothing to do but wait. The trees were young in this neighborhood, which told him what an upstart town it was. There were houses going up within his sight, though this house he'd rented looked older. It was three stories and painted a bland white, with a white picket fence out front, for heaven's sake.

Every now and then a carriage rolled by on the mostly quiet street. Some of them were rather grand, as if the Germans around town were trying to show off their success, acting as if they belonged in America.

It disgusted him. And it made the wait all the more irritating.

Thaddeus was a man who moved things, who shook things. He bought and sold. He squeezed money out of land and buildings and people. He wanted to get back to it. The wreckage of his fortune could all be put right if he could just get things settled with his lunatic wife. For now, all he could do was wait for his investigators to bring him word of Eugenia. He'd been waiting for four years, ever since the day she'd escaped from Horecroft Asylum and run away.

He hadn't laid eyes on her since.

Then she'd gone and fouled things up for him with the Pinkertons so they wouldn't work for him anymore. He'd heard the Pinkerton agent, John McCall—who'd been with him that first year when he'd gotten close to getting ahold of Elizabeth—had blackened his name with Allen Pinkerton.

Thaddeus assumed Pinkerton wouldn't put the word of his far-distant agent ahead of the word of a good customer, but the man had balked. He was especially upset about the wanted poster Thaddeus had posted along the rail lines. Pinkerton claimed it was a crime, but Thaddeus considered his wife a thief.

Pinkerton attested that those wanted posters were about criminals who'd escaped custody, who'd been charged with a crime. Thaddeus told him it was just a matter of time before Eugenia was charged.

Of course, Thaddeus would never have her arrested. He'd just get his money and be done with her.

Nevertheless, Pinkerton wasn't interested in working for Thaddeus anymore.

Then that Wadsworth woman, Katherine Jones, had contacted Pinkerton. She'd been in the asylum and escaped with Eugenia. It sounded to Thaddeus like she'd been exactly where she belonged.

Either way, he'd had to give up on the Pinkertons and hire his own investigators who didn't work for the agency.

It had worked out in one way because they didn't charge as much. But in another very important way it hadn't worked out because his men hadn't managed to find his wife.

Now he lived in this wreck of a house, in a neighborhood teeming with foreigners. He hadn't gone outside since he'd arrived. It was humiliating to live amongst such rabble.

To make matters worse, he had to share the house with Sykes, a common thug. But the man seemed content to have the third-floor rooms for his own, while Thaddeus, with his bum leg, lived on the first floor. The second floor had five bedrooms, but Sykes didn't try to impose himself there.

Thaddeus had found a bank with safe-deposit boxes and put his money in there. It made him feel safer because he feared that Sykes might turn on him and steal the money. Thaddeus had never let him see it, yet Sykes wasn't a fool. Thaddeus had kept back a fair amount of the money because he was paying out to his investigators at regular intervals. He had to pinch pennies and hoard what was left. But only for now. Soon he'd get his hands on the madwoman he was married to. What a foolish decision it had been to marry her.

Of course, she was the wealthiest, most beautiful debutante in Chicago the year he realized it would be a smart business decision to marry. He remembered seeing her, wanting her, what with those dark curls and bright blue eyes. He had no way of knowing her mind was unsound. And her being so naive and kindhearted had made it very easy to fool her.

Though he didn't think of himself as charming, he'd

worked hard at convincing Eugenia he truly loved her. All he had to do was picture the bags of money she'd bring into the marriage and the charm followed, natural-like. He'd already been successful when he met her. In fact, he got along quite well without a wife. But other men of his stature were married, so he figured he should be married, too. Besides, he'd wanted *more*. He wasn't near the level of his in-laws' wealth. Eugenia's dowry had been a temptation he couldn't resist.

The fact that it was *her* dowry that had boosted him into the upper echelons of Chicago's wealthiest families mattered not at all, nor *her* inheritance he was after that would restore his fortune. When a man got married, his wife's property and cash became his—all she brought with her, and all she inherited, his. That was the way things were. He knew it. Eugenia knew it. Eugenia's parents knew it. So they had done him wrong when they'd cut him out of that inheritance.

He suddenly felt a powerful need to ride to the bank and make sure his money was still there. "Sykes! Get down here." Thaddeus looked at his suit. It was getting old, and he'd gained some weight recently so that it no longer fit right. Well, he wasn't going to spend money on new clothes.

Sykes came into the sitting room. "What can I do for you, sir?"

"Go hail a cab. I need to go to the bank."

Just the quickest flash of interest lit Sykes's eyes. No doubt he was hoping Thaddeus would bring all his money home so it was within his henchman's grasp.

Without delay, Sykes turned and was gone. He was the last one left who obeyed.

He thought of his daughter's money. That should have been his, too. She'd still been unmarried when she inherited it. As a married woman, the money belonged to her husband now. He saw no way to retrieve that wealth, and Elizabeth had gotten the lion's share from her grandparents.

Eugenia, however, had gotten plenty. And *that* money was Thaddeus's, pure and simple. Which meant his wife was a thief.

6

Dakota had his coffee and cobbler with the O'Tooles and with Jake's family.

He needed to hit the trail and get his horses sold, but he couldn't pass up Fiona O'Toole's good cooking. He didn't blame Bruce Collins a lick for marrying her.

He now knew better than to say that to Maeve.

"Jake, I've got to ride to all the neighboring homesteads. I can't go straight to Alton." While the cabin was a bit crowded, having people around him filled an empty place in Dakota's chest. He got mighty lonely out on his land.

"If a train comes," said Jake, "we'll hop on it. I'll leave word where you can find us. Chances are we'll be a few days waiting in town. I don't know the train schedule."

"A train arrives every few days." Dakota hunted around inside his head for any knowledge he'd gained about the trains. Truth was, he didn't go to town much. He glanced around the room. "Can we talk in private for a bit?"

Jake nodded, and the two of them stepped outside to be out of earshot of those in the house.

Dakota quickly told Jake about the attack and the letter he'd found. His jaw tight, he added, "I'll stay away from your family if you want."

Jake gave Dakota a clap on the back. "I want you along with us, Dakota. I'm sorry about this trouble dogging you. After we face Ginny's troubles, we need to talk to the sheriff in Alton. Tell him to keep an eye out."

"I will, but what happens if he sees someone hop off the train who looks like he's kin to Vic Darnell? There ain't much he can do."

Jake frowned. Then his eyes went sharp, and he snapped his fingers. "When we get back, I'll bring you over a couple of our puppies."

"You still get a litter every spring?"

"We gave the first batch away. Then our dog had another litter, and they must be half wolf 'cause there ain't any male dogs around. These latest litters have gone fast. We got more last spring, and they're all gone. Joseph handles it with Bruce's help. We'll save a couple of 'em for you next spring."

"If I can get back to my meadow alive, it gets mighty quiet in the wintertime. No one's gonna come huntin' when there's twenty feet of snow on the ground. The dogs are a good idea. Thanks." Dakota gave a grim laugh with no humor in it. "Who knows, maybe I can live to an old age on my quiet ranch."

Jake clapped him on the back again. "If we get things solved with the Darnells, maybe you can see about a wife and a family. It's a fine thing to have both."

"Maybe. Someday. Sure as certain not now."

"We'll figure something out, Dakota. You should come

and live in Hidden Canyon with us. Chances are the Darnells won't be able to find you there."

"So you aim to solve Ginny's problems and finally be clear of your need to be hermits, but then you'll turn right back into hermits to hide me? Because if you come and go openly from that canyon, you're gonna wear a trail and it won't be hidden anymore."

"You're right about that. Well, we're going to do something, Dakota, I promise you. Seeing Ginny face her troubles head on and fight makes me want to do the same for you."

Dakota felt the constant tension he lived with ease a little. He stayed alert, practically on a razor's edge, at all times. And for now, he needed to keep doing that. But maybe something could be done about his troubles. The thought gave him hope. "All right, I'll see you in Alton. The horses usually sell fast."

Jake looked around, then leaned in close and said, "We aren't telling anyone, but if we're gone, come to Cheyenne."

Dakota appreciated the show of trust. "I'm gonna hit the trail now," he said and hurried off. He hoped to sell the rest of his horses on his way to Alton. There was a shortage of well-trained horseflesh in the West. If he didn't sell them, he'd either have to let Jake go on without him or pay to ship the horses by train and bring them along. He knew Fort Bridger was on the way to Cheyenne, and the cavalry would buy every horse he had. It would cut into his profits, but he'd get enough to make it worth it.

Alton was situated on the old Oregon Trail route, with the railroad having chosen a different town in which to build a depot. That decision had been like a death knell to a lot of western towns. Later, though, they built a train spur to Alton, putting the Union Pacific a whole lot closer to Dakota. He'd heard rumors that spurs were planned for all the way to Boise. When that day came, Dakota would be an hour's horseback ride to the train, and he could rush all over the country selling horses if he had a mind to.

Yet he preferred to do business with his neighbors. He knew the price he charged for one of his horses, set at twenty-five dollars a head, was fair. He might get as much as ten dollars more if he drove a hard bargain. Either way, it gave him a sense of satisfaction to provide something badly needed to his neighbors.

Dakota rode on, winding his way between homesteads, and was three days on the trail to Alton.

Beth was weary when they reached Alton. They shouldn't have stayed so long at the O'Tooles' place, but it was so encouraging to see their old friends again. It helped them remember what freedom meant. It was a reminder that what they wanted was worth fighting for.

Mama rode beside her, with Jake on the other side of Mama. Maeve was on Beth's left. Oscar and Donal followed close behind. Now Mama guided her horse close to Beth, then closer still.

Beth saw the fear in Mama's eyes as she looked around the bustling little railroad town. It seemed like anything the railroad touched, whatever it was thrived.

That Alton had gotten a spur to the main Union Pacific line had saved the town after being bypassed by the

Transcontinental Railroad. Many became ghost towns when they were bypassed. The spur helped Alton to double in size. The streets were full of horses and wagons, people gathered in small clusters, including women and children.

"So many people," Mama said in wonder. "It's almost overwhelming. To think I once lived in Chicago . . ."

Beth reached across to rest a hand on Mama's arm. Jake came up beside her. Oscar and Donal closed the distance from behind. Even Maeve rode closer.

Maeve, Jake, and Beth each had a babe in their arms. Mama, with her hands being shaky, had said she was afraid she might drop one of them. They surrounded her now, everyone's eyes peeled. Beth realized she was actually looking for her father. But of course he wouldn't be here. He'd send minions to do his dirty work.

Surrounding Mama was exactly the right thing to do.

Oscar said, "Let's go get you registered at the hotel, Ginny. I'll guard your door while Jake sees about the train schedule. Maybe we can get out of here without spending the night. In the meantime, you need somewhere safe to rest for a while."

Oscar looked at Donal. "Can you wait until we find out when the train is coming through?"

Donal was a fully grown young man now and as tough as any pioneer. "I told Ma not to expect me until she sees me. I've got supplies to buy and a few other errands, but I'll stay close if you'd prefer it."

"Run your errands, but don't head home just yet." Jake had eyes sharp for trouble, and Beth felt as safe as was possible given the circumstances.

"I-I do feel exposed." Mama shook her head. "I used to ride around Chicago in a carriage whenever I chose. My goodness, I don't even know myself anymore. I feel like a terrible coward."

"It's not cowardice, Mama," Jake said, "to recognize you're in danger and to be careful. That's wisdom."

"But I'm not in danger, not really. There's no way Thaddeus could know I'd appear out of the wild in this town right now."

"Truth is, Ginny, he could know." Oscar swung down from his Morgan horse. It was a draft animal, but not huge. "This is the town he visited the time he found Beth. The O'Tooles and Dakota both said they've been questioned about you. He'll be more likely to have someone here watching for any one of us than anywhere else."

Jake dismounted, Lydia in hand, and strode over to a pillar that supported the roof of the entrance to the Alton Grand Hotel. He ripped a piece of paper down from the post.

Beth didn't ask about it. The only real question was, had the picture been of Mama or of her?

Jake crumpled the paper in his fist and shoved it into his front pocket. Oscar had Jacob Jr., but even with holding a toddler, he helped Mama off her horse.

Beth got to the ground before a man had to assist her, then snagged Lydia from Jake. "Go buy tickets while we get inside."

He nodded, looked around the street in the lowering sun, then hurried away. Donal headed for the general store. Oscar escorted the women inside, and Beth trailed after, carrying two of the children.

"I'll sign the registry book for us." Oscar waved them toward the dining room. "It looks like they're still serving a meal. Go on in and get some supper. You ladies get something for Jake, Donal, and me."

Mama nodded, still shaken and looking pale. She'd known what Jake had torn down. Almost certainly it was a wanted poster, offering a ten-thousand-dollar reward for Eugenia Rutledge.

They paused before they stepped into the dining room. Mama murmured to Beth and Maeve, "I've seen the picture your father used. It looks very little like me nowadays. My skin had hardly ever seen the sun back then, and I wasn't wearing a calico bonnet."

A blue calico bonnet sprinkled with white flowers, tied under her chin with a blue ribbon. Her dress was made of the same blue fabric. It was Mama's best dress.

Beth had on a similar dress in red with yellow flowers. Both showed a year of washing. Honestly, Maeve's green gingham dress was newer and nicer than the ones they wore.

"I had on a fine dress when that picture was taken. My hair was done up in a lovely style. Like an idiot I saw nothing wrong with allowing my lady's maid to spend an hour once or sometimes twice a day fixing my hair." She shook her head in disgust. "And I changed dresses at least three times a day. A morning dress fine enough to welcome company, a walking dress so I could stroll through the park or have lunch with friends, and if we had an event in the evening, which was several nights a week, a silk gown. But even if we weren't going out, I always changed into an even finer dress for dinner."

"Can you believe how much time we spent on vanity?" Beth grimaced to think of how they'd wasted their lives. "You look better now, Mama, because you're happy and it shines out of you, even with knowing the danger you face."

"We didn't have much to do besides primp and go out to lunch or an evening at the theater."

"Now, Mama, we both worked for the church and served on committees that tried to help the poor. We raised money to improve the hospital. And Grandma and Grandpa did great work for the frontier missions, which we supported generously. We did more than drink tea and fix our hair."

Nodding, Mama said, "Yes, we did. But now we work from sunrise to sunset just to care for the children and feed the men and keep the clothing washed and mended and the cabin clean. And if Lydia is in a mood, you work through the night. It's a hard life, but it's a better one. One I believe God finds more pleasing to Him."

"You could say that both of us are more sane than before you were locked up."

"You're both fine, rational women, and no one could think different." Maeve seemed to think that settled everything.

Unfortunately, it didn't.

"Let's hope a judge agrees with both of you." Mama gave her a solemn look, then squared her shoulders and strode into the dining room. The evening meal was mostly over. The few people still eating glanced at them with the attention they'd give any stranger before going back to their meals.

By the time their plates of fried chicken had arrived, Oscar was sitting with them, and Jake was entering the dining room. No sign of Donal.

The children were fed mashed potatoes, and the older two each clutched a chicken leg in one hand. Maeve sat between the twins, helping them drink a bit of milk along with their meal. Lydia, with four shiny white teeth now, got bits of chicken mixed in with her potatoes, and she gnawed on a biscuit between bites Beth fed her.

Soon the last diner left the room until their group was all that remained. Then an older lady and gentleman walked past. The lady looked at them a bit too long, then walked out.

Beth fought down nerves, wondering if the woman was on her way to study that poster, wondering why it was gone. Were there other posters in town?

Jake took a seat and said, "The train heading east passed through yesterday. We're going to be here until at least Monday—if the train is on time. And the train being late is more common than its being on time."

The adults exchanged looks. This town wasn't where they wanted to linger. Every day, even every hour, they stayed here meant a greater chance of being noticed, and of someone passing the word on down the line to Father.

"Maybe we should go back to the canyon for a few days," Oscar said. He bit into a biscuit with some temper showing.

"A full day's ride to go home, a full day back. For a three-day wait?" Mama had furrows of worry on her forehead that looked deeper than they had when they'd ridden out of the canyon just this morning. "No. We'll stay put. Send Donal home with the horses like we planned."

Which trapped them in Alton. But they weren't about to make a run for it no matter what happened. If trouble caught up with them here, they'd just have to face it.

Jake said quietly, "I went around town and tore down four more posters. I didn't see any others. I told Donal to keep an eye out."

The chicken dinner, which was delicious, was suddenly like a stone in Beth's stomach. It was Thursday. It was going to be three days in Alton at the very least, and danger drew nearer with every hour Ginny was out of the canyon, not yet set free of the taint of madness.

7

Dakota rode into Alton without a single horse remaining besides the one he'd ridden there.

His pockets were flush with money. He could now afford to buy a few more head of cattle, although he was also rounding up longhorns that'd gone wild and lived in the mountains just as the mustangs did. So he was building a herd that way, too. But then putting all his money toward cattle would certainly speed things up.

He had one bitter thought of the Darnells hunting him and wondered what the point was of growing a herd if he'd never have a safe and peaceful home?

Dakota reached Alton to find the train hadn't arrived yet. Jake's family had been here a few days, so he'd caught up without trouble. He stabled his horse at the livery. "Where are Jake Holt and his family's horses?"

With a kindly gleam in his eye, the stableman answered, "Some young Irishman took them away. Said he'd bring them back when the family returns."

Donal. He must have ridden to town with the group and

then taken their horses back to his place so they wouldn't have to pay to board them. Dakota didn't want to leave his horse behind and find himself on foot when they climbed off the train, so he paid to stable the animal with the intention of bringing it along in the stockcar. He hadn't seen Jake yet and was glad about that because Jake liked to pay for everything.

Jake had invited Dakota to come along and help protect Ginny. Dakota knew Jake's wife, Beth, had a lot of money. She'd brought it with her when she traveled west, and they'd found little to spend the money on, locked away as they were in the canyon. Jake didn't want the trip to cost Dakota anything, but Dakota liked paying his own way. So he went to the train station to pay for his ticket and space in the stockcar for his horse. Ticket in hand, Dakota headed for the hotel just as Jake was stepping out onto the boardwalk.

"I got you a room," Jake said.

Dakota shook his head. "I'd prefer to pay for my own."

Jake laughed. "Too late. Already paid for." Jake came up and patted Dakota on the shoulder. "Thanks for going along with us."

"A room of my own? I've gotten used to solitude, so I appreciate not having to share."

"Yes, a room of your own. I rented out the whole second floor, so no one has reason to get too close. You need to get yourself a wife, Dak. Solitude isn't all it's cracked up to be."

The whole second floor? He knew this hotel and had stayed in it. A room for Beth and the children and Ginny because Ginny needed someone with her. A second for

Oscar and Jake. The hotel rented a number of rooms on the second floor. Yep, Jake was spending too freely. But maybe it was worth it to have empty rooms on both sides of them.

Dakota couldn't come up with a smile over Jake's teasing about marriage. "You know I can't be getting a wife. It wouldn't be safe nor fair to bring a woman into my life."

Jake's expression turned somber. "I know. Sorry."

Dakota nodded. "I'm bringing my horse along on the train," he said, wanting to talk about something else, and quick. "When we get back, I'll ride out to the O'Toole place and send Donal in with your horses. How long will we be gone?"

"I don't know if we're going to be away for two days or two weeks or two months. It all depends on a lot of pieces of this puzzle fitting together. We're going to try to slip in, get a judge's ruling on Ginny, and slip back out, hopefully without getting a glimpse of Thaddeus Rutledge. We know he's out there hunting for her."

"I've been to town plenty of times since I settled here. Folks are still hanging the wanted posters and asking questions. That Rutledge is a fool to have spent so much money trying to track down his runaway wife. I'm sure if he gets ahold of her, he hopes to torment her into handing over her inheritance to him. And maybe she'd even do it now that Beth's money isn't at risk. Rutledge should just keep his hands on what he already has and consider it a fair enough deal."

Shaking his head, Jake said, "It's about the money, but only in part. Thaddeus isn't a man who likes to be thwarted. He decides what he wants, and he doesn't stop his pursuing till he gets it. The word *no* never comes into play. He was cut to ribbons by Yvette when he caught up with Beth that first year we came out here, but even that didn't make him quit."

"Kat and Sebastian said he was limping bad, most likely from being cut. Then he broke his arm being thrown off a train when he tried to get his hands on Kat to shake information out of her in his search for Ginny. Kat said in a letter that his arm didn't heal right. She also said he'd salted money all over Independence, Missouri, to get out of kidnapping charges and a long stretch in prison. That didn't stop him either." Dakota gave a grunt of disgust.

"Beth thinks a man who gets as rich as her pa is likely to be ruthless, though she says her grandfather was a wealthy man and a kind one. The way Rutledge acts, well, his isn't a life any decent person would want to live."

Dakota laughed. "*Decent* isn't a word Rutledge has any interest in being tagged with."

"Yep," said Jake, "the man's safe from ever being called that."

"You know, even with men around watching for him, Rutledge can't get out here that fast to try to stop us—not if we get to where we're going, quick get the ruling, and ride back home. Am I right?"

Jake gave Dakota a grim smile. "That's our wish for a fact, but we're on the lookout for trouble just the same. The train has made a huge country mighty small. Nothing like the vast land you and I used to guide a wagon train across for months."

Dakota hesitated. "I hope I don't bring more trouble to you than I'm worth."

Jake's eyes flashed with concern. "Getting out of the territory for a week or a month, however long we're gone, might be the best thing that could happen."

Dakota didn't say it, but nothing about what lay ahead sounded like the best of anything. He wondered if the same people snooping around looking for Ginny Rutledge were out to earn themselves some extra money searching for him. He'd tried to move around quiet-like, yet he'd been found twice. The whole Darnell clan were apt to catch up to Dakota someday, maybe all at once.

Dakota followed his old friend into the hotel and almost stumbled in shock.

Maeve stood in the doorway to the dining room. He knew Donal had already headed for home. He'd forgotten about her.

"What are *you* doing here?" Maeve jammed her hands on her hips.

Apparently, she hadn't known he was coming.

Dakota turned toward Jake, who had ignored both of them and headed straight into the dining room. It was about high noon, and here Dakota was facing another clash with the face-slapper. He narrowed his eyes and stayed well out of range. "I'm coming along on the trip to help protect Ginny."

"No, you're not." She stormed right up to him, and he stepped backward until he hit the now-closed door with his back. Somehow he'd ended up alone with her in the hotel lobby. Was she aiming to slap him again?

With no idea of what to say, instead he just stood there staring at her, breathing her in. She smelled nice, though he couldn't say like what exactly. He'd never given much thought to what a woman smelled like, but to him Maeve smelled like a purely full-fledged adult woman.

She wore a pretty green dress with white lace at her wrists and neck. The color made her hair glow like fire. He wanted to warm himself on the fire of her hair.

He finally found his voice. "You're going because they need your help. That's my reason for going, too."

She looked a little stunned. And then for no good reason Dakota could see, she moved closer. Their gazes locked together. It reminded Dakota of when they'd first gotten to know each other on the wagon train—they'd looked at each other a few times too many. He'd felt drawn to her. He'd known he was headed west for the last time.

Dakota lifted his hands and rested them on her upper arms. He drew her even closer, and she let him. "Maeve, if you want—"

"Maeve! Can you come in here, please?" Ginny's voice slapped aside whatever wild notion had taken over Dakota's mind.

Maeve jumped, then backed away from him, wide-eyed. "What are you doing?" She shook her head almost violently. "What am *I* doing?"

She didn't wait for Dakota's answer, which was just as well since he had no idea of how to respond. Instead, she whirled around and raced into the hotel dining room. She was gone, but Dakota still felt the warmth of her.

Jake came to the dining room doorway just as Dakota was about to go outside and throw himself into a water trough to clear his head.

"Can you come in now?" Jake asked. "They're serving the meals, and they want to get it all handed out at once."

It wasn't a water trough, but it'd do as a distraction. Besides, Dakota had been living mostly on hardtack and beef jerky for the last few days. A couple of people he'd sold horses to had fed him, but then he'd pushed on, hoping to get to town before Jake left.

Well, he'd made it. But things were a lot stranger than he'd ever imagined. Sure, he wanted to help keep Ginny out of the clutches of her indecent husband. And sure, he liked the idea of putting a lot of miles between him and the Darnell clan. Even so, was saving Ginny and his own life enough to convince him to put up with Maeve?

His thoughts turned all mushy then, as he couldn't come up with a solid answer. Later, he decided, then yielded to the temptation of fried chicken, mashed potatoes, and a bowl of creamed peas. The hotel cook had baked loaves of soft bread that were still warm, and there was apple pie with sweetened cream and all the hot, strong coffee he could drink.

Dakota focused fiercely on the food in hopes Maeve would vanish instead of sitting there so sweetly, bouncing a baby on one knee, in that pretty green dress.

8

The train didn't come for a week. The Monday train was late, and no amount of nagging at the train station had changed a thing.

Maeve knew this to be true because she'd witnessed a fair amount of that nagging by Oscar when she walked around Alton with a fussy, teething Lydia.

By Wednesday, Jake had taken to pacing and muttering. Ginny had begun hiding in her room, only coming out for mealtimes, and twice she asked for a plate to be brought up to her. Though the hotel didn't offer such a thing as room service, they let Beth carry a meal upstairs as long as she brought the dishes back to the dining room promptly.

With Ginny hiding, Jake pacing, Oscar nagging, and Beth serving meals, Maeve had to admit this job had been no random bit of kindness. They really needed her, and she was earning her keep and every penny of the wages they'd offered even though she'd refused to accept. If they offered again, she might just change her answer.

Maeve felt the tension. Everybody was afraid that the

Pinkertons or a crooked lawman or some bounty hunter or Rutledge himself might turn up at any moment.

Maeve and Ginny slept in the same room, often with the twins tucked in bed with them. Sometimes the little tykes wanted their ma or pa and kicked up such a fuss they'd disturb Beth or Jake through the thin walls of the hotel room. When they did so, Beth or Jake would hurry over and fetch them.

Maeve listened for the train. She'd never been on one before, so she was looking forward to it. Despite the fear that Rutledge or his minions would turn up to try to drag Ginny away before she could have her day in court, the advantage to the wait was that Jake and Beth were sending telegraphs.

Kat and Sebastian Jones were coming to the trial from Cheyenne.

Of course, Jake wasn't telling any of them just where they were going. But he had to tell Sebastian and Kat, so the secret was only as good as the honor of the telegraph operator. The one here in Alton, and the one in Cheyenne where Kat and Seb lived.

There was a bench just outside the hotel. During the daylight hours, Dakota, Oscar, and Jake stood watch over everyone who came and went in town. Whichever one of them wasn't out front was out back. The third man got a break.

The fear that someone might turn up with plans to kidnap Ginny and haul her away to Chicago and throw her back in the asylum was so real it almost hummed between all of them. Beth, Ginny, and Maeve kept busy wrangling children, although sometimes one of the men would bounce a child on his knee while he sat outside. The two older children especially liked a chance to run and play.

It was early in the morning on their tenth day in Alton when the train whistle finally blasted. Maeve about jumped out of her skin.

From the second the whistle blew, Dakota was moving. He didn't have much, and what little he had, he packed up every morning. Now he took his bedroll and satchel to the station and left them there, turning back to fetch his horse.

He jogged down the train platform just as everyone else was coming out of the hotel. The train still hadn't pulled in, yet they were all eager to leave Alton behind them.

The train pulled to a stop with a loud whistle and squealing brakes. Steam blasted out of the engine as the clacking wheels rolled to a stop and passengers began disembarking.

Dakota strode out of the livery with his horse. He watched the family climb aboard, then headed for the stockcar. A conductor rolled the doors open, and with a grating rasp of metal on metal, the station agent shoved a ramp up to the door. His horse, a well-trained critter not bothered by the racket or the hollow echo of his hooves on the wooden ramp, was easily loaded.

Dakota was the last to get on. It was nicer than the last train Dakota had ridden, which was the first year the train made the trip to Utah. He'd spent the winter in Oregon after his wagon train had arrived. Then he'd headed out early enough in the spring to reach Independence before it was time to roll out.

It was a strange thing, crossing the whole country in just a few days by locomotive going east, only to take five months to go back west on a wagon train. The railroad had come close to ending wagon-train travel. A few still crossed the country that way, but it was a dying business. There were more wagon masters and trail guides than there were available jobs. Dakota had seen that coming, and he had quit his wagon-master career the same year Jake did. Both of them had plans to homestead near each other, and Jake had already claimed a piece of land and built himself a cabin on it.

Then Jake had met Beth and turned off from the wagon train in Idaho. He'd told Dakota to go change the claim to his own name and live in the cabin. It'd taken a year, but Dakota found homesteading didn't suit him. He'd decided to find his old friend and turn to taming wild horses. But after he'd headed out to find Jake, he'd run into trouble and found himself locked in a feud with the Darnells.

Mulling over the mess he was in, he stepped into the rearmost passenger car, where he'd seen Jake's family enter. He found them all settled in their seats for the trip ahead. There was one seat left empty, all the way in the back, with one other occupant right next to it.

Maeve.

Well, two occupants, for she had Jacob Jr. in her arms. Beside her waited the only empty seat in the passenger car.

His stomach twisted when he thought of how pretty she was. She had on her green dress again today, and it was hard for him to look away.

She wasn't having any trouble, though. She had her gaze fixed on her little toddler friend. It was as if he were invisible.

Dakota tossed his satchel and bedroll on the floor and sat down. He forced himself to remember the sting on his cheek after she'd slapped him, and the sting on his other cheek from when a bullet had grazed him. The two stings ought to be more than enough to keep his feelings in check.

Jake needed help, and Dakota was happy to stand beside his friend. Add to that, getting out of Idaho for a while was an idea with merit. But he sure wished Maeve wasn't coming along.

Dakota scanned the other passengers with a knowing eye. None of them seemed to pay the least bit of attention to the riders who sat in the back. There were at least three dozen people packed onto the train besides Jake's family. Dakota couldn't judge much from staring at their backs. He readied himself for trouble, just like every minute of every day, and turned to see Maeve glaring at him.

And from her expression, and the fire shining out of her blue eyes, she looked as though a two-hundred-pound, stinking polecat had taken the seat beside her.

The train whistle blasted, and with a jerk of iron and the chuffing of the engine, the train slowly began its journey east.

Dakota watched the little town of Alton slide away until they'd left it behind. The rolling hills of Idaho now filled the car windows. Green and lush, they rushed along through the southern part of the Snake River Valley. Some said it was as rich and fertile of soil as could be found anywhere in America.

To give himself something to do, Dakota plucked little Jacob out of Maeve's hands and hoisted the little guy up until his head dangled over his own. A deep chuckle rolled out of the tyke, and out of the corner of his eye, Dakota saw that Maeve was smiling. He'd gotten that grumpy look off her face, at least for the moment.

"Hey, Junie. I think I'll call you Junie for Junior instead of Jacob. That's an old man's name."

Jacob's chuckles turned to squeals.

Just ahead of him, Jake sat beside Beth, holding a sleeping Lydia. Jake twisted to look over his shoulder and growled, "We're not calling my son 'Junie.' Stop it before it sticks somehow."

Dakota grinned and hoisted the little guy again. "Um, how about Chip then?"

"No, that sounds like a broken coffee cup."

"Little Jake." He lifted the boy up high, then lowered him, getting a laugh each time. He glanced at Jake and saw amusement on his face, though it was slight. Jake had been wound up tight for days. Dakota kept playing with the little one just to give the family something to think about besides the fight they were taking on. "You can be Big Jake. Or Young Jake and Old Jake? That sounds good to me—Old Jake it is."

Beth bumped Jake with her shoulder. "Old Jake? Does that suit you?"

"No."

"How about Jay, or maybe JJ?" Maeve's voice was light, almost musical. She'd relaxed a bit. "I think I'll start calling him JJ. That sounds like him."

"We call him Jacob so he's got a different name than me."

"But you got the nickname. A child needs a nickname. Good thing old Uncle Dakota stopped by or you'd've hung an old man's name on him from birth. So JJ, Lyd?" Dakota nodded at Lydia.

"Not Lyd, for heaven's sake." Beth rolled her eyes.

"And . . ." Dakota glanced at the back seat across the aisle from him, where Oscar and Ginny had Marie. "Mare? Nope, sounds like you think your child is a girl horse. Mary? Is Mary a nickname for Marie?" Dakota asked Jacob, who giggled.

"How about ReeRee? JJ, ReeRee, and Lyd."

Beth said, "Call them whatever you want. We'll just go back home after all this and call them by their real names, and you'll be remembered as that odd, eccentric old Uncle Dakota who calls them by weird nicknames."

"I can live with that." Dakota lifted JJ up high and down low, enjoying the feeling of having a baby in his hands. He'd always liked kids.

Marie, calmer than her twin, Jacob, but an active little thing just the same, sat on Ginny's lap and looked up at Oscar. She chattered so fast that Dakota couldn't understand a bit of it.

Ginny was a married woman, and there was nothing improper between her and Oscar, but Dakota could see that Oscar was in love with her. To Dakota it appeared it wasn't really romantic love. It was more like a devotion on a plane far higher than romance.

Oscar had worked in the stables on the Rutledge estate in Chicago, and he treated Ginny like the fine lady she'd been back then. It wasn't obvious, and Ginny wouldn't put up with him acting as a servant, but it was there.

On Ginny's part, she treated Oscar like a true and loyal friend.

Dakota didn't see how there could ever be more between them than that. At least not as long as Thaddeus Rutledge was alive. But regardless of their relationship, those two were like grandparents to Beth and Jake's children.

As Dakota played with JJ, he glanced sideways at Maeve. "This one reminds me of my little brothers," he said.

"All of them? You said there were five of you."

Dakota shrugged and stood JJ on his knees. The little boy bounced and started saying "J-J-J-J-J-J" while Dakota held tight his chubby fingers.

Beth and Jake were distracted by Lydia's waking up, howling. Dakota hoped they didn't get tossed off the train for being annoying.

Marie was keeping Oscar and Ginny busy. In the crowded car, sitting next to Maeve, even with a bouncing toddler, Dakota found himself alone with Maeve. He'd somehow managed to avoid her all week.

"JJ reminds me most of the youngest. I helped tend them all. Ma wasn't a real hardy woman. Having babies took a lot out of her."

"My ma was always out of bed on the same day a baby came." Maeve frowned a little as she spoke of her mother.

Dakota was quick to turn her attention away from her ma. "It's different for everyone, I guess. When Ma died, Grandma, my pa's mother, stayed with us awhile. Then Grandma found a neighbor to be a wet nurse for Jeffrey. And because there wasn't room enough, Grandma took the baby, little Jeffie, who slept at her cabin at night. Her and Grandpa came over every day. Grandpa worked with Pa a lot. They shared farming equipment. Once Jeffie was sleeping through the night, Grandma started leaving him. They had a small one-room cabin, and there was no room for him. Besides, Pa wanted him to know where his home was. By then Grandma was feeling her age. She died when Jeffie was two. I was twelve at the time. We all spent a lot of time doing chores, but caring for those little ones fell heavily on me. Jeffie was just a little younger than JJ here. Johnny was five. The next two were older and helped out. I ended up being their teacher, too."

He clamped his mouth shut and listened to the rushing wind outside the passenger car. The clacking of the churning wheels. The rest of the railroad car was quiet. Lydia was busy drinking from a bottle of milk Beth had brought along, and Marie was cuddled up against Ginny, listening to her grandma read.

Dakota looked at Maeve. "Sorry, I got to blathering away. Never did much talking to a woman, not ever in my life. Guess I don't know what I'm doing." And he clamped his mouth shut again, harder this time. Because he still didn't know what he was doing.

Maeve said hesitantly, "I've worked alongside Ma all my life. And now she sends me off on a trip so she can marry another man than my da." Maeve gave her head a violent shake, then dug in the satchel she had at her feet. She pulled out a book and waved it in front of JJ. "Would you like me to read you a story?"

Dakota had never seen a book with pictures. The cover had a drawing of three bears on it. They were standing in a circle and holding hands—in a way no bears would ever act. *Fairy Tales* was printed with black letters on the yellow cover.

JJ might be a little whirlwind, but it seemed he liked books. He dove at Maeve. Dakota helped move him onto her lap. As he got the boy settled, he brushed against her arm and her side and her hand. He sure didn't mean to. Then he got a look of annoyance from Maeve before she opened the book to read in her Irish lilt.

Dakota leaned his head back against the wall, gazing across Maeve, JJ, and the book at the scenery rushing by, and enjoyed every word of the fairy tale. The land Dakota had passed through with his wagon train was now sprouting with homesteaders. He'd heard several small towns had sprung up along the railroad line. Every fifteen miles or so, there'd be a town where the train could stop to refill its tanker car with water. When there was no town, a lone water tower stood, a windmill beside it, ready for the train to draw from.

The tension they'd all been living with eased a bit. The steady chug of the train's engine, the clickety-clack of the iron wheels, and the wind whistling past the windows all had a soothing effect. Of course, the tension didn't fully disappear, and wouldn't until the situation with Ginny was resolved.

But they'd gotten out of Alton without anyone bothering Ginny. For now, at least, they were free.

Which gave Dakota too much time to think.

As he stared out the window, he thought of the fresh grave on his land, and it made his heart ache. He'd decided to get far away from there, sell his horses, and maybe wander a bit. It seemed wrong to stop being on full alert, but Jake was a tough man. Oscar too.

Dakota leaned forward and whispered, "I'm going to try and sleep awhile. Wake me at any sign of trouble."

Jake, looking back over his shoulder, nodded. Yet the quietly spoken words weren't so quiet they didn't earn Oscar's notice. Oscar nodded as well. Dakota knew Oscar was thinking any trouble would be aimed at Ginny. But Jake knew there could be something more and aimed straight at Dakota.

Even with the disturbing presence of Maeve O'Toole, Dakota let the chugging of the engine and the clacking of the wheels lull him to sleep.

9

"Train travel is a wonder." Maeve couldn't believe how far they'd come and so fast. In less than a day, they'd traveled a distance that had taken the wagon train almost a month to travel.

And now they were disembarking in Cheyenne, Wyoming. The town was a hive of activity. It was the territorial capital and looked to be growing as fast as the townspeople could build.

"I telegraphed ahead," Jake said, picking up his haversack while balancing his son in one arm. The man had done this many times before and looked to be a master at it. He slung his rifle over top of the haversack, safely away from the little one.

"Did you pick Cheyenne for a reason?" Maeve had heard it was hard to get a fair trial in the West. Wealthy men often tried to pay off jurors to get the verdicts they wanted.

She'd heard talk of the minions who roamed these parts in search of Ginny. The hope was that they'd get a ruling deeming Ginny to be sane, declared so by a judge. She'd then carry that document with her whenever she left the canyon, accompanied by a few strong men like Oscar, Joseph, Jake, and probably that Ma-stealing snake, Bruce. But with a legal ruling on her sanity, Ginny would be free to go wherever she wanted. Her husband would have no power over her.

Beth had told Maeve that Wyoming was unusual in its favorable treatment of women. That must've been the deciding factor in why they'd hold the trial in this territory. And if a declaration of Ginny's sanity was in fact declared, they'd take that declaration home with them. Ginny's safety depended on it.

"We picked Cheyenne because this is where Kat and Sebastian Jones live," Ginny said. "We hope that knowing someone locally will be to our benefit. Kat, if she's called upon to do so, will testify in my defense. She's very familiar with the conditions in that asylum."

"How does she know about the conditions there?" Maeve couldn't quite believe that Kat had worked there.

"You've never heard that Kat was locked up in the asylum with me?" Ginny shrugged and added, "No, I suppose you haven't. I've been closemouthed about much of what went on in the asylum, and Kat's stories are hers to tell or not tell. She escaped from the asylum with me."

"The same woman who saved my family with her level head, quick actions, and doctoring skills—she was judged to be insane?"

"Kat accused a powerful man, her husband's uncle, of killing her husband. When she wouldn't quit accusing him, he had her locked away. But marriage protects you from anyone accusing you of such things. Now she's got Seb for a husband, and her uncle discovered he'd made a big mistake. He regretted not believing her and changed his will to leave her everything. She sold out of all the Wadsworth family holdings and moved to Cheyenne. She's a wealthy woman, and Seb is a respected inventor. Besides that, she's done a lot to establish herself and Sebastian in Cheyenne by supporting churches and charities, even donating to a few local politicians."

"Not to mention," Maeve said, "living her life in a kind and wise and utterly sane way for years."

Ginny smiled. "Yes, not to mention that. Her word may hold a lot of weight in the courtroom, and I'm much obliged for her help."

Oscar smiled, though there wasn't much about this he liked. "Wyoming's motto is Equality for All, or something like that. They've granted voting rights to women, to freed slaves—all black people, in fact—and to native folks. It's a territory run by wise folks. A good place to fight this battle. We have hopes of finding ourselves in the hands of someone who believes in the fair treatment of women. There are several women serving as judges in Wyoming—the first territory in the Union to allow it."

"Women judges?" Maeve could hardly believe it. "Does Idaho have that?"

"Nope." Oscar shook his head. "Only Wyoming so far."

Maeve furrowed her brow. "Whyever not?"

Ginny patted her on the shoulder. "It's something we can work on when we get home."

Dakota came from the stockcar, leading his horse. "Now, Ginny," he said, "don't you get started with that *women-voting* fuss. Except for your husband, who did you wrong, men take care of women. Especially in the West where woman are treated right."

Ginny said, "That's a very big 'except,' Dakota. I admit I haven't given much thought to women voting. I've been busy being locked up and then running away in a desperate bid for freedom. But it does feel like I wasn't given rights as an American citizen. It's wrong that I can be locked up just on the say-so of a husband who's got a lot to gain by treating me wrong. It might be harder to do such a thing if women had some kind of equal power to men. I mean, where is the law that says a wife can lock up her husband? That seems like a very simple example of unequal treatment, and for no good reason."

Dakota nodded. "You're right, Ginny. There are some lousy men in this world."

Somehow the way he said it drew Maeve's attention. He seemed to be thinking of someone specific when he spoke of lousy men. And someone he knew, not the tyrant Thaddeus Rutledge.

"There's Sebastian." Jake pointed. "He said he'd arrange for us to have rooms in the hotel. There are too many of us to fit in his house."

Maeve saw Kat smile and wave. She loved Kat Jones. She had the knowledge that helped save Maeve's family. They would have all died if it hadn't been for Kat and her medical training.

And Kat had been locked away, too? Maeve felt a stirring deep inside to fight for fairer, more equal laws. Sebastian was at Kat's side as they wove through the crowd at the train station. Kat came straight for Ginny and hugged her almost desperately. Then Beth got a hug, and it was Maeve's turn. They greeted each other like long-lost sisters.

Once all the hellos were finished, Maeve took Lydia. She was sleeping, but in all the bustle, the twins became overwrought. They took turns crying and wanted only their ma and pa.

Maeve sympathized with them. They were all used to a slower pace and a quieter life.

10

Dakota remembered Sebastian from the wagon train. A quiet man.

He had barely exchanged a dozen words with Sebastian, and Dakota had made it a point to get to know the pioneers on each train. Instead, the man had kept to himself mostly, even when others were around.

Now it looked like they were teaming up to stand guard.

"Been a long time, Sebastian."

"Dakota. I'm glad you came along. Beth had written us that you were ranching near Hidden Canyon, but I didn't know they'd pressed you into riding here with them."

They shook hands, but neither of them did much relaxing considering the danger that might surround Ginny.

Dakota, leading his horse, strolled along with the others—rifle slung over one shoulder, six-gun in his holster, eyes scanning the crowd constantly. "Did you know they were coming?"

Sebastian nodded. "Kat's done a lot to prepare for this. She's hunted up a good lawyer, an honorable man who will know how to talk to a judge and jury. I knew they were coming, but I wasn't sure when. I thought they might put it off another year. Beth said they were urging Ginny to put it off forever."

"I can't say as I blame the woman for not wanting to have to hide for the rest of her life."

Sebastian shuddered. "We got snowed in the first year we came west. I about lost my mind, being stuck in that canyon, and I don't say that lightly considering Ginny and Kat spent time in an asylum."

Kat came up beside them, her arm linked with Ginny's. "Seb and I have hotel rooms for you. And once we got your telegram that you were coming, I contacted Ginny's lawyer. He's talking to Cheyenne's justice of the peace to arrange a trial as soon as possible."

It sounded good to Dakota. They could get in and out of Cheyenne fast, and Ginny could get back to Hidden Canyon. Of course, the whole point of all this was to not have to go back into hiding.

Dakota had a hard time believing a judge's ruling would do much to discourage Ginny's cruel husband. "We stayed in Alton for over a week, waiting for a train to come through. It's made us all a little edgy."

Ginny nodded. "There was plenty of time for word to get out that I had emerged from hiding. Thaddeus could be on his way here even now. But would he know to come to Cheyenne?"

"Sure he would," Dakota said. He was a watchful man at all times, but right now he was even more alert than usual. "Jake sent a telegraph to Sebastian. The telegraph operator in Alton and the one here in Cheyenne both knew we were coming. Besides that, someone in Alton could have followed us here. Or someone could be here waiting for us. Once they saw us step off the train, one of Rutledge's investigators would waste no time wiring your husband your location. No doubt Rutledge will be on his way to Cheyenne by the end of the day."

Beth came up, holding her daughter, and slid a protective arm around her ma's waist. Jake and Oscar followed close behind Ginny, there as a human shield. Dakota and Sebastian moved in front of her to protect her from that direction. Kat and Beth remained on either side of her.

And still she wasn't safe. She wouldn't be either—not until they had a judge's ruling about Ginny's soundness of mind. Which seemed about as dumb as anything Dakota had ever heard. Just one look at her, or better yet, one conversation with her, would tell anyone with half a brain how clearly sane Ginny was, and that all of this was nothing but a fool's errand.

Yet somehow her husband had managed to get the asylum to lock her up.

They reached the hotel just as Lydia stirred in Maeve's arms and began to whimper. They stepped into an empty lobby. Once Dakota judged the place to be safe, he plucked Lydia out of Maeve's hands. Sure, he wanted to help with the care of the little ones, but mostly he just loved babies.

It'd been a long time since he'd been around them much. Once in a while there'd been an infant on a wagon train; there'd even been a few born during his many journeys. But it was a busy job being wagon master, and he got very little chance to spend time with a baby. Of course, this chubby little thing was hardly an infant anymore. She'd be walking and talking soon. He hoped he'd get to see her take that first step.

The rest of their group entered the hotel just as the sun was setting.

Gasping, Maeve said, "Look at that!"

Dakota turned to her, then followed her line of vision to gaze out the hotel's grand picture window. A colorful sunset painted the western horizon, the kind that would soften the hardest of hearts. The sky was cast in a vivid red, and thin clouds shone blue and purple across the red. It was a stunning sight.

"Surely this is a sign," Ginny whispered, as if they were standing in a holy place. "It's God's way of greeting us and telling us we've come to the right place."

A tall, brown-haired man stepped out of the hotel's dining room. "Welcome, folks. I'm Bill Whitmer, and I own this hotel. We get a telegraph letting us know if a train is coming so we can keep the dining room open. Mr. Jones has already arranged rooms for all of you. We can offer you a meal if you want one."

Dakota thought it was about the friendliest welcome he'd ever heard, and he reached out to the stranger to shake his hand. "A meal would be welcome, Mr. Whitmer, and a bed for the night. Thank you."

"Come on in. I've got stew simmering. It's left over from the evening meal, but it gets better with each passing hour so you're in luck."

Dakota saw a Cheyenne newspaper lying on a table in the dining room. He couldn't help but notice a headline in huge print: *Jay Cooke Declares Bankruptcy*. He read the words but didn't pay it much mind.

Ginny saw it too and snatched up the paper. "Jay Cooke?"

Hearing the word *cook* turned Dakota's attention to the stew cooking in the kitchen. It smelled so good his mouth watered, and his stomach growled.

Ginny stood reading the article, her eyes growing big.

Mr. Whitmer rushed into the kitchen and was out with three plates in seconds. The plates were covered with chicken stew with biscuits on the side.

The group took their seats, Dakota somehow ending up next to Maeve again.

Beth took the newspaper from Ginny to take a look for herself. "Jay Cooke is one of the richest men in America. Or at least he was before this. My father used to talk about him with absolute envy. Cooke's bank going under is going to harm a lot of people."

"It says there," Ginny said, referring to the article, "that he gave out loans for hundreds of millions of dollars to fund the building of a northern line for the Union Pacific. It was supposed to span the Territory of Dakota." She glanced at Dakota. "Aren't you from there? Have you heard of this, a railway track going across that part of the country?"

Dakota shook his head. "I'm from there, but I haven't been home in an age. I heard there was a southern route planned across Texas and Arizona. Following the Santa Fe Trail. I can't imagine they'd need another one, let alone two."

Ginny gestured toward the paper, still in Beth's hands. "The whole of the eastern half of the United States is crisscrossed with train tracks. Thousands of miles of them connecting nearly every city. It stands to reason they'd want to lay a lot of tracks in the West, too. But now with Cooke going bankrupt, it'll crash the entire financial market."

Dakota wasn't sure what it was she was talking about so he didn't comment, but one look at Ginny, one moment listening to her somber tone, and he could tell it was bad. Just how rich was this Cooke anyway?

"It'll cause a recession," Ginny added.

Another word Dakota didn't recognize. As long as it didn't bother the wild mustangs on his land, he couldn't see how it could hurt him. "What's a recession exactly?" he wanted to know.

"Jobs will dry up," she answered, "in New York and all along the railroads. And if New York has a recession, it will damage every big city in this country, and plenty of little ones. Lots of banks will fail. Very likely including the banks here in Cheyenne. When jobs are lost, the people who had those jobs aren't earning money anymore, which means they aren't spending money. That hurts everybody." Ginny shuddered, looking more and more grim. "Before long, it'll affect every town in the country."

Mr. Whitmer returned carrying three more plates of food. "I've got more, so all of you have as much as you want. And there's milk for the little ones, fresh-brewed coffee for the grown-ups. Go on and eat. I'll fetch your drinks, another bowl of stew, and more biscuits. There's custard pie, too. Enough for everyone to have a slice." He smiled, then hurried back toward the kitchen.

After Whitmer had left, Oscar said, "You know, there

was talk that Rutledge was overextended, even before we left to come west."

Ginny blinked. "There was?"

"Yep, and that was before the fire. I didn't see how it affected him, but it must have."

"I heard the rumors, too," Kat said. "Nearly every building he owned burned to the ground. Of course, he'd have them insured, and he started building again immediately. But if this news"—her expression said she didn't know who Cooke was either—"stirs things up badly enough, Thaddeus Rutledge could be wiped out entirely."

Oscar growled, "Might make him even more desperate to get ahold of you, Ginny, and your money."

"Or if this thing hits your husband hard enough," Dakota said, "maybe he'll finally have to quit hunting for you. He won't be able to afford to pay all his agents."

"No, he'll be more determined than ever." Ginny frowned as she chewed. Then she looked at what she was eating and brightened. "This coq au vin is perfectly cooked."

Dakota nodded, a bit confused. "If your husband is so overextended, how could he find the money to be 'more determined'?" Dakota wanted to hear all the details of Ginny's troubles, but right now he wished he could concentrate on this stew. It was nothing like any chicken stew he had before. And the sauce was about the most flavorful concoction he'd ever tasted.

"A man as ruthless as my husband will lie, cheat, and steal before he'll pay what he owes and accept his newfound poverty. He'll use slippery accounting practices, if need be, to hide his trouble. He can get the bank to extend him credit or mortgage any property he has to finance whatever plot he's got going on. He'll leave bills unpaid for purchases while he spreads his money around to various investigators. His creditors are used to waiting patiently when dealing with Thaddeus because he has always in the past paid up. Even if he's broke, I can promise you, he'll find the money to hunt me down. So let's try to have the trial tomorrow, and then we can get back home."

Mr. Whitmer approached with a coffeepot and several tin cups. He poured steaming hot coffee, left the pot on the table, then rushed away again. Soon he was back with three cups of milk.

"This is the most delicious thing I've ever eaten," Dakota said.

Whitmer grinned. "I got the recipe from a man who owns a diner in Pine Valley. He calls it coq au vin. We're having chicken parmesan for the noon meal tomorrow, along with crème brûlée."

"Thank you," said Ginny. "We certainly picked the right hotel."

"Did I hear you say something about a trial?" the man asked.

"Yes. I've got some legal troubles I'd like to bring before a judge."

"Something came up just today," Whitmer said, "and our judge headed west and will be gone awhile. We have a justice of the peace here in town, but the cases stack up. You'll have to wait your turn."

"A town as big as Cheyenne only has one judge and one justice of the peace?" Kat sounded a little put out.

"We're fast-growing, ma'am, but still mighty new. We sometimes have to wait awhile for cases to be heard."

This was going to slow everything down. Even though Dakota didn't know Thaddeus Rutledge and didn't consider him much of a threat—not compared to the men hunting him—still, he sensed the hot breath of Rutledge like the steam from a locomotive.

Thaddeus directed his gaze out the window at the busy people on the street. He sat in the closest thing to a comfortable chair, his leg propped up, a constant ache in all his joints, and contemplated owning Omaha.

It wasn't Chicago. Not a real city, but there was money to be made here, and idleness had never suited him. His head buzzed with ideas for buying up property. Renting out tenements. Chances are he had enough money to put a down payment on something. But first he'd need to find a banker who wasn't well connected to the financial world outside of Omaha.

He'd use the first banker by telling a few tall tales, delivered with the cold confidence he'd always been able to summon when talking business. Soon the banks around town would know they were dealing with a man of consequence, and they'd fall over themselves loaning him enough money to finance properties all over Omaha.

Thaddeus would rebuild his wealth by leveraging his iron will and sharp skills. It tasted sweet to think of doing it on his own, without his fool wife's money. He could then let her go, and good riddance. He'd make a life for himself right here in Omaha. In such a backward place they'd be grateful that a successful man with as much knowledge and experience as Thaddeus Rutledge would deign to settle in their midst and help them run the town right.

He could be among the most influential men in town before long. For he knew how to present himself as much richer than he truly was. No banker would look at him for more than a minute and not see he was dealing with a rich, powerful man.

At the thought of what kind of impression he'd make on a banker, Thaddeus glanced down at his suit. He'd brought it and one other when he'd left Chicago. Both were a bit stained and worn and sadly out of date. He hadn't been to a tailor in a while. In Chicago, the one he preferred had become obstinate and downright rude about extending credit. And there hadn't been time for such a thing as finding a good tailor here in Omaha.

Thaddeus knew he looked a bit ragged these days, which was another thing he blamed Ginny for. His hair had gone white as the years passed, and the burden of searching for her had curved his shoulders downward. Pain had carved lines into his face. His hair could use a trim, as he'd neglected barbering for some time now.

Maybe he should get himself a new suit and a haircut to project the right image. Then he'd just see about settling into this cow town. He could do it. Be a big man around here.

His eyes landed on a newspaper next to him. He'd been exhausted since arriving in Omaha—the trip had been a terrible strain—and he'd been paying little attention to the outside world. It wasn't until today that he felt rested enough to contemplate such things as taking over this backwater of a city. His eyes scanned the front-page headlines:

Jay Cooke Bankruptcy Rocks Financial World
Wall Street Panic-Stricken

Jay Cooke! Thaddeus knew him . . . that is, Thaddeus knew *of* him. Jay Cooke was one of the top men in New York. He'd borrowed millions to build a railroad and had been seeking additional millions from his European connections.

Now bankrupt.

Thaddeus wasn't surprised to read that Wall Street was in a panic. He relished the thought of an arrogant man like Cooke having gone bankrupt. Thaddeus always enjoyed it when other people faced hard times.

The amusement didn't last more than a few moments, though, because Thaddeus knew what was likely to happen next.

Jay Cooke was too big, too powerful. When someone like him went under, he dragged lots of others under with him. No doubt this news would kick up a recession that might very well set the whole country back. Banks all over the nation would struggle to remain open.

Thaddeus's pulse sped up. He had to get to the bank here in Omaha before it failed. Get his money out. Once those doors locked, the money would be gone for good.

He'd go today. Get as much gold coins as he could back into his possession. He'd make it. It would take a bit of time for Cooke's troubles to reach out this far, but it would get here. Omaha's banks would soon close, and when they did, there would be no mortgages given. And that would put to death his plans to build his own wealth in Omaha.

His stomach twisted, for the way out of his financial

malaise had just vanished, as if some magician had done a trick and made his future prospects disappear.

He remembered how Eugenia's father had invested his money. It had been managed conservatively, and there was no debt he knew of to be called in. No mortgage held by a collapsing bank that would drag the Wyse fortune under with it. In fact, just as Eugenia had come out of the Great Chicago Fire richer than ever, she'd now possess one of the few solvent fortunes in America. Wyse hadn't held debt, and he hadn't held stock for any company that might go out of business.

All of his wife's wealth would survive, probably double. He'd liked the idea of wheeling and dealing his way back to wealth on his own, but those plans had just gone down in flames along with Jay Cooke. Getting his hands on Eugenia's money was now Thaddeus's best chance to build a promising future for himself. A financial panic could drag on for years. He needed the money Eugenia had stolen from him. He had to find her.

His scheming cut off as he glimpsed a man striding down the street, who turned at the walkway leading to his rented house. The man wore a long leather coat that looked to have been made by hand. His hat was one of those Stetsons. He had a holster strapped low on his hips with a pistol riding by his right hand.

What could this stranger want? What business did he have here in Omaha?

Had Thaddeus's Chicago creditors tracked him down? Had they sent one of their men to demand a reckoning? His heart started racing again.He eyed the pistol and considered the fact that he lived in a far more lawless town out here in the West than when living in Chicago. And he hadn't made any arrangements, as he had in Chicago, to make a quick and quiet escape if the need arose for one.

A hard rap at the door jerked Thaddeus's head around, and he braced himself to leap out of his chair and run. But he was a man who ran too slowly these days.

It was only seconds before Sykes emerged from the back of the house. He paused in the doorway to the sitting room where Thaddeus spent his days.

"Find out who it is," Thaddeus said, "and what it is he wants. I don't care what he says—I won't see anyone."

Sykes nodded and moved to the front door.

There was the low murmur of voices, for far too long. He heard Sykes speak only one word loud enough to understand: "Where?"

Thaddeus began to itch from the wait and considered rising from his chair to see what was going on. Before he could get up, the door closed and Sykes came back into the sitting room. Thaddeus watched their visitor walk away from the house, then disappear from sight around a corner. He turned to Sykes and knew what he was going to say just from the shine in his eyes.

"They found her. Mrs. Rutledge is in Cheyenne, Wyoming."

Thaddeus felt a rush of excitement, quickly followed by irritation. "Cheyenne, Wyoming?"

Sykes walked over to a stack of papers they'd brought with them and tapped his finger on the map he'd pulled to the top. He looked at Thaddeus, the shine in his eyes even brighter. "Cheyenne is right on the railway line now. Only a day's travel away. Two at the most."

With great effort, Thaddeus got up and went to the map. He hurt. His arm, his leg, nearly every joint in his aging body. All that hurt turned to anger at his wife.

He grabbed a sheet of paper and jotted down a note. "Send this telegraph. Wait for a reply. Then hurry back here. Based on what answer you get, we'll know when to leave. I've got one errand to run besides the telegraph. I'll tend to that while you're at the telegraph office. Summon a carriage for me before you leave to send the wire."

He'd put the money in the bank quietly, without Sykes there. And he'd take it out the same way.

"Before the end of the day, we'll buy train tickets and head west. I'll soon be reunited with my troublesome wife. And it's long past time."

11

Brand?" Nell Nolte, justice of the peace of Pine Valley, Wyoming, waved a telegraph at her husband. He rode into town with her most days, then came in again to escort her home.

They'd just reached town on a warm Monday morning, and there'd been a telegraph waiting for her. Going by its address, it looked as if they'd sent this same telegraph to every justice of the peace in the territory in a desperate search for someone to come lend a hand.

School wasn't in session and so their ten-year-old daughter, Michaela, had stayed home. Brand would ride straight back and barely be gone half an hour most days. But today he had a few errands to see to, which was a good thing. Nell caught him before he headed home.

Brand was just stepping out of the general store with a gunnysack of cornmeal in one arm and his little tyke son in the other. "What is it?"

"I want to go to Cheyenne. I'm running low on fabric, and I—"

"Sure, sounds like fun," Brand was quick to reply.

Nell blinked a few times. She realized she was always rushing to explain herself to Brand—a bad habit left over from her days with her first husband, who had to be wheedled into doing anything.

She gathered her thoughts and continued. "The telegraph has been sent all around the territory, looking for a justice of the peace. They had trouble with the judge and the justice of the peace in Cheyenne and are shorthanded. It's a good chance for us to go to Cheyenne and do some shopping."

"What case do they need help with?" Brand asked.

"Doesn't say." She looked down at the extremely short telegraph as if some further explanation might appear. Which of course it did not. "I don't care honestly." She grinned at her handsome husband. "The idea of having such a good reason to go to Cheyenne just seems providential. I have to let them know right away. They'll take the first judge who contacts them. We'd have to ride on horseback to the nearest station and catch the train. But we can get to Cheyenne fast—if a train comes through in a timely manner, of course."

Brand nodded. "Let's go right now and see if you can make it in time." They hurried toward the telegraph office.

"This has happened before," said Nell, "and I think they have a hard time getting anyone to travel. I suspect I won't have any trouble getting there in time."

Once at the office, she sent the wire and then got a reply almost as soon as the telegraph quit clicking on her end. She read it quick. "They say I've got the job and to get there as soon as possible."

"Does it say how long they want you for?"

Nell shook her head. "Most trials take a day, maybe two, so we shouldn't be gone long."

Both of their older girls were now married and to brothers. The three families shared work all the time when help was needed. Leland and Samantha and their two little ones might move out to the Nolte homestead while Nell and Brand were away. All three homesteads were within a short distance of each other.

"Head home and start getting ready," Nell said. "Michaela should come with you. She'll like visiting Cheyenne, and she can help me pick out fabric. I'll pack my robe and gavel and a change of clothes. I just finished making a new dress. Tell Michaela to pack her Sunday-best blue dress and her pink gingham. And some clothes for Buck, too. I'll tell Mariah what's going on. I should be ready by the time you and Michaela get back to town."

Since it was before the noon meal, her friend Mariah Roberts would be over helping Clint in the kitchen, so it would be easy to pop in there with the news of her travel plans. Nell grinned to think of how fast a body could race across the country since the train had gone through. Though it was a long horseback ride to the nearest train station, it was nothing like coming all the way here from Missouri in a covered wagon.

"I'll be back in an hour, and we can hit the trail." Brand jogged toward the horse he'd just rode in on, swung up into the saddle, and galloped out of town.

Nell had just recently realized a second baby was on the way, but she hadn't told anyone yet. Brand tended to get nervous, as he'd lost his first wife when Michaela was born. Now she was glad she'd waited and didn't have to listen to any fretting about whether she should go for a long ride through wild country.

As she rushed to the diner, she wondered what case was so important they couldn't just leave whoever they'd arrested in jail until the judge was available. She hoped it was something interesting. More than that, she hoped it wasn't anything too nasty. She'd never had to sentence anyone to hang.

Once the Deadeye Gang had been cleared out, they'd found their little part of the world to be a law-abiding place.

With a silent prayer asking God to give her wisdom in her judgments, she entered the diner. The place was quiet now that the breakfast crowd had mostly finished. A few stragglers lingered over their cups of coffee.

Nell hurried into the steamy kitchen, struck by the aroma of whatever delicious breakfast Clint had cooked up.

Mariah was herding her son and had her daughter in her arms while still managing to help clean up the kitchen.

"I've got a special request to see to a case in Cheyenne. Brand and I are riding for the train as soon as he gets back to town. He's going to bring Michaela if she wants to go." Very rarely did any of them do such a thing as travel. Nell half expected Mariah to ask to come along. Instead, she seemed content to listen to Nell telling her about it.

"And you don't know what case you'll be hearing?" Mariah asked.

"No, but it sounds important, or they wouldn't be sending wires searching for a justice of the peace. I suspect it will be an interesting case."

Mariah smirked. "You just want to go shopping in a bigger town, admit it."

"Just good timing. Do you have anything you need? You could make a list."

Mariah looked at Clint. He smiled. "Nothing for me. My garden is producing. My animals are thriving. I can't think of anything in the world I need that isn't right here in this kitchen." He went to Mariah and slid an arm around her waist and hugged her briefly. Then he dashed back to the stove to block their youngest from playing with the nice red-hot coals.

Mariah said, "Well, you can get me some bright blue wool fabric. I want a new dress for winter."

Nell almost jumped up and down with glee. She so enjoyed sewing pretty dresses. "Oh, Mariah, that color will look beautiful on you! If you think of anything else you want, let me know."

"Most things can be ordered through the general store, so we have no great needs." Mariah scooped up Buck as he tore past her. She kissed him noisily on the neck while he giggled and squirmed. "Have a good time in Cheyenne."

Nell hoped to find a wide selection of fabrics, and she hoped this wasn't a case that would cause her any misgivings.

12

It echoed in Maeve's ears—as well as in her heart and soul—that Ginny's case was going to change the world. And Maeve would be here to witness it.

They had to put an end to the law allowing a husband to commit his wife to an insane asylum. As it was now, the law decreed that a judge and a doctor needed to declare a person insane before they could be locked up—with the exception of wives. If a husband declared his wife to be insane, no law prevented him from having her locked away. At least that was the case in Chicago. In Wyoming Territory, where women had more rights than in any other place in the country, they would plead for a judge to hear Ginny's case and rule that she was indeed sane. Her husband couldn't take away all her rights as an American citizen without a ruling in a court of law.

Of course, it had helped that Kat and Sebastian were in Cheyenne. They'd been able to write letters and make arrangements. Ginny had the moral support of a pair of highly respected local citizens, who could find a lawyer to represent Ginny at the trial. Kat and Sebastian had hired a doctor to examine Ginny. The doctor would act as a witness, giving his expert opinion in court about her sanity.

It was all so infuriating. A person should be *assumed* to be sane. If someone claimed she was not, they should have to prove it. Instead, because of the cruelty and injustice of the law, it was the opposite.

But maybe not after they had the trial. Maybe it was just the first time, and maybe it was just in a small way, but this trial could change the world. And it would set Ginny free to live her life without fear. Then, once free, she wanted to help other people who'd been committed to an asylum unfairly.

Seven days they'd been waiting in bustling Cheyenne. In that time, Beth had insisted they all carry guns on them, Maeve included. She had something Dakota scoffed at and called a "peashooter," which she had in a holster strapped around her ankle. She'd even taken some shooting lessons.

Ginny kept a gun in her reticule, but she was so tied up in knots that she could barely think. The whole idea had been to get their case heard and ruled on without Thaddeus Rutledge finding out about it. But he had men everywhere, and the days seemed to be passing so slowly.

The waiting was nearly over, however. Word had come that a justice of the peace was on his way to rule over the trial. Maeve hoped they'd be done and out of here very soon. She stepped out of the hotel and looked around. The sun was shining in Cheyenne, a beautiful day in late September. Maeve had on her green dress, and she always felt good when she wore it.

New buildings were going up everywhere. The state

representatives were in town for the territorial session. There was a strong sense of growth in town, the feeling of a bright future ahead for everyone. Rumors of a train spur spreading out from the main Transcontinental line had been circulating among the townsfolk, although Ginny said all that talk would end with Jay Cooke's bankruptcy.

Maeve had a hard time believing that one man's financial woes could harm a whole country. But Ginny seemed to know such things, and Maeve had to admit she didn't.

It was Monday morning. As she studied the town, staring in wonder at all the activity around her, a light breeze that hinted at the approach of fall mussed her tightly bound hair just enough to let a few of her corkscrew curls free.

People rushed along in wagons and on horseback. Mothers walked their children to school with quiet chatter, their footsteps echoing off the boardwalks that lined the businesses along the street. A bell rang, out of sight but not far away, and the children picked up their pace and ran toward the sound, leaving their mothers behind. Wagons and horses stood idle where they'd been tied to hitching posts.

Someone had told her more than two thousand people lived in Cheyenne. Maeve had passed through some big cities on her way west. They'd first come ashore in America in New York City, and the size of it had overwhelmed her. Da had headed straight for a livery and purchased a wagon. Before long they'd put all the hectic activity behind them.

It wasn't her only look at a city. They'd left Ireland from Dublin, the port nearest their home, and Dublin teemed with people. So many of them on the same trek away from the hunger of their homeland.

From New York they'd trundled their way to bustling St. Louis and from there to Independence, Missouri. There Da had outfitted their two covered wagons and bought the oxen and supplies they'd need to head west on the wagon train. Because Da had pushed so hard, they'd been in the first wagon train in the spring. The wilderness had shocked her with its contrast to New York City and St. Louis. Maeve had felt so alone in their little caravan west.

But the crowds that had pressed against Maeve during her long journey here hadn't done so for long because she and her family were always traveling on. Now, though, they'd finally stopped. And it felt good to settle on a homestead, in a new land, and to stay in one spot.

Cheyenne amazed her. Over two thousand people, all living and working together, somehow managing to get along. Within sight of their hotel, she saw a general store, a dry-goods store, a carpenter shop, a land office, a post office, a blacksmith shop, a store boasting of leather goods right beside a dress shop with a ready-made dress hanging in the front window. It might have been that very shop where Beth had bought her pretty new dress.

Customers bustled in and out of the shops, calling out greetings to friends, waving with friendliness to those who passed them. Beyond everything already built, there was construction in progress everywhere and talk of a courthouse and a city hall being added to the splendid city.

Maeve was curious about it all. She'd like to walk the streets of Cheyenne and act as if she had somewhere to go and was far too rushed to pay attention to the other folks jostling and sweeping past. She'd like to wander slowly by the windows displayed with goods, even go inside and touch fine fabric and smell spices and leather and perfume.

While she enjoyed all this life and activity, at the same time she itched from the delay in the trial. She missed her quiet life back in Idaho. She wasn't sure how those two went together. But when she thought of back home, she remembered her ma remarrying and didn't want to go back.

Was it already over with? Would Maeve return home to find Bruce living in her house? And find Donal, who was younger than Maeve, married and settled into adult life?

Maybe she should stay right here in Cheyenne. She wasn't looking forward to returning home only to find her life so completely changed. Here in Wyoming, she could find a job. Perhaps Kat could help her with that.

Maeve had never had much schooling, and her reading and arithmetic skills were minimal, which meant she couldn't be a teacher. Still, there had to be something she could do to support herself. Except she missed her family and wanted to go home. Except she'd find her ma married and find her home invaded.

Shaking her head as if to clear her jumbled thoughts, she looked over her shoulder just as someone emerged from the hotel. They'd been informed that the substitute judge would arrive today on the train, and then they'd finally have the trial. Maeve had heard a train come through just a bit ago and had hoped it was the one carrying the judge. Yet it had come from the east, and the judge was said to be coming from the west.

As Mr. Whitmer served them breakfast, he told them the westbound train had pulled over. Cheyenne was a town equipped with a spur track. The train coming from the west had passed any town with a spur line, so it had right of way this time.

Maeve sent up a prayer of gratitude that the judge would arrive soon. The trial would be held, Ginny's case settled, all without Thaddeus Rutledge getting here to try to stop the trial.

They'd gone to church yesterday after finding out the judge would arrive on Monday. Maeve had prayed fervently for today, as she was sure they all had. She prayed without ceasing. Today they'd fix Ginny's problems and head back to Idaho.

And Maeve would face up to the changes she'd find back home. As she marveled at the frantic pace of Cheyenne and prayed for God to hold them with His protective arms, Ginny came to the door of the hotel and saw Maeve already outside.

"As you know, the judge is to arrive in town real soon," Ginny said from inside. "When the menfolk are done eating, we'll go down and see if my case can get on the docket—if not today, then as soon as possible."

Maeve nodded and leaned against the outside wall of the hotel, enjoying the sunshine. "For your sake, I hope we can have the trial today. Get this over with."

An enclosed buggy rolled up to the hotel, stopping right in front of Maeve and Ginny. Thaddeus Rutledge erupted from the coach and rushed at Maeve. "You there. You're the one I saw with Beth." Then, charging up the steps of the hotel, his eyes landed on Ginny. He reached through the open door with cruel victory etched on his face. "I've got you now." He grabbed her arm.

"Thaddeus, no!" Ginny screamed.

Thaddeus dragged her down the steps toward the buggy. With none of the menfolk outside yet, Maeve threw herself at Rutledge.

"Get your hands off her!" Maeve hit him with all of her strength.

Rutledge, roaring threats, went down.

Maeve jumped on top of the man and punched him squarely in the nose. "Run, Ginny!"

Thaddeus Rutledge had a viselike grip on Ginny, who had tumbled to the ground along with them. She rolled aside and shouted, "Oscar, Jake, Dakota, help!"

Straddling Rutledge, Maeve punched him again and again. He caught her right hand, but he was holding Ginny with his left, so Maeve could keep up her pounding. She struck his chin, his ear, his nose again. Swinging with everything she had. When she hit his nose a third time, she heard a satisfying crunch.

Maeve shouted for Ginny to run while Maeve held him down, but he wouldn't let her go. Finally wrenching herself free, Ginny leapt to her feet and kicked her husband in the head, then the side, trying her best to stop him from hurting Maeve.

"Run, Ginny!" Maeve screamed. "He doesn't want me—he wants *you*."

"No, I'm not letting him hurt any of us again." Ginny kicked Rutledge in the leg, hard.

His roars of anger turned to a cry of pain. He heaved Maeve off him and scrambled away, clutching his leg.

Then the buggy driver entered the fray.

"Get her, Sykes! Get my wife."

The driver wrapped his arms around Ginny and dragged her toward the buggy.

Jake stormed out of the hotel dining room, Beth right behind them. Both had a child in their arms. Oscar was next, holding baby Lydia. These were not people who could offer much help.

Then Dakota came out. He didn't have a baby.

He roared, "Sheriff! Get out here!"

Ginny was almost inside the buggy when Dakota dove off the boardwalk and tackled the driver called Sykes. Both of them went down in a heap. Ginny, holding on to the buggy to keep herself from being taken, stayed upright.

Dakota slammed a fist into Sykes's face. Ginny broke free of the fracas and dashed away toward Beth.

Maeve staggered to her feet as Dakota and Sykes rolled toward her and knocked her down again.

A man wearing a silver star came running down the boardwalk.

"She's my *wife*," Rutledge protested. "I have a right to take her home with me." Still clutching his leg, he struggled to get to his feet.

Sykes, a rough-looking customer wearing two guns, tossed Dakota aside and advanced on Ginny. Oscar caught her arm and tucked her behind him.

"Get inside the hotel, Ginny." Dakota lunged to his feet and dodged in front of Sykes.

Thaddeus limped toward Ginny while Sykes became occupied fighting off Dakota, who wasted no time punching Sykes in the face again, then again. He went down hard and knocked into Rutledge, who fell over.

Sykes clawed for his gun. Dakota reached out fast as a

striking snake and yanked both of his six-guns away and tossed them under the boardwalk.

Oscar thrust Lydia into Beth's arms, moved Ginny so she was behind Jake, then rushed down the steps with a look of near-savage glee. Rutledge had just regained his feet. Oscar plowed a fist into Rutledge's belly and knocked him down.

Maeve grabbed Ginny and towed her into the hotel.

Mr. Whitmer set down his armload of tablecloths and came to Ginny, whose torn sleeve was dangling around her wrist, her hair twisted into dusty knots around her shoulders. "What's going on?" he asked.

"That man, the older one," Ginny said and pointed out the window. "He's my husband. He tried to kidnap me right off the streets of Cheyenne. I told you I've had legal trouble, and I wanted a trial to solve it. Well, the legal trouble is that man and his abuse of me."

"Sit down right there." Mr. Whitmer pointed to a table that still had plates of food on it, pretty clearly abandoned by Oscar, Jake, Beth, and Dakota.

Ginny, shaking, said, "He'll take me with him. No judge can stop him."

Maeve took both her arms and turned her to look out the large front windows. They watched the sheriff put shackles on Sykes while Dakota hauled Rutledge to his feet by the back of his neck. Oscar slugged Rutledge one more time, even though the fight was clearly over.

Dakota stepped between Oscar and Rutledge. He was saying the time for punching was over. At least for now.

Maeve noticed that Dakota hadn't been any too quick about stopping Oscar.

The whole group headed for the jailhouse.

"This is Wyoming, ma'am," Whitmer said. "Here, no man touches a woman in violence and claims it as his right. Possibly for the first time ever, a wife has as many rights as her husband. You've come to the best place in the country to solve your problems."

Ginny stood and burst out crying. "Can that be true?"

Watching her husband being hauled off to jail, she said to Maeve, "Is it possible?" Then more quietly, her voice breaking, she added, "I still could be proved insane. And now Thaddeus is here to tell his lies and twist things to his advantage. He is a powerful man with . . ." Ginny fell silent as her eyes darted to a third man, who had just emerged from the buggy. Her face went white, and Maeve caught her before she collapsed.

Maeve eased her into a chair. "What is it, Ginny?"

"That man is one of the most respected doctors in the country when it comes to matters of insanity and caring for people who are proclaimed to be mad."

Maeve looked at the man. He was small of stature, his nose very firmly in the air as he followed Rutledge and Sykes toward the jail. Determination in every step. "Who is he?"

"Dr. Maynard Horecroft," Ginny answered. "He kept me locked up for three years, and he'll testify that I am furiously mad. Add his testimony to Thaddeus's money, and I'm doomed." She bowed her head and wept.

13

Dakota was as mad as a rabid badger.

Rutledge had knocked Maeve to the ground. She'd refused to be shoved aside to let them take Ginny, and they'd been rolling on the ground, fighting.

A quirk of a smile almost escaped. He was pretty sure Maeve had broken Rutledge's nose. Good for her. Then his anger swept back through him. It couldn't be allowed to stand. "I think we should hang them."

The sheriff pushed a shackled Sykes into the jailhouse. Dakota had Rutledge and enjoyed forcing him to walk across the busy streets of Cheyenne to be thrust into jail.

Beth walked with Jake, carrying three babies between them. Oscar, looking furious and ready to swing his fists a few more times, brought up the rear.

Except, no, he didn't bring up the rear. There was one more member of their little parade. A short man, with a bearing that said he was someone to be reckoned with. He'd stepped out of that carriage after the fighting was over. Now he'd followed them to the jailhouse.

At Dakota's perfectly reasonable suggestion of a hanging, the short man sniffed as if Dakota was talking nonsense. Or maybe as if Dakota smelled bad.

He hadn't fought. He hadn't spoken. But he had an arrogance about him and had stood by while Ginny and Maeve were attacked. Dakota thought that made him part of this crime, and he'd've liked to see him in a pair of handcuffs.

The thug Sykes was muscle-bound, dark-haired, and dressed in a suit that didn't look natural to him. Sykes didn't sniff at Dakota's recommendation of a hanging. In fact, he looked downright scared.

The sheriff shoved Sykes through a door behind his desk, into a room with two jail cells. He put Sykes in one while Dakota pushed Rutledge in the other, slamming the door shut with a loud clang of metal on metal. The sheriff twisted the key in one lock after the other, and the men were detained.

Dakota took a long look at Rutledge. He was surprised at just how old the man was. Ginny was a youthful woman who'd passed herself off as Beth's older sister on the wagon train. Dakota had found it believable. But Rutledge wasn't just old, he was ancient. He limped badly, especially favoring one leg, and Dakota had heard he'd been stabbed by Yvette. Rutledge had survived, but not unscathed. He also favored one arm, holding it close to his body every chance he got. He'd sustained injuries that either weren't treated right or had been serious enough he hadn't fully healed.

Dakota thought of Joseph, who was back in Hidden Canyon with an arm he favored. Joseph didn't spare himself much when it came to work. Had Rutledge had an injury like that?

His hair was bone-white and had receded badly. He had a paunch that swelled out, along with a few extra chins. His shoulders were rounded as sometimes happened to old folks. His face was lined with wrinkles that seemed deeper than could be accounted for by age, though Dakota didn't know Rutledge's exact age. But his wrinkles cut deep along lines set by frowning.

Ginny's husband. The man she'd been hiding from for years. He didn't look all that dangerous to Dakota. He'd been losing a fight with Maeve, after all. Still, a man could do harm that went beyond using his fists. Dakota had known men like that. And it was clear that Ginny was terrified of the man.

It wasn't just Ginny either. Oscar had helped Ginny hide, which meant Oscar took Rutledge seriously. Beth and Jake had agreed to their isolated life, so they'd concluded the only safety to be found was in hiding. Ginny might be overly afraid of her husband if he'd abused her, while Oscar looked like he was on edge enough to start shooting.

Jake kept a hawk eye on all three of the newcomers. The little ones had all been brought along to the jail because Ginny was badly shaken and not up to caring for them right now. Maeve too. Both women had been roughed up in the fight, each getting knocked to the ground. Had they been injured? Dakota would make sure they were all right.

Before he could leave, the third man, the short one who hadn't been knocking women to the ground, said, "Mr. Rutledge has done nothing wrong. He is concerned for his wife's well-being. He's been trying to find her ever since she ran away from treatment years ago. His intention is to see her brought back to rational life or, failing that, to see that she is kept safe from her own madness. I believe it isn't possible for her to regain her sanity. Her mind is too badly broken. But Mr. Rutledge has never given up hope that his wife will one day be well again."

The man looked at Rutledge—broken nose, bleeding, coated in dirt from rolling around in the street—and added, "That redhead who attacked him has obviously got her own problems. I've had many occasions to see a woman lose her composure in such a way that she attacks. It's always a sure sign of madness. As a doctor, I can see she's as insane as Ginny. Does Wyoming have proper facilities for the mad? I'd be glad to speak with anyone in a position to commit her. She needs round-the-clock care and to be locked away. She poses a danger, both to herself and to others."

Jake grabbed Dakota's arm just as he swung a fist. A fierce tug ended with Dakota subsiding, glaring at Jake. "No one talks about Maeve O'Toole like that."

JJ bounced in Jake's arms and reached for Dakota to hold him. Jake moved his body just a bit so Dakota couldn't take the little boy. Probably a wise decision.

Beth was holding Maria and Lydia. "No one talks about my mama like that either." Her eyes flashed with anger.

Dakota wondered if Jake was going to have to wrestle his wife next.

Beth said, "I only regret I'm not the one to give you that broken nose, Father. You have had that coming for a long time. I'll go thank Maeve as soon as we're done here."

"Another madwoman," the sniffing man said. "Her father has said she's showing signs of her mother's broken mind."

"Sheriff," Beth said, interrupting the diagnosis, "are you going to keep these men locked up?"

"I am for a fact. You said the trial concerning Ginny is later today. Once that's done, she'll be safe from these sidewinders." The sheriff thrust out a hand to Dakota. "I'm Rex Peters, sheriff of Cheyenne. I appreciate your help getting these men under control."

"Thanks for coming so fast, Sheriff. We all appreciate you stepping in." Dakota shook his hand firmly.

The jail was as new as the rest of the town. Dakota thought the bars looked sufficiently sturdy. He could still smell the raw wood and see sawdust in the corners. Behind the sheriff's desk, a row of guns were locked in a rack on one side of the room. The cells took up the back of the jailhouse.

"I'll unshackle you now that you're behind bars," the sheriff said.

Sykes offered his hands through the bars as if he'd done it a few times before and knew exactly what was expected of him. Dakota studied Sykes more closely. He was a man hired to be the strong arm of Rutledge's will. Who was he? What lay in his past that had trained him so well how to behave behind bars?

Sheriff Peters unlocked the handcuffs. He'd only had one set and used them on Sykes, a decision Dakota approved of, although seeing Rutledge shackled would've been real satisfying.

"I want a doctor. That is, if this one-horse town has such

a thing." Rutledge touched his nose gingerly, then his lip. He pulled out a kerchief to stanch the bleeding.

"He's gonna take one look at you and tell you your nose is broken. Broken by a one-hundred-pound woman who was trying to pull you off your wife when you attacked her. The doc's not gonna do much for you. Waste of his time."

"I demand medical attention, Sheriff." Rutledge slammed the side of his fist against the bars. He flinched and cradled his arm.

Sheriff Peters turned to Horecroft. "Didn't you say you were a doctor? You tend him."

Horecroft sniffed. "I'm not that kind of doctor."

"I am going to make you sorry you locked me up, Sheriff," Rutledge said. "I've been searching for my wife for years. She's a danger to herself. I did *not* attack her. I took her arm, and then that little vermin tackled me with no provocation."

"I suspect she had plenty of provocation," Beth snapped. "Like hearing my mama scream and cry for help and watching her fight my father's hold on her."

Oscar shook his head. "Ginny's been living on her own for years—like you just said, Rutledge. You admit she's been away from you while you searched for her. She hasn't been in a bit of danger—until you showed up." Oscar sounded grim as death. "She's worked hard to cook and sew, to care for her own home. She's as rational as any woman alive, and no doctor can be trusted in his assessment when he's being paid to rule her insane."

Dakota wondered if they should get the children out of there.

"Who's that old man, Mama?" Marie asked.

"That's your grandpa, honey." Beth sounded weary. "Don't expect anything from him. He's not nice like your grandma is."

Marie, with her round, blue eyes, said, "Hi, Grandpa."

JJ bounced in Jake's arms. "Grampy! Grampy! Grampy!" He struggled to get down while Jake held on tight.

Rutledge focused on the little girl, then on the boy in Jake's arms. "You managed to produce a son, Elizabeth? I'd've thought no woman in your mother's line could do that."

"Don't get your hopes up, Rutledge," Jake said. "We're raising him up to be a rancher. He's not going to be interested in being a robber baron or whatever you call yourself."

"Robber baron's about right," Oscar said. "I've heard tenement owner, slumlord, thief, tyrant, cheat, and plenty others."

Rutledge glared at Oscar, then turned back to the sheriff. "I did not harm my wife. I was delighted to see she was alive and well. And because she's run away before, I caught hold of her to take her back with me to a place where she can be properly cared for."

"You mean the Horecroft Insane Asylum." Beth handed Lydia to Oscar and hugged little Marie tight. "A place of horror where my father put my mama against her will without any kind of hearing as to her mental state. My mama, Eugenia Rutledge, is an intelligent, sensible, utterly sane woman. Father's decision to lock her away was because she had inherited money from her parents in such a way that Father couldn't touch it. His cruelty was all based in his demand that she hand over her money to him.

She might have given him the money in exchange for her freedom, but he also demanded that she hand over the money I inherited. She refused and so he locked her up with no trial, no doctor's examination, no proof of her being insane. I would have handed over my inheritance, but I didn't realize that was what he wanted. And I don't think that's all he wanted. He mainly just couldn't stand a woman defying him, so he decided having her own opinion meant she was insane."

"I examined her. She's completely mad." Horecroft checked his watch as if this conversation was a waste of his valuable time.

"Examined her how?" Beth asked. "What tests was she given? I've lived with my mother for four years now, and she's calm and wise. She's a woman to trust and depend on, a woman with a strong faith. She's a hard worker and has a fine intelligence. What tests could you have given her that would say otherwise?"

"I've made sufficient observations. You're in no position to question a well-respected doctor with years of experience."

"We are all going to question everything about you, Horecroft." Beth plunked one fist on her hips while swaying with little Marie in the other arm. "You're a man who's grown wealthy denying citizens their rights. That shouldn't be allowed, and I'm going to see that it's not. In a few years, men like you will be the ones locked up. And in case you haven't noticed, right this moment my father is the one locked up."

Rutledge made a purely rude sound. "Your mother hasn't told you the whole truth, Elizabeth. She needs constant care." He touched his swollen nose again. "That little redhead, probably Irish trash, attacked me. I'll expect her to be arrested before this nonsense is over."

Dakota thought the fool was lucky to have bars between himself and the rest of them. He was glaring at the jail cell and contemplating getting his hands on the key when Sebastian Jones walked in.

14

Kat rushed into the hotel's dining room and went straight for Ginny.

"I saw Dr. Horecroft on the street." Kat sounded frantic as if she might grab Ginny and run.

Maeve couldn't decide whether to stop her from making a run for it or help her. Bruised and filthy, Maeve's green dress was torn at the shoulder and bloodstained. She was pretty sure it was Thaddeus Rutledge's blood, and she rather liked knowing that. She and Ginny were both disheveled, their hair in a tangle and loose when they usually had it bound up.

And they were both coated in dust from tumbling around on the street. In a physical fight. Maeve had never so much as shoved her sister or brothers prior to this. She was still shaken from having attacked Rutledge and punching him. Her hand ached as a result.

Ginny wasn't quite so hurt, but she was pale and shaking so badly that she could hardly breathe. Maeve wasn't so frightened. It was the fury that made her tremble.

"Yes," Ginny replied. "Dr. Horecroft is here with Thaddeus to take me home."

Kat shuddered and pulled out a chair from the table. Maeve, and even more so, Ginny, had been shaking too badly to risk the stairs. Mr. Whitmer had kindly offered to help them to their room. He'd seen how upset they were and knew they would need assistance. They'd asked if they could sit in the hotel's dining room for a while, and he'd left them alone once he was sure they were all right.

Kat angled her chair to face Ginny and sank into it. She rested her hands on Ginny's shoulders. "I know what it took for you to come out of hiding and face the accusations against you. And that was without your husband being involved."

"If anyone knows what it took, it's you, Kat. Having you here in Cheyenne, knowing you'd be able to contact people and make arrangements for me, helped give me the courage to face a judge."

Kat brushed Ginny's bedraggled hair back with gentle hands. "I'll tell you what I told Seb when a man came to our house and tried to kill us."

Ginny gasped and hugged Kat firmly. "You never told me that."

"It's been hard to include everything in a letter. I gave you the highlights."

"And a killer coming after you wasn't a highlight?"

Kat gave a little shrug. "The man ended up dead, and I thought I might be tried for murder. His gun went off while I tried to get away from him. The bullet ricocheted and killed him, but the law only had my word on that.

Thankfully, the law in this state is very kind to women, and it turned out that there was no question I'd be charged for what happened. We also knew—because the man had said so with his dying words—more gunmen would be coming for us. I told Seb we could either stay here and be on our guard for the rest of our lives, or we could turn tail and run back to Hidden Canyon."

Ginny managed a weak laugh. "You two hated that canyon. Beautiful as it is, neither of you are suited for such an isolated life."

After one winter they'd stopped to visit Maeve and her family on their way out. On their way to getting married. Beyond that, they had no idea where they were headed.

"Or," Kat said, easing back in her chair and looking Ginny in the eye, "we could go to Independence. We figured the gunman to be from there, as Seb had told only his lawyers where we were. So we could confront his lawyers, demand to know if they were behind our troubles, and if not them, then who was."

Ginny drew in a shuddering breath.

After a long moment, with Kat holding Ginny's gaze, she went on. "We chose to face our troubles. We decided we didn't want to hide in that canyon anymore. Nor did we want to live on edge for the rest of our lives. We decided to fight back. And you're here because you've chosen to do the same. I'm sure you hoped to get through the trial and receive the obvious and only possible ruling handed down by the judge, deciding once and for all about your sanity. But now Thaddeus is here, and you'll have to carry on with him directly opposing you. Add to that, you'll have to face that awful Dr. Horecroft."

Ginny stared at Kat as if absorbing strength from her. Maeve remembered Kat from their journey west on the wagon train. A quiet woman, Kat had been the one who knew just what to do when they had the accident with the O'Toole wagon. It was Kat who'd gotten Ma breathing again. Others, copying Kat's movements, had gotten Bridget and Conor breathing again.

They'd been too late for Da, but not for lack of trying. Maeve remembered the day well, every last detail—kneeling at her ma's side, working over her as Kat gave instructions. Sebastian had watched what they were doing and rushed to work on reviving Da, but to no avail.

Kat was quiet, though underneath she was strong. While Ginny drew on that strength, Maeve found herself doing the same, or rather finding strength of her own.

"It's an ugly business, Ginny," Kat said, "but you'll find a way to face up to it. I know you will."

Maeve watched Ginny's shuddering stop, her spine stiffen, her shoulders square. Then fire flashed in her eyes, matching Kat's.

Kat gave Ginny all the time she needed. She looked at Ginny with eyes that searched deep. At last, the strength of that gaze changed to satisfaction.

"You'll face up to it and you'll win," Kat added. "I'll stand beside you, add my voice to yours about how you were mistreated in that asylum. And I'd be honored to swear before a judge that your kindness and strength helped many women cling to sanity while Dr. Horecroft did his best, day after day, to drive us all mad."

Ginny rose to her feet.

Maeve was delighted to see how steady she was now.

Before Kat had gotten there, Maeve wasn't sure Ginny's shaking knees would have allowed her to stand.

With a sigh of pleasure, Maeve knew Kat had done some doctoring here in this hotel dining room. If only those women still locked away as they were in the asylum could be given the wisdom and care of Kat Jones. She should be a doctor. In fact, she should run that asylum. And, Maeve suspected, Kat's first act would be to let most of the women there go on home.

"I'm going up to my room now to wash up, fix my hair, and put on a clean dress. You're right, Kat. It's time I face up to Thaddeus and his ill-treatment of me."

Kat was dressed beautifully, though in a comfortable blue calico dress. But it was clean and unfaded. No ripped seam or bit of dust anywhere. She wore no bonnet, leaving her golden hair to gleam in plain sight. It was tied back in a neat bun, not a strand out of place—a strong reminder that Ginny and Maeve weren't so presentable. No decent woman would step out in public in such disarray.

"No." Kat shook her head. "Let's leave you coated in dirt. I think the sheriff needs to see you like that." She turned to Maeve. "And your dress was torn? I heard there was a tussle, but we got there after everything was over, and I've heard no details of what occurred. No woman here has been mistreated in such a way as you two were, not in Cheyenne. Sheriff Peters needs to see both of you just as you are."

The jailhouse door flew open. Ginny led the way in, striding straight into the back room. Eyes flashing, Maeve came in right behind her, Kat next.

Dakota wondered what had happened. Ginny seemed all right now, while only moments ago she'd seemed near collapse. Her skin had been as pale as milk. Her body was racked with shudders, and her eyes were brimming with tears.

Now she looked like she was leading soldiers into war. Her cheeks were flushed and pink, her hands fisted as if she were looking for someone to fight.

Maeve was still dusty from the tussle with Rutledge. Her left sleeve was torn nearly off at the shoulder. She had blood on one fist and a splatter of it on the front of her dress. With cold satisfaction, Dakota knew none of that blood was hers.

Ginny ignored everyone in the room and walked right up to the iron bars confining her husband. "I'm glad you're here, Thaddeus."

Dakota jumped. Everyone in the room jumped except Kat and Maeve, but then they probably knew what had happened to transform a terrified woman into a warrior.

Oscar's fists clenched.

Rutledge's eyes went wide. "You are?"

"Yes, I am. I have allowed your cruel treatment of me for too long. Today we settle things once and for all."

Oscar's fists unclenched. Satisfaction shone in his eyes.

The whole back room of the jail was crowded with Jake's family, three little ones included. Add in Kat and Sebastian, the two prisoners, Dr. Horecroft, and of course Sheriff Peters. There was barely enough room to move. And yet Ginny had cut through the crowd like a razor-sharp knife. Her only goal to look her husband right in the eye and stand strong against him.

"Today I will be found sane, Thaddeus. Today your time of ruling over my life like some cruel despot is over. Today you will be sent home to Chicago, and we will see each other for the last time." Ginny's eyes narrowed as if she were just now really seeing her husband. "What happened to you? You look terrible. And it's not just your bleeding face."

Dakota had noticed, too.

"What's the matter with your arm?"

Kat, standing just behind Ginny, her arms crossed, said, "He broke it when Seb tossed him off a train."

Ginny glanced at Sebastian and nodded, pleased with him. She turned back to Rutledge. "And what's wrong with your leg?"

His lips twisted into a snarl.

"I was told he was already limping when staying in Independence," Kat said. "That was last year. I did some investigating into your husband. He came back from his trip to Idaho sewn up in a dozen places and with his leg cut up badly by Yvette."

"Yvette did that to your leg?"

Rutledge remained silent, glaring at her, his eyes angry.

"Well, good for her," Ginny said, her focus still on her husband. "Your suit is too tight. You've gotten fat, Thaddeus, and your hair has gone all white. Your shirt is dirty, too. I suppose it got stained when you attacked me the moment you saw me, and you ended up on the ground. But it's more than stained. Your suit looks worn and shabby, and your shoes are scuffed. I've never seen you with other than perfectly polished shoes. This isn't all the result of a scuffle with my little Irish friend." Ginny gave Maeve an approving nod. "I do believe you've fallen on hard times, and not just since Jay Cooke's bankruptcy little more than a week ago."

Rutledge finally piped up. "It's been a bad time financially, but nothing unusual. And things will come around for Cooke—he's too smart a man to be kept down for very long."

"I'm sure in time Jay will recover, but what about you? Have you convinced yourself that whatever financial ruin you're facing will come right?"

"Of course it will come right, you fool woman." Rutledge took a step closer to the bars. His limp was pronounced. "You can count on it."

Kat moved to stand beside Ginny, shoulder to shoulder. The two of them faced Rutledge together. Kat said, "You've shut yourself away from the world to hide from this wretched man?"

Ginny nodded.

Sebastian drifted forward to be with Kat, making it a foursome, all of them staring down Rutledge.

"Well, I haven't been shut away," said Kat. "I have friends in Chicago. Your husband has for a fact fallen on hard times. He's lost nearly everything. His creditors came calling a month or more ago. He ran."

Oscar nodded and said, "Word has it he was on shaky ground even before that. I'm not surprised to hear he's used up all his chances. Chicago burned nearly all the way to the ground two years ago. Several of your husband's tenements went up in smoke."

"I was insured," Rutledge sneered. "I rebuilt."

"Right," Kat went on, "and he rebuilt using shoddy

material. He crowded in as many tiny, badly ventilated rooms as he could and with no regard for the fire laws, which Chicago has now. Then he raised rents even higher. Even with insurance to help, he ended up with buildings mortgaged to the hilt. His creditors forced him to sell, but even then he was left drowning in debt. He lost his shares in nearly every company he was invested in. His own home burned to the ground."

Ginny gasped and took a half step closer to Rutledge. "Our beautiful home burned down?"

Dakota thought she was too close and opened his mouth to warn her, tell her to move back a bit.

"You were never going to be allowed to live in it again." Rutledge narrowed his eyes. "Now, that's enough about my finances."

Kat ignored him. "He built himself a larger mansion, no shoddy construction there. Only the best for Thaddeus Rutledge. The biggest house in the best part of town. It's also heavily mortgaged. I heard he left town through his back door while his creditors were howling at his front door."

"You've got no business prying into my financial affairs." Rutledge reached through the bars with a sudden, violent motion. He latched on to Kat's arm and dragged her toward him.

Kat cried out and stumbled into the bars, banging her head against the iron with a sickening thud.

Sebastian leapt forward and wrenched Rutledge's hand away from Kat.

Ginny shoved at her husband, shouting, "Get your hands off of her!"

"Stay back, ladies. We can't trust him to behave decently." The sheriff pushed in between the women and Rutledge. He faced the women, his back to Rutledge.

"I'll not have that woman gossiping about my personal life to anyone who'll listen."

Sebastian grabbed Rutledge by the front of his stained shirt and pulled him hard against the cell door. Rutledge's head gave a satisfying thud to match Kat's.

"No man around here puts his hands on a woman like that—not without *consequences*." Sebastian gave Rutledge a forceful shove back into the cell.

Dakota looked at the sheriff, who seemed unconcerned about what was going on behind him with his prisoner.

Oscar came to Sebastian's side. Jake urged Kat and Ginny to step back a few more paces.

"If she spreads such lies about me," Rutledge growled, "she'll come to regret it. No decent woman would say such things."

Sebastian balked at Rutledge's statement. "There is no more decent woman in Wyoming than my wife. And if you dare to say different, you'll be begging Sheriff Peters here to keep you locked up because a jail cell is the only place where you'll be safe from those consequences I mentioned."

The sheriff tipped his hat to Sebastian. "Nicely put."

Maeve smiled, and Dakota watched the tension ease in Kat's face, then Ginny's. Maeve slung an arm around Ginny and whispered loud enough for everyone to hear, "You did a terrible job picking a husband, Ginny."

A laugh escaped from Ginny, and she hugged Maeve back. "I did for a fact."

Kat went right back to sharing her tales of Rutledge's money troubles. "Chicago was on its way to being rebuilt, but now Jay Cooke's bank failed. It will throw everyone into a panic. Banks are closing all over New York and Chicago. They'll no doubt fail in San Francisco, St. Louis, Philadelphia, Denver, and Boston. They're calling it the 'Panic of '73.' They're going to stop building the railroads because Cooke was funding all of that. Men are losing their jobs left and right. Whole towns will fold up and die. Your husband, with very little left, will lose the last of his wealth."

Kat turned to glare at Horecroft. "You can only be here for the money. Well, I can promise you, Thaddeus Rutledge doesn't have any. He's probably told you he will get lots of money when he regains control of his wife. He will *not* gain control of Ginny, and he will *not* get her money."

Dr. Horecroft sneered. "Why on earth would I take the word of a madwoman like you, Mrs. Jones? Your husband may be willing to put up with an asylum escapee. I've heard women are scarce out here in the West, so he may feel like he can't do any better."

Sebastian took an aggressive step toward Horecroft, who ducked behind Sheriff Peters.

"But when we have this trial," Horecroft said from his hiding place, "you can be sure I'll have ready the testimony and paperwork necessary to get Mrs. Rutledge back to a place where she can receive the best care. And that's the Horecroft Insane Asylum in Chicago." Horecroft turned his attention to Rutledge. "Now, I have matters to prepare for the trial. I will see all of you in court."

Rutledge nodded with such confidence that Dakota felt his first qualm of worry. What did these two have planned?

Horecroft left the room in double-quick time as if he was a very busy man. Dakota thought it looked more like he was running away. But to where?

Kat shot Rutledge a look. "You should've been locked up after you kidnapped me in Independence. But that was two years ago, before the fire. Back then you could still afford to buy your way out of trouble. And that was in Missouri. You should know we take a much dimmer view of men assaulting women in the West. I think this time we should just toss you in the territorial prison, along with Mr. Sykes here—who was involved in my kidnapping—and let you both grow old and die in there."

"This man kidnapped you, Mrs. Jones?" The sheriff's bulldog face turned back to scowl at Rutledge.

Kat nodded firmly. "He most certainly did. And he paid off lawmen and judges and politicians all over Missouri. He contacted the governor and donated generously to his next run for office. He managed to stay out of jail. But he can no longer afford to bribe the authorities. His crimes are now catching up to him. If he tried to kidnap Ginny and assaulted Maeve, and this man Sykes helped him in doing so, they should both be locked up, just as Mr. Rutledge here formerly locked up his wife."

"Sounds like he's made a habit of kidnapping women," Maeve said, frowning at Rutledge. "He shouldn't be allowed to walk around free. Nor should Mr. Sykes be free."

Sykes blanched. Here was a man who knew trouble with the law could cause a man heaps of pain. Yet Rutledge just narrowed his eyes and looked at all of them with great contempt.

Dakota didn't like a bit of it.

15

"You folks go on out of here now." The sheriff gestured toward the door. "Your mister will be kept locked up, Mrs. Rutledge."

Thaddeus Rutledge coughed as if to get everyone's attention. "I insist on being allowed to attend the trial. I came all this way, and now my wife is making a mockery of the care I've provided for her. The trial can't go on without me there to tell my side of what's happened. Dr. Horecroft is right now searching for a lawyer who will represent me. I *will* be at this trial."

Sheriff Peters, his arms crossed, studied Rutledge for a long moment. "All right. I reckon you should be at the trial. I'll go along and stand guard. It'll be good practice for you for when your own trial date comes along. Maybe we can get this same judge to sentence you to prison as long as he's here."

Rutledge didn't even blink. "Good. And it appears I'm the one who needs to be guarded in this town. I'll welcome your protection, Sheriff."

The sheriff rolled his eyes, then turned his back on Rutledge and walked with the rest of them the few paces it took to reach the door. "You folks don't go far. I may have more questions for you."

Beth quietly said, "I've asked at the hotel if we can use the dining room to gather because none of us has a room large enough. Mr. Whitmer has been very generous."

Maeve had seen a few coins pass from Beth to the hotel owner yesterday. She suspected it was Beth who'd been so generous.

While the sheriff gave them a few more warnings, Maeve remembered Rutledge's accusations about her tackling him, which she had. But he was trying to kidnap Ginny. It had to be legal for Maeve to step in to prevent Rutledge from hauling Ginny away against her will, even if force had been needed to do it.

If they couldn't accuse the man of assaulting Maeve—since she had most certainly assaulted him first—then they'd accuse him of kidnapping. Was it legal to kidnap your own wife? Being an honest woman, Maeve hadn't had much experience with the law. The law seemed so confusing at times like this.

Maybe it wasn't too late to arrest Rutledge for kidnapping Kat back in Missouri. Could they prove that Rutledge had made a habit of kidnapping women? Surely that was worse than doing it just once. Yet even once was a hanging offense, wasn't it? And Rutledge's man Sykes had helped, so that made him an accomplice. If they couldn't see them hanged, then the two men should at the very least spend the rest of their lives in the territorial prison. As long as they were at it, she wished they'd toss that arrogant Dr. Horecroft in prison, too.

Maeve's thoughts were in a turmoil as she walked with the others back to the hotel. Beth led the way into the dining room. Mr. Whitmer came and served everyone coffee and offered them cobbler. They thanked him and accepted the coffee, but no one was up to eating.

The men hadn't finished their breakfast, which was still half-eaten on the table. Whitmer cleared the dishes away and left them alone.

"I'm going to change out of this dress and get my hair back under control." Maeve got a few nods, then left the room. She barely noticed Dakota following her out. At the base of the stairs, she stopped and looked at him. "What are you doing?"

"I'll just walk upstairs with you, make sure the room isn't occupied. I don't know where Horecroft went, but you could be in danger."

Maeve looked past Dakota's shoulder to the open door to the dining room. Whispering, she said, "I got mixed up in that fight, but all the trouble is aimed at Ginny. I think instead of worrying about me, you should stay down here and guard her."

"Horecroft is likely looking for a lawyer for Rutledge, but then we have only a dishonest man's word on that. I don't trust Horecroft, not after the way Rutledge talked about you."

"What did he say?"

"He questioned your sanity, of course. The man seems to go straight to that conclusion with any woman who gives him the least bit of trouble." A smile crept onto

Dakota's face. "I saw with my own eyes how many times you punched him. I'd say that qualifies as trouble."

Maeve nodded. "Well, the man deserved it. I was happy to break his nose. Someone needed to, after the way he's treated Ginny."

"Yep, you didn't leave much of him for Oscar, but enough. Oscar hit Rutledge as if he'd been saving it up for years. I've never seen him so angry."

"I'm glad he got a chance to work some of that anger off. And you took care of Sykes. We all held up when trouble came, didn't we?" She looked up the stairs. "Do you really think Horecroft might be up there with evil plans for me?"

Dakota shrugged one shoulder. "You or Ginny. You share a room. Let me just check to make sure it's safe."

Maeve nodded and led the way upstairs. "Rutledge mentioned me, did he? Before I got there?"

"He said something about you being redheaded Irish trash."

Maeve, outraged, turned on Dakota, who flashed a wide smile even as he held his hands up as if in surrender. "Don't look at me like that. I didn't say it—Rutledge did."

She stormed up the rest of the steps, stopping outside her room and rather grandly gesturing toward it. "Go on and check, Dakota, and don't forget to look under the bed. A rodent like Horecroft might be hiding there."

Dakota stepped forward. When he was even with Maeve, he said quietly, "You're ten times the person Rutledge will ever be. Calling you names and pegging you and Ginny as insane is proof he's a foolish man. He's been throwing his money away searching for his wife. He's been hurt three times now as he searched for her. He's too arrogant and, honestly, too stupid to just give up and admit the money he wants to steal from Ginny isn't his to take."

"Ten times?" Maeve looked up at Dakota and remembered, before Da had died, there'd been a bit of interest that passed between them.

"One hundred times. You're a fine, smart, hardworking woman. This country needs you more than it needs Rutledge."

He reached out for what had to be a rat's nest of hair and tugged on one of her many corkscrew curls. "And I love your red hair and the pretty Irish lilt in your voice."

Swallowing hard, Maeve had to force herself to step back from him and the kind look in his blue eyes. "Thank you. Now get on in there and toss out any intruders so I can tidy up. I must look a fright."

Dakota shook his head and smiled. "I'm not frightened."

He went into her room and was back out in a matter of seconds. "All is clear—nobody in there. I'll wait out here for you."

Maeve thanked him again, deciding she appreciated his protecting her.

When they got back downstairs, they joined a quiet bunch.

"Any word about the judge?" Maeve asked.

Beth shook her head. "We've been listening for the train whistle. Kat and Sebastian left to get word to the lawyer she hired that it was time to get to work. She should be bringing him back here soon."

Maeve settled in with a cup of steaming-hot coffee and

listened for the sound of an approaching train. She'd rinsed the blood out of her dress and brought along her sewing notions to reattach the sleeve.

The judge was coming.

Would they get a fair judge? Or one who would be influenced by Dr. Horecroft's arrogance and Rutledge's wealth?

Maeve saw Ginny's hands shake as they lifted her coffee cup. The white cup had a lovely pattern with delicate blue flowers and small green leaves on it. Ginny raised the cup a few inches, then set it back down with a hard click when it became clear she couldn't get even a single sip of coffee without spilling. Ginny had stormed into that jailhouse a confident woman. Right now she looked anything but.

"Should someone be watching Horecroft?" Dakota seemed calm compared to the rest of them. But his eyes were watchful as he assessed every person who passed by the window, came into the hotel, or rode a horse within his sight.

He was more vigilant than the rest of them, but then he was a man who'd been in charge of a wagon train on several grueling trips. A man used to taking charge and dealing with trouble with steady nerves.

Maeve, as she considered the man and mended her dress, realized Dakota had been like this since the day he'd joined their group. Did he have more experience with danger than she was aware of? She wanted to have a long talk with him, ask him what all he'd been through to make him into the man he was today.

16

At last, a train whistle blasted, and half the group jumped up from their chairs, the others looking around nervously. Dakota went cool, maybe cold. He was icy calm, as if a gunman were coming after him. But it wasn't that. His trouble with the Darnells would probably wait for him to get home. None of them knew he was in Cheyenne.

Right now it was time to get on with this trial.

The clock on the dining room wall had ticked away the morning until now it was afternoon. Folks had come in for the noon meal, and the hotel was full of activity. But no one paid much mind to Jake's family.

Dakota said, "You okay here, Jake? I think I'll walk over to the train station, meet the passengers, find the judge and bring him here."

"We don't know who the judge is. He'll walk right past you."

Dakota shrugged. "I need to move around. Sitting tightens me up. I need to stay loose to be ready for trouble. If I miss the judge, I'll head right back here."

He stepped out into a warm September afternoon. He was tempted to go visit Rutledge in jail to make sure he was still behind bars. Another whistle blast, on top of the screeching of iron wheels, drew his attention back to the train. He turned away from Rutledge and headed toward the station.

He reached it just as the locomotive drew to a full stop. Steam shot out of its sides. A conductor jumped out of a passenger car and pulled down a wooden step.

Dakota considered himself a good judge of character. He studied each disembarking passenger. The first one who descended caught his attention. The man had the look of the Darnell family. It was an old man with a beaked nose and a hairline that peaked on his forehead just like most of his kin. He was stringy thin, and his eyes were a shade of black Dakota rarely saw.

With no idea if the man was one of his enemies, Dakota tugged the brim of his Stetson low over his eyes to shade his face and moved closer to the station to lean against a post, keeping his distance from the stranger. He was careful not to stare, for a man could sense when he was under observation by someone else.

Instead, he watched passengers alighting from the train, and there were only a few. He also watched out of the corner of his eye the tall, lean stranger, stomping down the station steps and heading for a train car. At the man's approach, the car's door rolled open and a ramp was shoved up beside it.

More travelers exited the train. A few couples. Would a

judge bring his wife along? Dakota didn't think so. Men alone stepped down, most of them dressed in western attire, not the clothes he would have expected a judge to wear.

The last people off the train were led by a blond woman wearing a beautiful blue dress. A man came close behind her, the woman's husband most likely. He was carrying a little boy in one arm. A half-grown girl, as blond as her ma, brought up the rear. When as a unit they'd left the station platform, and no one else alighted, Dakota gave up his looking for the judge.

He reckoned he'd expected a man to step off the train wearing a judge's robe and carrying a gavel. He stayed where he was, however, until the man who might be a Darnell claimed a horse that had been led down the stockcar ramp. Dakota watched as the stranger mounted up and rode off.

With that, he headed back toward the hotel. A few moments later, as he approached the building, he saw the stranger who might be a Darnell tie up his horse and then stride into the hotel lobby. Waiting for the man to register his name in the hotel ledger, Dakota saw him climb the stairs. He gave the man plenty of time to get to his room before entering the hotel himself.

Dakota had a decision to make. He couldn't leave Jake's family here alone. He could possibly convince them to move to a different hotel, but he'd need to explain himself or at least come up with a reasonable excuse.

Surely the trial wouldn't take long. It should be over and done with in a single day, and then they could all catch the next train and head back home. Except a train had come from both directions just today, so it'd be a while before another one came along.

He looked around and found the lobby empty. He went to the hotel registry and read the last name in the book.

Ezra Darnell.

He'd written that letter to the man Dakota had killed. This man had declared war on Dakota and summoned every male in his family to go fight and kill. Dakota was afraid this wouldn't end until he was dead—or every Darnell in their clan was dead. He'd become the target in a feud.

Dakota had killed Vic Darnell, the young and wild grandson of Ezra Darnell. He'd had no choice in the matter. Later, he'd stood before the sheriff and a judge and was found not guilty of any crime. The Darnells were not in agreement with that judgment.

After taking a look at Ezra's scrawling handwriting, Dakota checked the hotel ledger and saw the page showed only Oscar Collins's name written there, with all the rooms rented. Oscar had done it to keep Ginny's name off the registry. He had kept Dakota's name off, too.

He realized they were using only four of the six rooms. Jake and Beth in one, along with the children. Maeve and Ginny in another, and more times than not they ended up with one of the children in the room with them. Oscar had his own room, and Dakota had his. Yet Oscar had rented out the whole second floor. Paid full price for two rooms they didn't use just to keep strangers at bay. Kat and Sebastian rode back to their own home every evening.

Ezra was on the third floor; there were several guests on that highest floor. Since most guests ate their meals in the hotel's dining room, so long as Ezra was staying here, Dakota would need to make himself scarce at mealtime. Or he could urge the family to eat early and retire to their rooms. It might be a good idea anyway.

Dakota strode into the dining room, wondering how long it would take for Ezra to figure out who and where he was. Other than Kat and Sebastian, the whole family was there, sitting together and talking quietly, as if this were the front room in one of their homes. Most of the other tables were filled with guests. He decided he'd discuss his troubles with Jake, but not in front of everyone.

"The judge wasn't on the train," Dakota began. "Leastways not that I could tell."

"But he was supposed to arrive today!" Beth had nearly wailed her reply.

Dakota couldn't blame her. Ginny's hands tightened on her pretty coffee cup until her knuckles turned white.

"Most everyone I saw climb down off that train was dressed in western garb, or they were couples traveling together. There was one family with little ones. Not a one of 'em looked like a judge to me." Dakota went to Maeve and eased the sleeping baby out of her arms. He'd had all younger brothers and found himself particularly eager to cradle a little girl.

It hurt him to think he should leave town, and soon. And he probably shouldn't go home. Would he have to let go of his nice stretch of land he hoped to buy? All those years of backbreaking work. It looked like he'd need to find his own hidden canyon, start over, build himself a new ranch.

Maybe so, but he couldn't leave Jake's family—not

today of all days. Ginny was in the very danger he'd been asked to come along and help protect her from.

But then Ezra Darnell might come at Dakota, blasting away and putting Ginny and this precious baby and Jake's whole family plus sweet, feisty Maeve in more danger than they were currently in with Thaddeus Rutledge.

Had Ezra somehow tracked him here? Or was it just chance that Dakota's enemy had arrived in Cheyenne?

With no idea of what to do, he paced while cradling Lydia in his arms, making sure to stay well away from the dining room door and the front window. The family had taken to gathering here, and the hotel owner hadn't objected. In fact, he'd been quite generous, refilling their coffee cups and such.

Dakota wondered what all Rutledge might get up to in trying to take Ginny back to Chicago. They should have run for Hidden Canyon the second they saw the man.

Ginny, trembling, lifted her chin and looked through the wall as if she could see all the way to freedom. "I'll wait however long I need to," she said. "We need to put an end to Thaddeus's threats."

A youngster came into the dining room door and ran up to Oscar and thrust a note in his hand. Jake tossed the kid a coin, and the boy rushed out.

Oscar unfolded the piece of paper. "The judge says to plan on coming to the courthouse in one hour."

Dakota frowned. "He's here?"

"Sure looks that way. It's signed by a Judge Nolte."

Perceiving that he'd been distracted by Ezra, Dakota said, "My mistake. I didn't see anyone who looked like a judge, but now I realize a judge may not be recognizable.

Let's head on over to the courthouse right now—before Rutledge has time to arrange for more trouble."

Since no one seemed to object to that, they let Dakota decide. He wanted to get out of this hotel before Ezra came down from his room. Dakota had no idea if the old man knew what he looked like. Maybe he could sit right beside the man, even talk to him, and Ezra wouldn't know who he was. Still, two of Ezra's kin had found Dakota, so it seemed likely the family had fine tracking skills. It suited Dakota to leave the hotel, not wait around anymore.

The family stood and trooped out of the building on their way to the courthouse, which wasn't far off. Once the group had entered the courthouse, Dakota turned and was surprised, shocked honestly, when he saw the judge.

It was the blond woman in the blue dress who'd stepped off the train with her husband and two children. The husband and children were here with her. She now wore a black robe over the blue dress, and in her right hand was a gavel.

"A w-woman judge?" Dakota's jaw dropped open. A movement beside him drew his attention to Maeve.

Her eyes were wide as she stared at the woman. "I didn't know women could be judges."

Dakota looked closer at her. Wide-eyed, yes, but wide-eyed with wonder, as if she was right now concocting a plan to give up homesteading and go rule on crimes throughout Wyoming.

Oscar came up beside Dakota, his arms crossed, but a bright look of hope in his eyes. "I heard they granted women the right to vote in Wyoming. It's one of the reasons we chose this territory for Ginny's trial. Kat encouraged us to come here. A woman judge. I can't help but like it, especially if Rutledge behaves toward her like he does toward all women." Oscar snorted. "Toward all *people*."

Dakota knew exactly what Oscar meant. "I wonder if Horecroft will decide the judge needs to be locked up, too. He might call her insane just because he doesn't like seeing a woman in that position. That may influence her."

"Yep, we might find in this judge someone firmly inclined toward our side of things."

The lady judge turned to smile at them. "Come on in and sit down. I understand you've been waiting for quite a while."

Young and friendly. Dakota didn't know much about judges, but he'd suspected they were of a stern and gruff temperament.

Not Judge Nolte.

17

Maeve suddenly knew what she wanted to do with her life. Watching the pretty young woman judge was both shocking and wonderful.

Beth and Ginny walked the short distance up the center aisle of the small courthouse to a row of seats in the front. Maeve, with Lydia in hand, went along as if a magnet drew her.

The judge approached them and flashed a smile. "Am I hearing this right?" She looked at Ginny. "I'm supposed to hold a trial and rule whether you're insane or not?"

"Yes, Your Honor. In Illinois, a husband's word is all that's needed to have a woman declared insane and locked in an asylum."

The judge's eyes narrowed. Maeve saw the smile fade. She also saw an intelligent woman who looked like she wasn't afraid to take hold of a situation and run things right.

"You ladies sit down here at this table." She looked at Maeve and Lydia. "We'll need to keep the children out of the front row, but the little ones are welcome as long as someone is handling them."

"These are Beth's children, Ginny's grandchildren." Maeve nodded at her two friends. "I came along to lend a hand in case the children get riled up."

Judge Nolte glanced at her son in her husband's arms. "My little guy is about the same age as your twins. But he won't be staying for court because the child doesn't know how to sit still."

"I'm Brandon Nolte." Her husband took a step forward. "I'll be outside with the children. Come join me if you want. The judge"—he nodded toward his wife and grinned—"needs to give her full attention to her work." He looked down at the girl. "You can stay in court if you want to, Michaela."

"No, I'll come along. Ma can handle whatever happens in here, but you might need help."

The judge laughed and patted the little boy on the back. Her husband and the children headed out. She gave Ginny a long look and then said, "Be seated, ladies. We'll get started soon." It was more like being welcomed into someone's home rather than the beginning of a legal proceeding.

There was a solid oak desk at the front of the room with a fancy chair behind it, very official-looking. Beth and Ginny were directed to a table with three chairs facing the desk. There was an identical table across the aisle from Beth's.

Behind the two tables was a barrier that looked like the pillars along the front of a porch. Behind that barrier were four rows of chairs, five chairs in each row, then an aisle and matching rows of chairs. On the right side of the room, up front, two rows of six chairs each were lined up at an angle to the desk and rows of chairs. That must be where a jury would sit.

The judge seated herself behind the desk.

Maeve moved back to the row behind Ginny and Beth. She'd never been in a courtroom before. This one seemed very imposing. And apparently the city was building a bigger one. Cheyenne was the territorial capital, after all. As she walked back to where the men stood, Kat came in with an elderly gentleman. Sebastian was a step behind the two of them. Kat gestured at Ginny, and the elderly man nodded and headed for the front of the room, Kat with him.

Sebastian went to the gathering of befuddled men and motioned toward the chairs behind where Ginny and Beth were sitting side by side. Sebastian said, "You're blocking the aisle. Let's settle in, gentlemen."

They headed up front, boots thudding on the wood flooring. Dakota was holding Jacob. Lydia had nodded off, her face pressed against Maeve's shoulder. Dakota came in first, taking a spot next to Maeve. Sebastian waited for Kat to finish introducing the older gentleman to Ginny. When finished, she went in ahead of Sebastian so she was centered behind Ginny. Seb took a seat beside her.

Jake came in the next row and sat one chair in, Oscar beside him on the aisle seat.

"That's Mr. Curtis Etherton, the lawyer we found when Kat was trying to learn what she could about the insanity laws," Sebastian said quietly, pointing at the older man.

Jake nodded. "Thank you for finding a lawyer we can all trust."

"Etherton is sharp—he knows the law and is supportive of a woman's rights. In fact, he served with the governor for a time when the territory was legalizing suffrage." Sebastian watched as the lawyer approached the judge and offered his hand in greeting. He gave her a sheaf of papers and began talking, though none of them could hear what he was saying. "Looks like Etherton knows the judge and respects her."

"Did you know the judge was going to be a woman?" Jake asked.

Shaking his head, Sebastian said, "I'd heard we had a few in Wyoming, but no. Actually, Mrs. Nolte is a justice of the peace, not a judge. But Etherton told me she's handled some difficult cases and has earned the respect of the governor. It seems he's given her broad jurisdiction. I've never seen a woman justice of the peace before. This should be an interesting day."

Thaddeus Rutledge came limping into the courtroom, Dr. Horecroft a pace behind him. Maeve saw Rutledge's nose was swollen, he had an eye turning black, a split lip that was puffy, and a tear in the leg of his pants. She felt a surge of pride knowing she'd done all that damage to the man. She quickly fought it down, for too much pride was a deadly sin. Still, she was glad she'd stopped Rutledge from kidnapping Ginny. She patted Lydia, who was still dozing against her shoulder. Maybe she should be a lawman instead of a judge. Bring criminals to justice. Or maybe even a lawyer . . .

Seeing Judge Nolte up front with Curtis Etherton, and Rutledge bruised and limping, gave her all sorts of new ideas about what a woman could do.

No sign of Sykes, so maybe the sheriff had kept him in jail. Speaking of which, Sheriff Peters had walked into the room right behind Horecroft and sat down at the back as if to block any escape attempts his prisoner might make. Or maybe he was just bored, and this was the most interesting thing happening in his town right now.

Two other men and one woman came in and sat in the row behind Rutledge on what Maeve had begun to think of as Rutledge's side. Each held a pad of paper and a pencil. Newspaper folks?

Maeve saw the judge's husband through a window to her left as he rounded the side of the building, bouncing and rocking the little guy. The man walked back and forth just far enough from the courthouse so as not to let any crying disturb the proceedings.

What was it like being married to a lady judge?

Maeve, Dakota, and Jake were occupied similarly to Mr. Nolte, all holding babies, though theirs were asleep. Maeve wondered how long the trial would take. Brandon Nolte might end up with a crowd around him if every baby here finished their naps early.

The older man finished talking to the judge and then sat beside Ginny. He leaned over and talked quietly with her.

The judge picked up her gavel. But before she could rap it on the desktop, Rutledge surged to his feet.

"You're not going to judge this case. This is outrageous. I demand a real judge." Rutledge leaned forward over the table, touching the top with his spread fingertips as if he were in charge of a roomful of businessmen, none of them as powerful as him.

Horecroft remained seated, but his snooty nose was

tilted up. Dakota half hoped the man would offer a diagnosis that the judge must be insane to think a woman could do this job. Maybe he'd even offer to lock her up.

The judge rapped the gavel, then studied Rutledge for a long moment. "You must know I'm a real judge. Surely you're aware that Wyoming has women serving as judges these days. Why would you make such an insulting statement right at the beginning of a trial that might set me against you? Is that wise, Mr. Rutledge?"

Rutledge stared at her as if his strength of will could maybe get her to set aside her gavel and robe, get up, and leave.

At last, without making nearly as big a fool of himself as Maeve wished he would, Rutledge sank back into his chair.

"Now then, I am Judge Nolte. I have served in the position of justice of the peace for three years now here in Wyoming. I'm here to rule on a case concerning an accusation against Mrs. Eugenia Rutledge of being insane and needing the medical care offered by the Horecroft Insane Asylum in Chicago. A call went out three days ago, asking for help as Cheyenne is currently short of the services of a judge. I said I was willing to come, my offer was accepted, and here I am. I know very little about this case, as it wasn't mentioned in the telegram. But I do know the services of a jury have been requested. There's no time for that today. I will put the word out for jurors to be summoned, and we will meet again tomorrow. Today, though, I wanted to meet you and find out what is going on here."

"I'm Curtis Etherton, Your Honor. My client, Mrs.

Rutledge"—he gestured toward Ginny—"has been accused of insanity with no judge or doctor ruling on this."

"I'm a doctor, and I have ruled that she is insane." Dr. Horecroft pulled a handkerchief out of his pocket and dabbed at his nose.

"Dr. Horecroft owns the asylum in question, Your Honor. He has a financial interest in having Mrs. Rutledge detained in his care. We want a ruling from a neutral party and an appropriate time allotted to make our case before a jury. We're here to see that my client is ruled sane by the court."

The judge looked at Ginny. Maeve couldn't see Ginny's expression, as she was behind her. But she'd wager Ginny had the usual, very sane, kindly expression on her face she always did.

Rutledge interrupted Judge Nolte's quiet inspection. "We'll need several days to prepare for this trial, madam. My wife has been in the West for a time and planned this court appearance. I just barely got to town. I want to find a lawyer of my own." Rutledge gave the older man sitting with Ginny a dark look. "And we want to be involved in the selection of the jury."

"The correct term to address me isn't 'madam.' It's 'Your Honor.' I strongly suggest you use that title." Judge Nolte gave Rutledge a narrow-eyed look. "Several days is not going to be possible, but I can give you until tomorrow afternoon. Tomorrow at one o'clock we'll select a jury. Then immediately after that, we'll hear what you all have to say."

18

Maeve sidled up next to Dakota where he leaned against the wall, right by the swinging door that connected the dining room to the kitchen. "What is—?"

Dakota yelped and jumped as if he'd sat down on a tack. He whirled to stare at her. "Where did you come from?"

Maeve's eyes widened as she looked up at him. "I walked right up beside you." Privately she admitted she'd come from the side he wasn't paying attention to, quietly, just to see if he'd notice her. "Now I'll finish what I was saying, and I'm surer than ever I'm right. What is going on with you today?"

Dakota's cheeks turned just the littlest bit pink.

"You're blushing? You don't seem like a man who's given to blushing. When was the last time that happened?"

Dakota's eyes seemed to gaze into the past, and yet he kept looking at the door to the dining room that led to the lobby. Which was what he'd been doing all afternoon. They were on the far side of the room, while the rest of their group sat around a table near the lobby door. They were talking with Ginny's lawyer, Mr. Etherton.

"I might've been, um, thirteen," Dakota answered. "Betty Ellen Wallace came and found me and my little brothers swimming in a creek by our house."

"Why did that make you blush?" Maeve asked.

He was watching the door again. With a shrug as if it didn't matter, and yet he'd remembered it mighty fast, he said, "We were all in our . . . uh, that is, we were all five of us in the—" he cleared his throat—"the altogether, I guess you'd say. And she was a twelve-year-old girl. No matter her age, though, any girl seeing us like that would've brought on a blush at that age. Well, at any age." He proved it by blushing more deeply.

Maeve shook her head in a tiny yet aggressive manner. "Forget the swimming. What is going on with you today?"

Dakota saw someone move in the hallway and moved to investigate further. Maeve knew he had seen something because she was now riveted on the dining room door the same as he'd been. Dakota was standing by the door to the kitchen, and then he slipped through it and was gone. She saw the man, whoever it was, walk on past and go outside. Seconds later, she pushed open the swinging door to the kitchen and smacked Dakota in the face.

Startled, she stepped back and saw he'd had his eye pressed to a barely open crack in the door. He'd watched the man pass by the lobby, too.

He glared at her and walked back into the dining room, a red welt forming on his forehead.

"Sorry." She was sorry she'd whacked him in the face, but on the other hand . . . "Were you hiding?"

"No. I was checking the back door. The kitchen is usually empty this time of day, so someone could walk right in through that door."

Maeve stared at him for a minute, then said something she knew was outrageously insulting. She wanted to shock him. "And I say you're a liar, and a poor one at that."

Dakota sucked in a breath, straightened to his full height, which was quite tall compared to her, and nearly cut her to ribbons with his blazing eyes. "You take that back."

Calling someone a liar in the West was serious business. Herds of cattle, whole ranches, horses, and mining claims were traded or sold with nothing but a handshake and a man's word that he'd fulfill his side of the bargain. If a man couldn't be trusted out here, he was finished. He wouldn't be able to conduct any business, and he might as well pack up his things and head back east. Though the West was huge, it was sparsely populated. People knew people they'd never met by their reputation. Cowboys sitting around a campfire wove tales of all they'd seen, of men they'd known. A bad reputation could fly far and wide as if carried on the wind.

"Argue if you want, or admit you're not going to tell me, but don't lie to me." Maeve cut off whatever righteous defense he was about to make for himself.

She watched him wilt just a bit. His eyes darted to the lobby door, just as they'd been doing all afternoon, and then he gave Maeve an uncertain look—as if he wanted to tell the truth but was afraid. What secret was Dakota hauling around with him? she wondered.

"You're afraid someone's going to see you?" Maeve

finally concluded. She had a younger brother and sister. They were imps, so she had to think fast to keep ahead of their mischief. Add up clues, read their sneaky little expressions. She did that now with Dakota.

"It can't have anything to do with Ginny," she went on. "You've shown no fear of being seen by Rutledge or his henchman Sykes or that awful Dr. Horecroft. Who is in this hotel you don't want to see you? You don't strike me as a man who's afraid of much, which means you're hiding . . . to protect us?" Maeve couldn't figure out how that made much sense, but it was all that came to mind.

Dakota tore his eyes from the door and gave her a look of such horror that she knew she was very close.

"What trouble could your being noticed by them cause the rest of us? Who do you know in Cheyenne anyway?" From what Maeve understood of him, he'd been in charge of the wagon trains and later lived in his valley where he gentled wild mustangs. So how could he know anyone here in Cheyenne?

"Something happened during that year when you went to take over Jake's homestead." She was putting it all together like a puzzle.

"That's enough," Dakota said. "Yes, I've got a secret, and it's one I can't tell anyone."

"That's the *definition* of the word," she said, shaking her head. "Well, if it's true you're keeping a secret, you're not very good at it. So you may as well tell me what's going on."

"No. It's a secret for a reason. It could be dangerous for you to know. Let's just say there's a man in town who may intend to harm me. If I wasn't in town, surrounded by women and children, I'd go face him. But I'm avoiding him because if he sees me, if he figures out who I am, it could lead to a shootout. And that puts anyone standing close to me in danger. So far he hasn't seen me, or if he has, he didn't recognize me. I'm hoping we can settle Ginny's trial tomorrow, then head straight for home. That way this man will never see me. If he catches up with me later, at least there won't be bullets flying right past Jake's toddlers—and you."

"Go to the sheriff, Dakota. Tell him about your troubles and have that man tossed into the cell along with Rutledge and Sykes."

"Can't have him arrested if he's committed no crime."

Maeve frowned as she thought it over some more. It seemed her skills at staying ahead of her little brother and sister had stretched as far as she could make them stretch. "Please tell me what all this is about." She loved secrets. She had several she'd kept for a long time. Nothing important, mainly having to do with old friends back in Ireland, girls who'd sneaked out of their houses to meet the lads who'd sweet-talked them into taking a walk late at night. But Dakota's secret sounded like it would be a good one. "You know, I'm great at keeping secrets."

Dakota snorted. "I'm keeping this one for a very good reason. Not only could it put you in danger, but Jake might decide he wants no part of me here with you folks. And if he does, I can't be around to help protect Ginny. So the secret must stay a secret. You're exactly right—that's what the word means."

Maeve crossed her arms and studied him. "If I knew what it was that might put us in danger, I'd be on edge with you. I'd be better able to protect everyone."

"Just be on edge. You don't need to know why."

"Yes, but I want to."

A shadow passed over Dakota's face, and he looked away from the door. He focused on her in a way that made her realize he hadn't done that since she startled him.

"If I told you"—he looked back to the lobby door—"you'd hate me for it and stay far away from me."

"I wouldn't hate you, Dakota." Which wasn't a fair statement because she'd hated him for certain when her da had died and he wouldn't let them take a day away from their traveling to give Maeve a chance to say a proper goodbye to him.

Of course, that was a while ago, and she hadn't hated him lately.

"You *would* hate me, and you should."

"That makes no sense. Why should I hate you?"

Dakota didn't answer, but then the answer might be part of the secret. "You'd never allow yourself to spend any time with me, and if I paid you any personal attention, you'd stomp off and hide behind Ginny."

"I'd never allow you to pay any personal attention to me anyway."

That drew his full attention again. Despite the quiet voices across the dining room and that gaping lobby door, Maeve felt as though the whole world went silent. Dakota's eyes locked on hers, and she felt that gaze as if he were touching her. She felt his interest. She felt her own interest.

He reached out to gently catch hold of her wrist. He pulled her through the swinging door, and from one moment to the next they were alone in the empty kitchen. She had one split second to make sure no one was coming in the back door.

Dakota lowered his head and kissed her. Her first kiss.

She was lost in it, confused by it, captured by it. She was drawn to Dakota by the touch of his lips.

He eased back. "You allowed that, Miss O'Toole."

Shocked by such a rude statement, Maeve opened her mouth to shout at the big lunkhead. He stopped her by kissing her again. And by the great horn spoon, she kissed him back.

All she'd been through. All the stress of travel and her mother's announcement about Bruce and worrying about Ginny and what was coming toward her—all of it faded away to nothing. It was only her and this man, drawing her closer in the empty kitchen, tilting his head to kiss her more deeply. Paying her some very personal attention.

In truth she knew nothing of kissing. Deep kisses, tilted heads, encircling arms. It was all a great mystery that she would admit to having wondered about. And now that mystery was solved, and she was only left to revel in it. Sink into it, hoping it would never end.

No quiet voices, no danger, nothing intruded on their little cocoon of privacy. All she could see or feel or know was Dakota and his strong arms and this wonderful closeness. It was unlike anything she'd ever felt for a man before. Cracks in the parched desert of her heart that she hadn't known existed filled and healed there in Dakota Harlan's arms.

Finally, he eased her away, just a few inches, just enough

that she could see him. Except her eyes had fallen shut. She fluttered them open to stare into his blue eyes. Her arms were around his neck, his around her waist.

"Maeve, you are a pretty woman." He kissed her again, then wrenched his head sideways. He shook himself all over like a dog shedding water, then dragged her arms off his neck. Holding her hands by the wrists, he kissed the back of her fingers, then urged her through the swinging door back into the dining room.

She slumped against the wall. Only it wasn't the wall, it was the swinging door, and she almost fell through it.

Dakota caught her, kept her on her feet, and drew her to the side enough that she could lean against something solid. He drew in a deep breath, let it out slowly, and said, "And that's why I should tell my secret. You need to be reminded I'm no man you want . . . well, paying any personal attention to you."

Maeve was sorely afraid she did want the attention. There was ample evidence of that. But since she was afraid her voice might shake, she didn't respond, nor did she ask him again what his secret was. If she did ask again, would he take her back into the kitchen? she wondered. He was trying to make her see how drawn they were to each other. And yet he didn't want that.

Though her thoughts were muddled, she remembered he'd said she would likely hate him after he shared his secret. She most certainly didn't want to hate him and doubted she would no matter what kind of trouble had brought this man to town, the one hunting him.

What could it possibly be? Dakota wasn't wanted by the law. When she'd advised him to go to the sheriff, he hadn't reacted like someone afraid his face was on a wanted poster.

No, some man was hunting him. A man with bad intentions but who hadn't committed a crime yet. She couldn't imagine what Dakota could have done to bring someone after him with a grudge. And why would she hate him if the man was unjustly angry with him? Did that mean Dakota had harmed someone? In some way not against the law?

For a moment, she was tempted to ask him once more just because she hoped he'd slip into the kitchen with her and kiss her again. Just to prove to her why they should stay apart.

Instead, she clamped her mouth shut. Using the doorframe to stay on her feet, she watched the lobby door. When someone moved out there and Dakota slipped into the kitchen, she could now see he was still looking through the cracked-open door. When he came back, she let him have at whatever nonsense he was up to. She was far too busy trying to get her heart rate to slow and her thoughts to clear.

She stayed beside him for a few more minutes. Then he did one of his disappearing into the kitchen tricks. But this time a man came into the dining room. An older man, gray-haired, stout, and dressed in a fine suit of clothes. He walked straight to Ginny's lawyer, who rose and shook his hand.

Dakota returned to the dining room as soon as the man was fully visible.

Mr. Etherton introduced everyone to the newcomer, including turning to point to Dakota and Maeve.

"This is Dr. Lawrence Snider. He's a respected man of medicine here in Wyoming. In fact, he's the personal physician to the territorial governor. He's going to spend some time with Ginny to assess her mental state." Then, formalities over, the doctor talked to Mr. Etherton earnestly for a few moments.

Dr. Snider extended a hand to Ginny, who rose from her chair. For the first time, Maeve noticed the papers in Ginny's hands. Ginny did tend to write a lot. Maeve had seen her do so several times during this trip. Maeve had assumed Ginny was writing someone a letter.

But who? Ginny had cut herself off from the whole world. They'd written to Kat, but they were here with Kat, so Ginny wouldn't be writing any letters.

Now she took the papers with her, and Maeve couldn't guess what was on them and why she'd want to show them to the doctor.

Beth rose, too, but then the lawyer Etherton started talking rapidly to her. With a frown, Beth quickly reclaimed her chair.

Ginny and Dr. Snider crossed to the other side of the dining room. It wasn't that big of a room, yet Ginny left her family on the east side of the lobby door and went with Dr. Snider over to the west side. The two of them settled in to talk while Beth fidgeted in her chair.

The babies soon woke from their naps, which kept Jake's family busy. Maeve abandoned Dakota to help out. Meanwhile, Ginny talked with Dr. Snider for the rest of the afternoon.

19

Dakota had made it through the day without coming face-to-face with Ezra Darnell. Sure, he was trying to be sneaky, but mostly it was luck. Darnell had gone somewhere and not come back until after all of Jake's family had quit plotting and planning, eaten supper, and gone to bed. Maybe Ezra hadn't come back at all—Dakota couldn't say—but they'd tucked in for the night and he still hadn't been forced to face his past.

Now he had to get through the next morning, then the trial in the afternoon. His aim was to keep Rutledge away from Ginny.

After the trial was over, they could finally leave town and head home.

The morning went on like the afternoon before. The family gathered in the dining room. Mr. Etherton and Dr. Snider were present among them, both men talking to Ginny. Everyone else did the baby wrangling, except Dakota who kept watch and hid when necessary. He didn't know how else to get through this day without lead flying, and Jake's family in the middle of it.

They ate the noon meal early, which suited Dakota fine. They managed to be done and headed for the trial before Darnell showed himself.

Dakota reached the front door of the courthouse, looked at the large building going up nearby to replace it, and held the door for everyone as they filed past him. He noticed a small gathering of men on the street near the entrance and wondered if word had gotten out that the trial might be interesting and worth their checking out.

Maybe today they'd get a crowd.

Maeve had offered to watch over the little ones in the hotel, but Dakota didn't like that idea. None of them did. Those babies would be a powerful hold on Ginny if somehow Rutledge got his hands on them.

Rutledge came into the courtroom soon after them, with Horecroft and a second man at his side.

Dakota had a hard time believing the man wasn't planning something underhanded. As he took his seat in the row behind Beth, Ginny, and Mr. Etherton, Dakota heard Etherton draw in a sharp breath. He could see there was tension in every line of Etherton's face.

Ginny, sitting next to her lawyer, leaned over. "What is it?" she asked.

"The man with your husband is a Wyoming lawyer. He's deceitful, dishonest, and very smart. I wonder how Rutledge latched on to him so fast. Horecroft probably spent yesterday afternoon hunting up the low-down chiseler."

Dakota looked down the row beside him. Maeve sat next to him on his left with a sleeping Lydia. Jake was on his right, Marie snoozing in his arms. Oscar had Jacob Jr. napping. Kat was next to the aisle, Sebastian directly behind her. Sheriff Peters sat on the same side as Rutledge, alone in the back row.

Every one of them was studying the man with Rutledge. Dakota could see that Kat recognized the man. Chances were that in her search that had led her to Etherton, she'd come across the man with Rutledge.

Rutledge's lawyer stood from where he sat beside Rutledge and Horecroft and came over to look down on Mr. Etherton. "We meet again, Curtis."

Etherton gave a little nod. "Pritchard. Still picking the wrong side, I see."

The lawyer looked at Ginny. "Daniel Pritchard, ma'am. Your husband is very worried about you. He's here to see that you get the care you need."

Pritchard stood still, an amused gleam in his eye. Dakota had the urge to knock the smirk off his face and knew at the same time he thought of it that Pritchard intended just that.

The door opened behind them, and Judge Nolte walked into the courtroom. No one else.

Dakota glanced out the window to see the judge's daughter sitting on a bench across the street as Mr. Nolte paced back and forth with his sleeping toddler. Nolte wasn't there just to care for the baby. He could have done that in whatever hotel room they were staying in. No, he wanted to be close at hand. Even with two youngsters, he lingered nearby in case his wife needed him.

He prayed Oscar wouldn't pick this moment to punch Pritchard in his smug face. Because then the judge would see it and probably throw Oscar out of the courthouse. Possibly all of them. And that, too, would be just as Pritchard intended.

The judge strode to the front of the room, sat behind her desk, and rapped lightly with her gavel. "Please be seated, Mr. Pritchard. I was informed you are going to be the legal advisor to Mr. Rutledge and assist with his trial and also with the jury selection."

Although she sounded professional and calm, there was something about her tone that caught Dakota's attention.

Judge Nolte wasn't from around here, but it was clear she'd heard of Mr. Pritchard and knew of his reputation. "We've sent out word this morning concerning the need for a jury. There's a small group waiting outside to be considered."

The men Dakota had noticed.

"Sheriff Peters will act as bailiff today. Sheriff, let the first twelve men in. I'm hoping we can settle who's to be on our jury as quickly as that."

The sheriff nodded, then moved to call for the twelve to come inside. None of the men drew Dakota's attention overly, though a few looked to be downcast. Perhaps down on their luck. Loafers from the saloon maybe.

Dakota leaned toward Maeve. "I thought there might be some women on the jury, Wyoming being such a progressive territory and all."

Maeve shrugged and patted Lydia's little bottom while watching the men take their seats in the two rows of chairs at the front of the room. The judge launched into a speech about what was expected of the jurors. Afterward Mr. Pritchard asked if he could question each of the men.

Judge Nolte said, "I'll allow it, but keep it short. My understanding is neither Mr. or Mrs. Rutledge is local to Cheyenne or even Wyoming. No one here should be acquainted with them and therefore be prone to bias."

The twelve men took turns giving their names in response to Pritchard's questions. Two of them said they were out-of-work cowhands. Two worked at the saloon, cleaning up and such. The way all the men refused to make eye contact with the lawyers made Dakota wonder if they worked for whiskey.

Mr. Pritchard asked each man if he was married, if he was a churchgoing man, and if he believed a wife should obey her husband and accept his authority and protection.

Mr. Etherton asked if they were accepting of a woman's rights, including the right to life, liberty, and the pursuit of happiness.

Dakota looked from the jurors to Ginny's lawyer, from Pritchard to the judge. None of them gave much away. For his part, he didn't understand the selection of these twelve people. A jury of your peers? What did that mean? Was it the first twelve men who were summoned, simple as that?

Pritchard had no objection to any of them. Three were rejected by Etherton. The judge dismissed two. All of that was for no reason Dakota could understand. More men came in to replace them. One of them was soon excused.

Finally, they had settled on the twelve jurors. Judge Nolte tapped her gavel again and asked for opening statements.

Again, Dakota thought most of it was nonsense. How could anyone with one working eyeball think Ginny was anything other than sane?

Because it made no sense, and because Rutledge's lawyer had never met Ginny, Dakota didn't see how this trial could end any way except with Ginny being ruled fully sane. It was clear Ginny took it seriously, as did Beth, and for certain Rutledge. Dakota braced himself for trouble. If necessary, he was prepared to grab Ginny and run. He wondered if Oscar had thought to tie a string of fresh horses outside somewhere in the event of a bad outcome. He wished he'd've arranged this beforehand. That way all they'd need to do was mount up, ride hard for Idaho and Hidden Canyon, and tuck Ginny away again.

Dakota hoped it wouldn't come to that, for although Idaho was just the next territory over, they were big territories. And Rutledge would for sure send a posse after them.

Mr. Etherton stood beside Ginny and faced the jury to give his opening statement.

"My client, Mrs. Eugenia Rutledge, was locked away by her husband for no just cause. It was allowed because of a cruel, unjust law on the books in some states and territories—those not as reasonable as Wyoming—that women can be treated in such a way. In Wyoming we are wiser than that. In Wyoming we believe women are to be treated with decency and kindness. We put into practice those solemn words in this country's Declaration of Independence: 'We hold these truths to be self-evident, that all men are created equal, that they are endowed by their Creator with certain unalienable rights, that among these are life, liberty and the pursuit of happiness.'

"Those words are meant for *all* Americans. Not just men. This woman"—he gestured with some flourish toward Ginny—"has been denied those rights. We here in

Wyoming Territory know that a woman is rare and wonderful, to be cherished by all men, and especially by her husband. Mr. Rutledge instead treated his wife as if she had no rights, no value, and deserved no respect. She was denied the right to liberty and the pursuit of happiness. I'll prove before this judge and this jury that Eugenia Rutledge is fully rational, fully sane, and that her husband had her locked away out of the hardness of his heart, and out of greed because Mrs. Rutledge's parents had left the bulk of their money to Mrs. Rutledge's daughter, Elizabeth. Her parents had seen their son-in-law's foolish, wasteful ways with money and didn't want him—"

"That's a lie!" Rutledge surged to his feet. "I did it because she was mad. She was a danger to herself. She—"

Judge Nolte banged the gavel over and over. "Sit down, Mr. Rutledge!"

Rutledge's lawyer pulled hard to get Rutledge back in his seat. Pritchard whispered something to Rutledge, jabbing at the papers in front of him.

"I demand order in my courtroom, Mr. Rutledge. This proceeding will be run without any such outbursts. And when I tell you to be quiet, you will do as you are told, or I'll throw you back in jail and we'll have this trial without you. Is that clear?"

Whether the judge's orders or his lawyer's pleading got Rutledge back under control was hard to say. But he slumped back in his chair, a scowl on his face.

Mr. Etherton continued. "I believe once you've had a chance to listen to Mrs. Rutledge and witness for yourselves her fully healthy mind, you will see she is the very picture of feminine grace and decorum."

The lawyer let those words hang for a moment. Dakota thought it was to underline that one of the Rutledges in this room wasn't behaving well, and it wasn't Ginny.

"In the end, I believe you will agree with me and rule that she is perfectly sane." With that, Mr. Etherton gave a slight bow to the jury, then resumed his seat.

Dakota saw Pritchard stand and leave his place at the table. He walked up to the jury, looking them each one in the eye.

"Mr. Rutledge took vows to love his wife in sickness and in health," Pritchard began. "When he saw her mind take an unhealthy turn, when he saw her make irrational decisions and defy him, her husband and master, when he saw her behave in a way that revealed the fevered thoughts in her increasingly troubled mind, he stepped in to see that she received the care she needed. The doctor who cared for her at his asylum is one of the most respected physicians in Chicago. Mr. Rutledge did not act on behalf of his wife out of a desire for her money. He has plenty of his own. He wants her to be cared for properly so that hopefully she can be fully restored to a state of sanity. Yes, she can appear calm and rational for stretches of time, but Mr. Rutledge and Dr. Horecroft know her better than anyone else alive. They have only her best interests at heart. We intend to prove that and, with your help, return her to the safety and care she had before she ran away. Thank you." Pritchard returned to his seat.

"Please, gentlemen, hold up for just a moment." The judge rose from her chair.

The lawyers nodded graciously.

Judge Nolte went down the center aisle in her sweeping black robe to the back of the room and whispered something in Sheriff Peters's ear. Peters listened intently, nodded, then turned and left the courtroom.

The judge returned to her place behind the desk.

Shortly after Peters left, another man, also wearing a badge, came in and took the same seat Peters had been in.

Then the judge asked for witnesses.

Dr. Horecroft took the stand, looking smug and condescending as always.

Dakota didn't waste his time listening to Horecroft. Instead, he was splitting his attention between watching out the window for any sign of Ezra Darnell, and watching the door at the back in case Ezra came in that way, guns blazing.

20

As Dr. Horecroft approached the seat beside the judge's bench, Maeve saw Ginny go ashen and lean against Beth, who sat on her left and wrapped an arm around her mother.

Kat had grabbed Sebastian's hand, and her knuckles were pure white. Sebastian held her hand in both of his and drew her close. All of them looked nervous, uneasy.

Those quick impressions from the two women who knew him best kept Maeve riveted on every word out of Dr. Horecroft's mouth. She glanced at Judge Nolte and thought the judge noticed the women's fear too, though she kept a straight face.

Maeve had seen Horecroft in action a few times now—during the street fight and at the jailhouse. Horecroft had refused to help bind up Rutledge's wounds, saying he wasn't "that kind of doctor." Maeve suspected the man was no kind of doctor.

Mr. Pritchard, Rutledge's lawyer, gave the court a broad overview, starting with Horecroft's side of things. "According to Dr. Horecroft here, Mrs. Rutledge was a sad case. Her husband brought her to him and the asylum because Mr. Rutledge cared for his wife and wanted her to be restored to sanity. The world is a stressful and confusing place for someone with Eugenia Rutledge's delicate sensibilities. Her husband told of how she'd begun losing control of her senses. Shouting at shadows. She was tormented by nightmares and had terrors during the daylight hours as well. She needed a place where she could rest. Where all the stresses of life could be lifted off her fragile shoulders." The lawyer paused and turned to Horecroft. "Isn't that right, Dr. Horecroft?"

"Yes. My asylum is such a place."

Maeve looked to the front of the room to see the judge studying Ginny and Kat. Maeve had never seen Ginny shouting at shadows or heard of her being plagued by terrors in the daytime. She had nightmares, but as Maeve understood it, the *asylum* had been the cause of the woman's nightmares.

Horecroft went on, elaborating on his and Mr. Rutledge's oh-so-kindly tale of poor Eugenia. "She was brought to me in a state of near collapse, and I offered the care and protection of the asylum, which is dedicated to giving people like her the rest they so desperately need."

Oscar had worked for the Rutledges at the time, in the stable. He'd driven Ginny to the asylum, and he'd been so furious when he realized what Mr. Rutledge was doing to his wife that he'd ended up out of a job. Oscar told Beth where her ma was, and the two of them began to plan how to free Ginny from that awful place.

Horecroft cleared his throat. "Mrs. Rutledge was not

ready to leave when she ran away. The very fact that she ran is proof of that."

No, it was proof she wanted to get away, Maeve thought. *And not much else.*

"And here she is now, out in the wilderness. Afraid of the very ones, her husband and I, who want only the best for her. Mr. Rutledge has searched diligently for her for years. He's finally found her and wishes to take her home, back to a place where she can get well." His voice had turned calm and compassionate.

Ginny watched him with narrow eyes, as if every word disgusted her. Horecroft and his kindly tone might have convinced Maeve if she didn't already know that Ginny was perfectly capable of caring for herself. She figured the judge was properly skeptical, but what about the jury? Would they believe what Horecroft was saying?

Mr. Pritchard asked more questions, all of them similar, giving Horecroft a chance to put on his show of the good-hearted doctor. When finished, he said, "That is all, Your Honor. No more questions for the doctor." Pritchard returned to his seat.

Horecroft was about to rise from his seat when Ginny's lawyer, Mr. Curtis Etherton, jumped up and said, "Just one moment, Dr. Horecroft. I have a few questions."

Horecroft's brows arched, and his nose twitched. Maeve thought he bore an unfortunate resemblance to a mouse she'd found hiding under the kitchen cupboard. She'd dispatched it, and right now she'd've liked to do the same with the doctor. It was probably a good thing she didn't have a broom handy.

Horecroft settled back in his chair, adjusted the tidy

ascot tie he wore, and folded his hands like a prayerful man who was only there to help.

"How do you, in your professional capacity, judge a woman to be sane?"

Horecroft hesitated. Something flitted across his face that was hostile, then quickly hidden. "I find your question offensive, sir. I am a man of science. I've trained for years how to properly judge a person's mental state. But to try to explain it to you . . . well, I'm afraid it would be beyond your ability to understand and be a waste of this court's time."

"Nevertheless," said Etherton, "if you would at least give us some idea of what goes through your mind when judging a woman like my client either sane or insane."

Horecroft fidgeted for a few seconds, clearing his throat again. "I've made it my life's work to identify those women in need of the special care they can only get in a residential facility like Horecroft Asylum—one of the finest establishments for such care anywhere in the country. In fact, the state of Illinois has recently—"

"Yes, yes," Etherton cut him off. "I'm sure you're proud of your asylum, but how do you decide who needs that special care? I realize I don't have your years of training, but try and explain it to me anyway. Please—it's important that you do."

Maeve watched Horecroft's color rise, his cheeks turning a deep shade of red. His mouth pursed in disapproval, and his eyes flashed. The man was clearly insulted.

"I've spent countless hours talking with Mrs. Rutledge. It's clear her mind is quite addled. She refuses to even—"

Etherton stepped closer to where Horecroft sat. "It's

clear *how*? Did you give her any tests? Either medical tests or written tests? You claim to have spent countless hours speaking with her. So then, was your assessment based on a verbal test?"

Horecroft ignored the question. "There are steps a woman in her condition must take in order to get better. She was a very frustrating case, but I believe with a little self-reflection and a willingness to admit she is troubled and needs help, she could be improved. And yet, after living at the asylum for a while, I began to give up hope that she could be cured of her insanity."

"So you're saying that you tested her by talking to her—that's how you diagnosed her? Is that correct?"

"Well, yes, I imagine that is essentially correct."

"Essentially correct sounds as though it's not fully correct. If there is more, such as mental or physical tests, anything I'm missing, disclose them now, Doctor, while you're on the stand. Again, how do you judge whether a patient is sane or not?"

Horecroft tugged at the collar of his white shirt. He was dressed in much finer clothes than Rutledge was, but they were too tight. Maeve wondered if he'd gained weight but wasn't able to afford new clothes. He'd lost the income from Kat and Ginny, and of course Yvette. How many people were in that asylum? Were they all wealthy?

All that was happening with the financial panic back east might have cut into the asylum's finances. Wealthy folks paying top dollar to keep their embarrassing or just inconvenient relatives locked away might have decided they could handle things themselves, locked them in the attic perhaps, and left Horecroft with a reduced income.

"There are several symptoms I look for," Horecroft said, "and Mrs. Rutledge has all of them. She's overly emotional. Given to weeping and wild talking she can't seem to control. Obsessive behavior like reading improper novels. Slovenly dressed, uncleanness . . ." He looked at Ginny in her clean, tidy calico dress, albeit not the fashionable attire she'd worn as a well-to-do Chicago socialite. Horecroft, having found his bearings again, continued, "Those who are mad exhibit sullen behavior and a lack of cooperation, as well as inappropriate anger directed at the very people who are trying to help her, namely her husband and myself. Of course, I also rely on the testimony of loved ones. And Mr. Rutledge was clear that he thought she had lost her mind. She wasn't the calm, rational woman she'd been earlier in her life. A husband is a good judge of such things; his word is sufficient for a diagnosis to be made."

The clock on the courtroom wall ticked loudly as Mr. Etherton let Dr. Horecroft's last remark hang in the air for all to ponder. After nearly half a minute of utter silence, Etherton said, "Just to be clear, you're telling this court that Mrs. Rutledge's husband simply arrived at your door, told you his wife was insane, and handed her over to your care. You accepted her into the asylum based primarily on his claiming she was mad—that is, in exchange for a generous monthly check from him. That's the criteria you used to lock up a free, adult woman for three years?"

Once more, Horecroft's face grew crimson. "She is clearly *insane*."

Mr. Etherton turned to look at Ginny, who sat quietly

at the table, hands folded in her lap, composed and attentive. "It's not clear at all."

"You're not someone who's handled hundreds of such cases. I, on the other hand, have developed the skills necessary to determine a person's sanity or lack thereof. Furthermore, the state of Illinois and the government of the United States of America have given me the right to make that judgment." Horecroft huffed, straightened his tight suit coat, and fell silent.

Etherton shook his head slowly. "On the contrary, Doctor, for Mrs. Rutledge is as sane as you and me, probably more so. I've spent time with the woman in question, who's quietly sitting here now beside me, and I heard no irrational talk, witnessed no overly emotional reactions, no sign whatsoever that she's not fully able to direct her own affairs in a responsible and rational way. Your so-called diagnosis, Dr. Horecroft, was grossly incorrect. It was also immoral." Etherton turned to Judge Nolte. "No further questions at this time, Your Honor, but can I ask that the doctor be called to the stand again if I see the need for it?"

"You can, Mr. Etherton." The judge looked at the witness. "You can step down from the stand, Dr. Horecroft."

Horecroft stared at her for a moment, as if he couldn't believe he was being instructed by a woman judge, before giving his head a little shake, standing, and walking over to sit next to Rutledge. He was closest to the jury of anyone, and it drew Maeve's eyes to the twelve men, sitting there and watching the trial unfold. A couple of them looked at Horecroft with something she couldn't quite define. Almost like . . . like they knew him. But how could they?

Horecroft and Rutledge weren't from Cheyenne or even Wyoming Territory. No jury of folks around here would know the two men and therefore be biased for or against them.

Judge Nolte shifted her attention to Rutledge's lawyer. "Any more witnesses, Mr. Pritchard?"

"Yes, Your Honor. I'd like to call Mrs. Eugenia Rutledge to the stand."

21

Dakota, already tense from the stupid trial, knotted up even more to think of Ginny being subjected to a bunch of rude questions from Pritchard.

Ginny's lawyer rose from his seat. "My client does not wish to be questioned, Your Honor. It's her right to remain silent in a case against her."

"Ah, but what is she afraid of, Mr. Etherton?" Pritchard asked. "Why is a 'perfectly sane woman' afraid to answer a few questions?"

Mr. Etherton simply replied, "It's her right. She may be willing to answer questions later, after the case is more fully laid out, but for now she will remain silent."

The judge nodded. "Any other witnesses, Mr. Pritchard?"

"You should compel her to take the stand, Your Honor."

"Mr. Etherton is right that she is not required to testify against herself. Any other witnesses?"

Dakota watched as Pritchard churned with frustration. Finally he sat down and muttered, "No further witnesses."

Dakota tried to keep his sigh of relief silent. He exchanged a glance with Maeve, who looked equally relieved.

Judge Nolte turned to Mr. Etherton. "Does the defense have any witnesses?"

"We do, Your Honor. The defense calls Dr. Lawrence Snider to the stand."

Dakota turned and noticed the man who'd spent yesterday afternoon talking to Ginny. Dakota had forgotten about him.

Dr. Snider was sworn in and settled into his seat. He was tall and gray-haired and exuded a warm, easygoing demeanor. Dakota sure hoped the man had something to say that would help Ginny's case.

"Dr. Snider, you spent yesterday visiting with Eugenia Rutledge, is that correct?"

"I did, sir."

"And your goal was to determine if there is any sign that would point to Mrs. Rutledge maybe being insane. Can you tell me how your talk went?"

"Among other things, we went over some writing Mrs. Rutledge has done regarding her concerns for the other women in the asylum. She wants to work toward changing the asylum system. Her view is that the Horecroft Asylum and most likely many other asylums are the worst possible places for both the sane who have been wrongly locked away, and the insane who desperately need better care.

"Because I'd been notified beforehand that I'd be called on to examine Mrs. Rutledge, this gave me time to exchange letters with Dorothea Dix, a well-respected nurse who served during the Civil War and who has since dedicated herself to the humane care of the mentally ill.

Mrs. Rutledge's plan, once this trial is over and her sanity recognized, is to donate her time and money toward the closing of such cruel institutions as Horecoft Insane Asylum. I am in support of that and intend to lend my name to this cause. As the personal physician to our governor and the territorial representatives, I'm going to work hard for our territory—with its tradition of suffrage and equality for all—to recognize another group who has little to no voice: the mentally ill." He looked directly at Ginny. "You've inspired me, madam." Then he pivoted to the jury. "This country would be better if all people had the wisdom and clarity of mind I found in Eugenia Rutledge."

Dakota almost cheered at the man's words.

Rutledge was on his feet again. "You talked with my wife for one afternoon. You are no judge of her mental state." He turned to the jury even as Judge Nolte banged her gavel.

"Sit down, Mr. Rutledge, and remain silent."

"You can't believe any of this. My wife there"—Rutledge flung an arm in Ginny's direction as he talked over the judge—"is a madwoman. Out of my control, as no decent wife—"

"Mr. Rutledge! This is your last warning."

Rutledge dropped into his seat and crossed his arms in disgust.

"One more outburst like that and I will instruct the sheriff's deputy to take you into custody and hold you in jail until this trial is over. Is that clear?"

Rutledge only glared at the judge. His lawyer, however, responded on Rutledge's behalf, "It's clear, Your Honor."

Dakota wanted to offer to help escort Rutledge to the

jailhouse. He would if it became necessary. In fact, he'd enjoy it.

The lawyer sat and whispered something to his client, and sternly. Rutledge stayed quiet but looked very unhappy with how things were going.

Dr. Snider, who was watching Rutledge as he might examine a bug he'd found in his soup, turned back to Mr. Etherton.

"Now, Dr. Snider, I have a few specific questions."

The two men had an extended back-and-forth that bespoke Ginny's calm demeanor. They discussed in particular what Ginny had written in her own hand.

"I'd like to have my client's papers included as evidence, Your Honor. Mrs. Rutledge has been writing diligently for years while in her frontier home. She's added to her thoughts since we talked yesterday. I believe they are a good representation of an orderly and intelligent mind, and one that has been consistently so for years. The pages are dated, and I'd be willing to wait here quietly if you'd like to read through them now."

Judge Nolte nodded. "I may read them later, Mr. Etherton, after we adjourn for the day. Leave the pages with me and let's continue with your witness's testimony."

The trial went on a long time, and then Lydia woke up. Maeve rose with a fussy Lydia.

Marie was stirring in Jake's arms. Dakota caught Maeve's arm. "Wait." He looked at Jake. "Let me take her. I can stay with Maeve if you're all right in here without me."

Jake nodded, then glanced at Jacob, who was now being called JJ by everyone. The boy was still deeply asleep in Oscar's arms. Jake slid Marie over to Dakota. "Thanks."

Dakota left Dr. Snider and Mr. Etherton calmly showing the whole world just how sane Ginny was. Dakota figured they'd have the trial finished before supper. Now, he thought as he followed Maeve out of the courthouse, all he had to do was evade Ezra Darnell and get out of town without having to shoot anybody.

22

Maeve went over to Brandon Nolte, who stood in the shade across the street from the courthouse. He held his wide-awake son in his arms. The boy was more of an age with the twins.

Lydia was sitting up in Maeve's arms now, looking at the interesting, bustling town of Cheyenne. In her very short life, she'd never left Hidden Canyon—none of Beth's children had. Maeve wondered how it all seemed to the Holt children.

"Where'd Michaela go, Mr. Nolte?" Maeve had to wonder because his daughter had always been close at hand.

Dakota sidled up to Maeve with Marie in his arms. She was groggy and rubbing her eyes. That wouldn't last for long. Soon they'd be chasing her to keep her from running in front of an oncoming freight wagon. Brand's little boy looked at her and Lydia with fascinated interest.

"Call me Brand." He nodded toward a storefront just down the street—*Sadie's Dry Goods*. "Her ma has an order in for fabric. When she's not a judge, she's a seamstress. And a fine one at that. She's running low on calico and gingham, and she may even buy some lengths of silk. She's going to buy enough fabric that she can sell yard goods to women who sew for themselves. Michaela has a few things she wants. She's partial to ribbons, and Nell has taught her how to tat lace. She wants to learn to knit, too. So she'll need yarn, thread for the lace, and some embroidery floss to do needlework. Nell told her to go ahead and pick out what she wants. Michaela has sound judgment for such things."

Maeve wanted to hear more. "A judge *and* a seamstress, that's wonderful. Your wife is a marvel. And because you're making it possible for her to be both, that makes you a marvel as well."

Brand laughed. "I'm a hand with children, I reckon." He looked at Dakota, and the two men exchanged smiles as they held the tykes. "I raised Michaela and her two big sisters for a few years without a ma. When I married Nell, well, she's mighty smart about girls, and I was a lunkhead. But when it comes to baby wrangling, I've been at it a lot longer than she has."

Dakota said, "I was the oldest of five brothers, and my ma died when the last of us boys were born. I was caring for little ones from a young age."

"Life's full of hardships." Brand kissed his son on his blond head.

"I'd like to go look in the dry-goods store, Dakota." He looked around the busy town.

Maeve noticed that overly watchful expression of his, just like he'd had in the hotel dining room. Which reminded her that he'd kissed her then. That made her want to get well away from him and shop for yarn with Michaela, and do it quick.

"I'd better come along." Dakota nodded to Brand. "It's occurred to us that threatening these children would be a good way for Rutledge to get his wife to come along home with him."

"He'd do a thing like that?" Brand had a look in his eyes. A man who'd seen his share of trouble.

Maeve saw it in Dakota's, too. Maybe someone might think they saw that same look in her own eyes. "The way Ginny tells it," she said, "her husband has never accepted defeat in his whole life. Her running off kept her money out of his reach. But regardless of the money, she defied him, and *that* he can't abide."

"Down, Pa!"

Brand bounced his wiggling son. "He'll have to accept it if she's found to be sane by the judge."

Maeve glanced at the courthouse behind her and regretted leaving, but a crying baby had no place at a trial. "I am sorely afraid that judge telling him his wife is sane and that she must be left alone now won't serve the purpose Ginny hopes it will. Win or lose, she'll still be in danger."

Dakota had his own arms full with Marie, who struggled to get down and play. "And she loves these grandbabies. There's not much she wouldn't do to protect them. Because of that, I don't want Maeve wandering around alone."

Brand nodded his agreement, wrangled his son, and stared at the courthouse, all at the same time.

Maeve, feeling hunted more by Dakota and her memory

of that kiss than some unknown henchman of Rutledge's, headed for the store. She had very little money and no need for a new dress, but pretty fabric and silk embroidery thread were always a pleasure to look at and touch. Maybe Dakota would stay outside.

But no. As she went inside, the lumbering ox came right in with her. It was a woman's shop! He had no place here, and she'd bet anything he had no need of silk embroidery thread.

Glancing at him, Maeve said, "We need to find a safe place for Marie to run around for a while. Could you go ask Brand if there's a school playground or a churchyard nearby?"

Dakota shook his head. "I'll be staying close by you. After you've done your shopping, we can find a place for the young'uns to play. For now, I'll hang on to Marie. I can hold Lydia too if you like."

Maeve turned away. Clearly the man was going nowhere. She visited with Michaela for a bit. Dakota wandered the store as if he was in the market for calico. Michaela was studying tatting thread.

The older lady running the shop was friendly and made a fuss over the children. "Can I help you find what you're looking for?"

Maeve looked around the store, which was surprisingly large. From the outside, the place didn't look all that big. There were bolts of material lying stacked on tables, among them fine leather and silk, and printed fabric and solid-colored cotton that looked perfect for men's shirts. A set of drawers had the labels *Embroidery silk*, *Thread*, and *Yarn*. The needles and thimbles were displayed behind the glass-front counters that lined the room. And a number of books were available for customers to page through; one of them was open to a dress in a style Maeve had never imagined. It had ruffles and underskirts and wide, billowing arms gathered at the wrists. The store also sold bonnets and parasols, gloves and handkerchiefs, even shoes. Everything smelled so new, clean, and fresh. Maeve could stay here in this shop all day.

"You have so many lovely things," she answered the older woman. "I'll just look around for a while if you don't mind. Go ahead and help Michaela."

"Oh, you know the judge's daughter?" She gestured to a teetering pile of fabric on the front counter. "The judge is also a seamstress, and she's begun selling fabric to the ladies in her area who make their own clothes. She's quite the businesswoman."

Maeve smiled. "Yes, Michaela and I have met." Maeve decided not to go into detail about how or why.

Michaela returned and laid skeins of white yarn on a stack of fabric. Judge Nolte, as a seamstress, appeared to have made a good-sized order. Maeve wasn't sure where Pine Valley was, but she got the impression it'd been a long journey to get to Cheyenne. No doubt it was hard to find fabric this beautiful on the frontier.

The owner went back to the stack of fabric and began wrapping bundles in brown paper.

Lydia yelped and wiggled. Maeve was heading to the back of the store to tell Dakota they should probably go when Marie dove for the floor. Dakota was paying close attention and didn't drop her. He looked at Maeve and whispered, "I'm going to set her down for a bit. Not much breakable here, and I'll watch her close." He lowered her to the floor.

The girl darted behind a table overflowing with fabric. Smiling, Maeve went after her, only to find the little one gone. Maeve saw an aisle between tables and heard Marie jabbering. With Lydia in hand, Maeve followed the toddler and found herself in a back room. She caught up to Marie and reached for her hand.

Someone locked an arm around her neck and hissed, "Quiet."

He turned her in the direction she'd come to look right at Dakota. She heard the metallic click of a gun being cocked and noticed Dakota looking past her shoulder at whoever held her.

"Take the baby," the man said. "Set her on the floor and let's go. Come along quietly or I'll shoot the woman."

"Please, let her go." Dakota had his palms raised. "I promise I'll come without any trouble."

"Not another word or the woman dies. Then I start on the young'uns. I'd as soon get out of town, but then you and I are going to have us a showdown. As it is, I'm willing to leave the little ones behind and only take the two of you."

Maeve felt the man's hot breath blow past her ear as he talked.

This was about Ginny. Rutledge had hired someone to harm them, his purpose to get Ginny to give up her fight and go home with her husband. Go back to the asylum. But Rutledge would want them to take Ginny's grandchildren as well. She'd be much more likely to do as she was told if it meant saving her precious babies. Why would Rutledge think Ginny would be swayed by a threat to Maeve and Dakota?

Dakota's jaw clenched. Then he said, "Give me Lydia, Maeve."

Her stomach sank. Dakota was going to do as he was told. Marie was already wandering out of the back room. Soon Michaela would see her, search for Maeve and Dakota, then call for help.

They just had to stay alive until help came in the form of the whole family over at the courthouse.

Dakota took Lydia without any sudden moves. He crouched down to lay the little girl on the floor. She promptly sat up and then crawled for the wall, where she pulled herself to her feet. Turning to look at them, she smiled.

Maeve wanted to go, and go fast—before this man realized he should take the children. The arm tightened around her neck. He motioned with the gun in such a way that the muzzle was visible with her right eye.

"Out the back," he ordered. "Now. There are two horses waiting. You'll only be a step ahead of me and never out of my sight. Mount up, then wait for me and the woman."

Dakota walked right out the back door. Maeve was just a step behind him as they both emerged into an alley. The man holding her closed the door to the shop.

Maeve saw there weren't two horses, there were three. On the third one, a man sat with his gun drawn. Aimed straight at Dakota.

"Mount up. Let's get out of town."

Dakota glanced at Maeve, his jaw rigid. He swung up onto the horse while Maeve was tossed over a saddle. The man who'd grabbed her mounted up so fast she didn't have a chance to even think of fighting back.

The group rode away from the back of the dry-goods store, heading for the edge of town.

Maeve, sprawled across the saddle with a man whose face she'd yet to see riding with her, prayed as she never had before.

23

The door at the back of the courtroom slammed open.

"Something's happened!" Brand Nolte shouted. "Dakota and Maeve are gone. They left the children behind. They vanished. We need help."

Jake stood, whirled around, and thought the very worst. Rutledge had done this.

The gavel came down onto the judge's desk. "This trial is in recess."

Dr. Snider, being questioned now by Rutledge's lawyer, leapt up and rushed toward Brand.

Jake shoved past Oscar, who still held Jacob. The sleeping boy sat up with a start.

The deputy at the back of the room surged to his feet. "I'll get the sheriff." He jabbed a finger at Rutledge. "You're still under arrest. Judge, make sure he stays here."

To Jake's amazement, Judge Nolte drew a pistol and aimed it right at Thaddeus Rutledge. "Remain seated, sir."

The deputy nodded his thanks and ran outside.

Jake shouted, "Oscar! Stay here with Ginny and Beth, keep them safe. Sebastian, come with me."

Sebastian was hard on Jake's heels, who was outside before he realized Kat had come along. He had no idea how tough she was, but he wasn't going to take the time to argue with her. "Where did you see them last?"

Brand had come along. No child in his arms. Jake saw the judge's daughter across the street with three little ones surrounding her. She seemed to be handling things.

"Michaela, get yourself inside the courthouse." Brand said to Jake, "There's a livery right down the street. I already looked—they're not around, and they'd have never left the children. They've been kidnapped for certain."

Brand nodded, and Jake ran to get a horse under him. Brand and Sebastian kept up, with Kat only a pace behind them. Before they mounted, both Kat and Sebastian checked to make sure their six-shooters were loaded.

"They must've rode out by way of an alley so that no one would see 'em." Brand was talking as fast as he was moving. "Michaela was in the front of the store when she realized the children were loose and unattended. They can't have been gone long."

Jake looked at Sebastian. "You rent the horses. I'm going to see if there's anyone behind that store who saw anything."

He rushed to the back of the store and found a tinsmith shop right across from the back door. Jake hoped to find someone who could tell them which way to go.

Rutledge looked flustered. "You have no business stopping this trial, Your Honor. Whatever is going on out in the streets, justice needs to be served in here."

Ignoring him, the judge said, "The jury is dismissed. Please leave the courtroom, gentlemen. All of the trial observers, you can leave as well."

Mainly she was referring to a few newspaper reporters. As everyone filed out of the room, Nell shifted her gun, aimed at Rutledge, to her other hand, her eyes narrowed. He had to be behind this. "No offer from you, Mr. Rutledge, to let that young couple go if Ginny will agree to go back to Chicago with you?"

She watched Rutledge, his face flushed with anger, struggle to his feet. The man was old and battered. Why was he here searching for a wife he didn't want, had kept locked up for years before she found a way to escape? Because he wanted her money. That's the only motive that made any sense.

The deputy came rushing back in. "Judge, the sheriff wants me to mind the prisoner."

"Take him away, Deputy. I want him behind bars until all this is settled."

"Trust a woman to stop work the minute something gets in the way." Rutledge slammed his left fist on the table before him. She'd noticed he favored his right hand.

She needed him to talk. "Before the deputy escorts you back to jail, you get one more chance, Mr. Rutledge. Who did you hire to harm that young couple? How long before we can expect a list of demands in exchange for their safe return?"

"I know nothing about what happened to them. I don't

even know who those people are except that they're apparently tending my grandchildren."

"Thaddeus," Ginny piped up, her voice ice-cold, "no one else has a motive to want to hurt them. They're all strangers in this town. I will not go with you no matter what terrible thing you've got arranged. Now cooperate with the judge. You're not back in Chicago, surrounded by all your powerful cronies. You're not even in Independence, Missouri, where you could bribe officials so they wouldn't arrest you for attempting to kidnap Kat. You're in Wyoming. And if that couple gets hurt, or worse, killed, you're going to hang for it."

The back door of the courtroom flew open, and Michaela walked in with three children.

Nell looked at the deputy. "Please get him out of here."

The deputy strode forward and clapped shackles on Rutledge's wrists and led him out of the courtroom. The man snarled and protested the entire way out. His lawyer rushed to catch up with them, shouting at the deputy, while Dr. Horecroft followed along without a fuss.

Beth hurried over to Michaela, Ginny right behind her. They took the baby and the little girl. All of the adults exchanged looks.

Oscar asked Beth, "Are you armed?"

Beth, Lydia in one arm, pulled a Colt Peacemaker out of her reticule. Ginny took a derringer out of a pocket in her calico dress.

The judge, who already had her gun out, carefully aimed it away from the children.

Oscar went to Ginny, caught her arm, and said, "I'm going, but you be careful. Just because your husband is locked up doesn't mean he didn't hire someone other than whoever took Dakota and Maeve. I thought a few on the jury looked a bit too kindly at Rutledge and Horecroft. I hate to have to leave you, but I can't stay behind."

"We'll be fine," the judge said. "Go. You can catch up to them if you hurry. Sounded like they're riding to the west of town."

Beth said, "Kat and Sebastian live west of town. Maybe they're heading for land our friends are familiar with. We're going to the hotel. We'll wait there for you."

Oscar gave Ginny a long look. For a moment, Nell wondered if maybe he'd change his mind and not go. The man looked torn right in half. But then he whirled away and ran out of the courtroom.

Nell turned to the two women, then looked at Mr. Etherton and Dr. Snider, who were still there. The reporters had all run off when the judge ordered them to leave. They went so fast and with such enthusiasm that she suspected they thought there was a good news story beyond the courthouse. "Aren't you gentlemen going to help the others?"

Mr. Etherton shrugged a shoulder. "I'm not a great rider, nor am I a skilled gunman. But I will escort you ladies and the little ones to the hotel and stay there with you."

"I'll come along," Dr. Snider said. "I know a few lawmen who are in town. Once you've settled in at the hotel, I'll go tell them what's happened with the young couple."

Nell nodded. Her stomach twisted as she thought of her farmer husband involved in a gunfight. Yet he was a tough man who'd spent the last few years learning how to track and getting more comfortable with his gun. She prayed he'd get through this without harm coming to him. She caught herself running a hand over her still-flat stomach, then said, "Let's go. Everybody stay together and remain calm. Everything's going to be all right."

"We'll do everything just as you said, Judge Nolte," Ginny snapped, "with one exception."

Nell realized by her stubborn upwelling of annoyance that she was used to giving orders and having them obeyed. A bit too used to it, in fact. "What is the exception?"

"We're not going to the hotel. We're going to the jail-house."

24

Dakota was going to die.

He accepted that. Unless a miracle happened.

But Maeve. His prayers were all for Maeve.

Every fear he'd had about finding a normal life, including a wife, and bringing her under the Darnells' guns was happening right now.

The man with Ezra rode up beside Dakota and jerked his gun out of his holster. He kept his own gun leveled at Dakota. Being almost for sure a Darnell, Dakota figured him for a mean man willing to pull the trigger. In fact, Dakota was surprised they were bothering to get him out of town instead of just shooting him down and riding off.

They rode out of Cheyenne straight west. They kept the row of businesses that included the dry-goods shop between them and Brandon. Ezra clearly didn't want to gun Dakota down in the street. He planned to get him away from witnesses before he killed him. It didn't take long. They'd cleared the last building in town and were riding hard for the foothills he'd heard someone call the Laramies.

Ezra Darnell had Maeve and was hanging back as they galloped toward the hills. Ahead, Dakota saw boulders and thick woods, broken land, rises, and gullies. If they got in there just a few paces ahead of pursuit, they could get lost and never be found.

Not only would Ezra find plenty of places to hide but he'd also find places to take cover and shoot anyone coming after him.

Dakota prayed that Jake wasn't coming after them.

He would be. Dakota knew Jake well. He knew the heart of the man, the courage, the loyalty. Jake would come. But he shouldn't.

He shouldn't abandon his wife and Ginny, his children, not when they were in danger from Rutledge.

Riding up front like this, Dakota couldn't make a move without Ezra seeing him and harming Maeve.

The man who'd disarmed Dakota hadn't taken his only gun, just the handiest.

"Head for the draw between those two hills," Ezra shouted from behind Dakota.

Dakota looked back at the man who rode just behind him. "Are you Ezra's son?"

The man glared at Dakota with those same black eyes. Those eyes and that beak of a nose were strong traits in the Darnell family. "Grandson. Name's Raul. Vic was my cousin. C'mon, pick up the pace."

"Are you all outlaws?" Dakota was trying to think of something to say, but no brilliant words jumped into his head that would be just the right thing to stop them.

"No, we're not. I helped build the railroad. Then I worked in a slaughterhouse in Denver until my grandpa asked me to help him end this."

"Vic was robbing a bank," Dakota said. "I didn't set out to kill him. He was shooting up a town because he was cornered. The sheriff was trying to bring him in without bloodshed. Vic just wouldn't stop."

"Sounds like him." Raul shook his head. "Fool kid. He was the youngest of us." The man jabbed his gun at the approaching draw. "Through there."

"Why are you doing this? You have to understand that he was going to die." Dakota wanted to tell Raul plenty of bullets went into his cousin.

Picking Dakota out for their feud was a foolish decision. But if he said as much, told of other bullets, would they then seek revenge on others they might imagine had a hand in Vic's death? Dakota couldn't be responsible for that.

It wouldn't help anyway. They'd just kill him and then start in on those others.

"How many of you Darnells are there anyway?"

"Grandpa and I and one of Grandpa's sons, Uncle Mort, who's Vic's pa. And Vic's got a brother, too, Tyrus. Grandpa Ezra sent out letters when he heard about Vic. Grandpa didn't know where you were. But he caught your scent when he stopped to wait for me to get here from Denver."

Dakota thought that might mean Grandpa and Raul here didn't know he'd killed two Darnells already—besides Vic. Mort for sure, and was the other one Tyrus? He tried to think. His heart was pounding with fear for Maeve. It was muddling his brain.

What could he do? What could he say that would stop all this?

"I was the guide of a wagon train for a stretch of years. Did you go west on the Oregon Trail? You're from Kentucky, right?"

"Yep. Cumberland Mountains. I lived there through the War Between the States, then ran off west when living with Pa and his hard fists got to be more than a man could bear. I rode the Oregon Trail but not in a wagon. I headed for Denver, and there I stayed."

Dakota nodded. Raul didn't sound purely evil, not like a man who wanted to be a killer. He was a working man after all. "Are you married?"

"Nope, but I've got a sweetheart. I figured I'd be gone so long with Grandpa she wouldn't wait for me, though I asked her to."

"You're not a killer, Raul. Why do you want to start married life with a murder on your hands."

"Ain't murder if'n you deserve it." Raul squared his shoulders and thrust his jaw out. Dakota thought the man showed these signs of determination only because he was forcing himself to.

"It's murder all right. And it's the kind of thing that leaves a scar on a man's soul. You're going to go back to Denver and try to start a life with a young woman, but for the rest of your days you'll carry the knowledge that you killed an innocent man. You killed an unarmed man. You killed a man in an unfair fight. And you'll be harming your wife while you're at it. Remembering all that will wake you up at night. It'll make your spirit heavy. It'll change you, Raul. You don't have to do this."

"Sometimes a man's gotta stand with his family." Raul sounded bitter. "Even if it does add a weight to himself. Now keep your mouth shut and ride."

Dakota looked over his shoulder at the man riding a few paces behind him. His attention moved to Maeve, whose eyes were wide with horror as she looked at him.

"You know these men?"

"Face forward." Ezra leveled his gun on Maeve. "And both of you, shut up!"

They rounded a pile of boulders and a copse of trees, then were swallowed up by a land more rugged than Dakota would have expected from this part of Wyoming.

"They're heading toward our land." Seb rode hard beside Jake on his left.

Jake couldn't remember Seb being such a skilled rider. Hooves thundered as they pushed hard. Jake could see the tracks, but he knew he was taking a risk. The men who'd taken Dakota and Maeve might turn off, yet it made sense they'd run for a hideout, and on this stretch of flatland heading west, a hideout was going to be in the foothills ahead.

The trail split, but both paths went toward the mountains, growing ever taller in front of them. Soon they covered the whole western sky.

Jake pulled his horse to a stop, hopped down, and studied a well-worn trail and a smaller, rockier trail that led slightly northwest. Three horses. The tinsmith had said three, and the tracks confirmed it.

One of them was carrying double. A woman slung over the saddle.

"The tracks follow the smaller trail." Jake swung up onto his horse and looked at Sebastian. "Can you read sign?"

"I'm not bad, but Kat's better."

Kat caught up to them on Sebastian's left. Brand rode up on Jake's right.

Brand must've heard Jake's question. "I can read sign, too. I was taught by a former U.S. Marshal and his brother—two of the finest trackers in Wyoming. We won't lose their trail."

Kat said, "I spent the first year out here tracking an elk herd and got to be good at reading a trail." She pointed well ahead of them. "I think I see a bit of dust in the air. That has to be them."

She looked from Sebastian to Jake, then to Brand. "Do you see it?"

"I do. But this trail is grass-covered, and the wind is just enough that no dust would hang in the air for long."

"I'm relieved to be with two skilled trackers," said Jake. "And, Brand, we're as close as we are because of your quick thinking and fast actions." Jake felt like he should send Brand away, but the man looked determined and so Jake let it go.

"That dust, if it's from them, leads to a trail between those hills." Kat pointed ahead. "They'll go there. And the land is rugged past it. We need to close the gap."

"One of those three horses has Maeve and the kidnapper on it. That's hard on a horse. They won't make the best time."

Jake studied the ground, then looked at what he hoped was dust from those they were chasing. "Let's pick up the pace."

"Did you hear Oscar say he didn't like the way those men of the jury were looking at Rutledge and his lawyer?" Nell asked Beth and Ginny.

Beth nodded. "I thought the same thing a couple of times. Three of them gave Dr. Horecroft a familiar sort of look."

"I saw it. I noticed it, too, in the men I dismissed from the jury. But these men were more careful at first. But not careful enough afterward. That's why I talked to the sheriff. I asked him to check around town for those three on the jury. He knew who each man was. I asked him to see if any of them had flashed money around town the night Rutledge got to Cheyenne."

Ginny's jaw tightened. "I wouldn't put it past my husband to hand out coins to a crowd of men and tell them to go volunteer to serve on the jury."

Mr. Etherton and Dr. Snider escorted them toward the jail. When they reached the door, Dr. Snider said, "I'm going now to talk to the lawmen I know."

After he left, Mr. Etherton gripped the doorknob. He looked at Ginny. "Ready?"

She gave a firm nod of her head.

"Wait a minute." Nell wasn't quite sure what they were doing here. But there was something about Ginny giving orders that reminded Nell of her own mother. "Before we go in to see your husband, I assume to wring some admission out of him concerning your friends, you need to know that all your husband would need is for one juror to find you insane." Distracted by that thought, she added,

"Juries rule on guilt or innocence, not sanity or insanity. Strange business to have a trial like this. Bringing you before a judge and jury is called *habeas corpus*."

"What?" Ginny asked. "Corpus sounds like *corpse*, and I don't like the sound of that."

Mr. Etherton gave Nell a pat on the back. "You know the law, Judge Nolte. Not all judges do." He turned to Ginny. "Habeas corpus is an order for a prisoner to be brought before a judge. Usually it pertains to whether being imprisoned can be allowed to go on. It translates to 'produce the body.' More literally it means 'you shall have the body.' It's not corpse like a dead body, but *corpus*, which in Latin simply means 'body.' So a prisoner is brought before a judge for that judge to rule on whether he remains a prisoner."

"Horecroft Insane Asylum was very much a prison. But unlike a true prison, I had no trial, no judge or jury, just Thaddeus and Dr. Horecroft deciding my fate." Ginny sighed. "I got away, but part of the reason I came out of hiding is that asylum is still full of women. Some of them are sane and being kept there by cruel relatives."

Nell considered that. "If the sane ones are freed, won't they be sent home to their cruel relatives, the very ones who locked them up to begin with?"

Ginny turned tired eyes to Nell. "That's a good question."

"And if Horecroft's asylum treats the truly mad in a way that's wrong, then how do they get better treatment?"

Ginny and Beth exchanged a long look. "We don't know how to help those poor troubled souls," Ginny admitted.

Beth spoke up. Nell could tell she was hesitant. "One of

the other ladies from the asylum is living in our canyon. I think she would qualify as someone who is truly mad. She eats with us, comes to church with us, but she stays back. She's real wary. And if you touch her, she goes berserk. She once spoke of her husband, and he must've abused her until he drove her mad. Or maybe she was already mad. We have no idea. Either way, he had her locked away in the asylum. But living in the canyon, with no one touching her, might be healing her. At least she's not subject to further abuse.

"She lives in a cave with a hot spring in one room so she's warm in the winter and can take a bath. We keep her in dresses, and she sings along with us at our Sunday morning meetings. For the most part, she seems rational, though very quiet and withdrawn. It makes me wonder if troubled women like her just need a safe, peaceful place, some compassion and understanding." Beth looked at Ginny. "We could see about having Dr. Horecroft arrested, then go bring every woman in that place, the sane and insane alike, to our canyon. Let them live out their lives there."

Ginny sighed. "I'd like to rescue them all, but bringing fifty women, a good chunk of them unwell, home with us? We'd better consult Oscar and Jake first." She glanced at the jailhouse door. "Let's go inside."

The door to the jail swung open. Nell saw that, except for Mr. Etherton, every one of them had a gun drawn.

25

Maeve jerked her head up as high as she could raise it, considering she was draped over a saddle.

Dakota knew these men? What was going on?

They charged through a narrow pass dividing two hills. She'd heard the man riding with her call it a *draw*. She'd never heard the word used in that way before. The draw was so narrow, there was only room enough to ride single file.

Dakota took the lead, followed by the man who'd waited for them behind the store. Dakota had asked if he was Ezra's son, and the man said "grandson." His name was Raul. Which meant the man who had her was Ezra. And Dakota knew them somehow. From what she'd overheard, someone had died, kin of theirs, and they blamed Dakota for shooting him dead.

Dakota had told her he had men hunting him. These men apparently. And hunting him only—they had nothing to do with Ginny and her husband.

Maeve was torn between relief and wanting to scream. How many evil men were there? Why did they all seem to be after people she knew and loved?

Dakota had said she should know what followed him so she'd know to stay away from him, and she wouldn't want him paying her any personal attention.

Well, the man had certainly been right about that.

The draw opened into a rugged upward slope that was much wider but had no visible trail. Ezra and Raul pressed on regardless, dodging boulders as they climbed. The horses were growing tired from the treacherous ride, especially the poor animal she was riding double on.

Maeve spoke quietly, not wanting to stir up Ezra more than he already was. "Why do you want to harm us? What has Dakota done that has made you so angry?"

"He killed my grandson."

Maeve gasped. "That's terrible. Why didn't you get the sheriff to go after him instead of you doing it?"

"The law ain't gonna protect my kin. I plan to do it myself."

"The law won't help you? Have you talked to them?"

She felt a hard rap on her head. Not enough to knock her out, but it hurt plenty.

"Shut yer mouth. Yer man's gonna die. Then we'll prob'ly set you on foot, let you find yer own way home. We needed to get outta town so we could settle our feud without any witnesses around."

Maeve considered that, deciding right then that any further questions would be unwise. She herself was a witness. No one had seen these men grab her and Dakota and run. No one except her. She very much doubted they would go and kill a man in cold blood right before her eyes, then allow her to live.

That rap on the head had served to clear away her panic and her anger at Dakota. She felt an almost deadly calm wrap around her until she was able to think clearly.

She had to get away. Either that or overpower these two men. That wasn't likely to happen since they were both bigger and stronger than she was, and armed. Which meant she'd need to catch them off guard, by surprise. She had to outthink them. And since Dakota's life was in jeopardy, she had to take him with her.

Or did she? Would they put aside killing Dakota if she somehow got free?

One thing they didn't know was that Maeve had a gun with her. Beth had done her best to arm everyone. Because Maeve didn't carry a reticule with her, Beth had bought her a small handgun and holster in Cheyenne which could be strapped around the ankle. Beth then demanded that Maeve show her the gun, a five-shot derringer, every morning and prove to her it was loaded.

Of course, Maeve couldn't get to the derringer. Yet if she picked the right spot, threw herself off the horse, dodged behind some boulders or trees, and didn't die in her desperate attempt to get free, would they still kill Dakota? Or would they try to recapture her first?

It might be enough of a distraction that Dakota could get away, too.

She braced herself to take any chance she was given, no matter if it was reckless and dangerous and could maybe get her killed. But doing nothing was even worse.

She thought of her ma with a twinge of pain in her

heart. She'd like to see her again. Maeve dying would hurt Ma terribly.

Well, she'd apologize to Ma and Bruce if she ever saw them again, but for now she paid attention to what was going on around her. The man who'd kidnapped her. The landscape around them. She had to get out of this mess.

With a sigh, she thought of something her ma used to say: "*A woman's work is never done.*"

"I want to talk to Thaddeus," Ginny said.

The deputy, sitting in a chair with his feet up, lurched to an upright position, then leapt to his feet while clawing for his gun.

"Don't shoot." Nell stepped between Ginny and the deputy, with her gun quickly tucked out of sight.

Beth shoved her gun into her pocket only a second or two after Nell. "Mama, put your gun away. We're sorry, Deputy. We didn't mean to come in like we'd planned for a shootout. But we are, as you'd suspect, on edge."

The deputy, looking very nervous, finally relaxed and blew out a pent-up breath.

"Are Mr. Rutledge and Mr. Sykes well secured?" Mr. Etherton asked.

The deputy nodded. "They are, sir. Locked up tight."

"You understand that my client, Mrs. Rutledge, feels she's in danger as long as her husband is in town."

"They're right here in jail, so she's not in any danger. Their lawyer has tried to get them free, and Mr. Rutledge has been allowed to attend the trial, but under guard. He will not be allowed to walk free, not as long as the charge of attempted kidnapping of his wife, and the assault on his wife and Miss O'Toole, are outstanding."

"And where is Dr. Horecroft?" Beth doubted the man would spend his time hanging around this jailhouse.

"He isn't under arrest. He followed us back to the jailhouse, spoke quietly with Mr. Rutledge for a couple of minutes, and left."

"My husband, please?" Ginny asserted herself again, though not with her gun out this time.

The deputy looked to the judge, then the lawyer, then Ginny. He shrugged. "It's all right with me. Promise you'll stay well back from the bars, ma'am. The sheriff said Mr. Rutledge grabbed Mrs. Jones through the bars the last time you were here, so he can't be trusted."

"We think he had a hand in the kidnapping of the two people who are missing, the people your sheriff is chasing after, along with the men who came into town with us. I'm hoping my husband will tell us something that will help find them."

The deputy looked at the judge again.

"We promise to stay out of grabbing distance," Judge Nolte reassured him. She then turned to Ginny. "Won't we, Mrs. Rutledge?"

Ginny managed a small smile at the stern tone. "Yes. I've no interest in letting that awful man get his hands on me, not ever again."

A reminder to the deputy that Thaddeus Rutledge had grabbed her and tried to run off with her.

"Michaela?" The judge turned to her daughter, who'd come into the jailhouse with them, carrying her little brother.

"Yes, Ma?"

"Will you stay here and keep the little ones occupied? I'm sorry I've been making you watch Buck all the time. I hope to look around Cheyenne once this mess is sorted out. I heard there's a man in town who came to study how Clint cooks and has a fine restaurant here."

Michaela grinned. "I'd as soon watch a pack of children as see the inside of a jail. But I'm planning on being a schoolteacher in a few years, so I could use the practice managing children."

Once Beth and Ginny had handed over Beth's children, the deputy led the way to the door that shut the cells away from the rest of the jailhouse.

Thundering hooves from behind snapped Jake's head around. The sheriff was catching up just as they rode into the narrow gap between two rugged hills.

Seb said, "Pull up. We can ride in together."

Sheriff Peters and his two companions caught up. "Are you sure they went in this way?" Peters asked.

"We tracked them here, Sheriff." Kat turned her horse to face them.

"We have to keep moving. Lots going on in town, but we've no time to discuss it now. Let me go first. It's a treacherous business following armed men with bad intent into a rugged stretch. It's my job to face such danger, not yours. The men with me are U.S. Marshals."

Brand said to one of the Marshals, "I recognize you. You were involved in the troubles with the Deadeye Gang in Pine Valley. I'm Brand Nolte. My wife is justice of the peace in Pine Valley."

"Morgan Sawyer. I remember you and your wife." From horseback the Marshal studied the ground and said, "Three horses. The same ones we've been after since we picked up the trail. I'll go first, Sheriff, if you don't mind."

Jake knew he had competent men with him, and yet the itch to rush ahead nagged him something terrible. He was very much afraid they had no time for caution.

26

Maeve had no time for caution.

As they climbed, the rocks became packed in tighter, the trees closing in. Soon these men would pick a spot, kill Dakota and Maeve, and very possibly shoot anyone who was coming to rescue them.

They rounded a curve in the trail, and Maeve saw a boulder-studded cliff to her left . . . well, off in the direction of her dangling feet.

Dear Lord God, protect me. And if these are my last moments on earth, gather me to yourself in heaven. Because I trust in you, Lord. I believe in you . . .

She drew a long, slow breath as they reached the steepest part of the slope, then threw herself off the horse feetfirst and fell over the cliff. She screamed to cause a distraction and to make sure Dakota knew what she'd just done.

"Hey!" shouted the man who'd been riding with her.

Maeve plunged backward, skidded down the slope, twisting so her head wouldn't slam into anything hard she slid by.

But everything was hard. She shrieked as she skidded, tumbled, bounced, and rolled. She'd had one quick look at the fall before she jumped. It hadn't been a sheer drop, but it was steep enough. At one point she hit a boulder so hard, her scream cut off. She kept rolling with only the least bit of control—grabbing at the scrub, yanking small trees from the gravel and dirt. A firm grip on one of these nearly wrenched her arms loose from her shoulders and pivoted her so she was falling feetfirst again. The tiny tree she'd latched on to ripped through her hands, scraping and cutting her palms.

On and on she fell. A bullet whizzed past her. That horrible man was shooting at her! She heard shouting from overhead. She heard Dakota and more gunfire. Then a boulder the size of a man loomed ahead. She slid into it with her feet and came to a lurching stop—in position for the gunman shooting at her. She leapt to her feet, stumbled and fell face-first, but managed to crawl behind the huge rocks where she could take cover as bullets ricocheted around her. She gasped for breath, the wind knocked out of her, and inhaled the dust she'd kicked up. But there was no time to recover. Dakota might even now have guns leveled on him.

She hiked up her skirt, drew the gun from her ankle holster, got to her knees and peered between a crevice in the rocks. The man who'd been riding with her was coming fast. He'd jumped off his horse and pursued her, sitting and sliding down the slope, gun in hand. The rocks rattled beneath his boots.

He was almost even with her and in a more controlled fall. He would catch up to her within a few paces. As he slid his way closer, she pulled back the hammer on the derringer, aimed, and fired.

The man's eyes went wide, and he let out a groan. He stood up straight, as the impact of the bullet had stopped him in his tracks. Stumbling forward a few steps, he spotted the crevice she'd used to fire at him. Though wounded, he raised his gun to shoot at her through the space in the rocks.

But Maeve beat him to it. She shot him again.

"Hey!"

Dakota's head came around. He heard Maeve's voice. She was screaming! He heard rocks sliding, falling, some of them large.

Raul turned toward Ezra.

Ezra had jumped off his horse and run off, skidding over the edge of the trail.

Dakota kicked his horse, and in two fast leaps he left the Darnells behind. Once he was out of the line of fire, he dismounted, grabbed his gun out of his boot, and circled back around a twist in the trail.

Dodging the boulder that made the trail curve, he saw Ezra shooting at Maeve. He was distracted, but not Raul.

Raul had seen Dakota take off and was coming at a full gallop, his gun drawn.

Then a gun fired, but it wasn't Raul's or Ezra's. A split second later, Dakota heard the old man crying out in pain.

Raul wheeled his horse around and charged back toward his grandfather. He halted, leapt off his horse, and went sliding down the same cliff Maeve had gone over, kicking up a cloud of dust.

Dakota charged for the spot where Ezra and Raul had disappeared. He saw Ezra jerk back and stand up from his plunging slide, even as Raul began plummeting toward him.

Ezra brought his gun around to aim it at a pile of boulders.

Another shot rang out, coming from the boulders. Ezra's gun fell from his hand, and he pitched forward, then slid down the steep slope face-first and out of sight. Raul, skidding and fighting to slow his descent, clawed at rocks and shrubs as he made his way toward his fallen grandfather.

"Maeve, are you all right?" Dakota started down the slope—going too fast, but he had to get to her.

"Dakota? You're alive!" Maeve's voice quavered like an aspen in the wind.

"Yes, I'm fine. Maeve, did you get hit? Did the fall injure you?" Dakota picked up speed and was out of control by the time he reached the pile of boulders where Maeve was hiding.

She rose from her shelter and stepped out just as Dakota slammed into her. They both tumbled to the ground. A well-placed boulder stopped them or they might've slid all the way back to Cheyenne.

Dakota flopped onto his back. Maeve bounced, then sprawled beside him. Before Dakota could catch his breath, he heard a loud cry.

"Help!" Raul was out of sight below Dakota and Maeve—except for his hands, which clung to a brittle-looking pine tree. "Help me, please. Someone!"

Dakota looked at Maeve, knowing the man begging for help wanted to kill him. He swallowed hard. "Did he shoot you, Maeve? Are you hurt bad?"

She shook her head. "Not bad, no. Now go. Get to the top of the cliff and ride out of here. Fast."

Dakota didn't argue with her. Headed downward again. In control finally, but it was a treacherous stretch all the same. He reached Raul just as the pine he was clinging to ripped free from the man's hands. Raul screamed for help, and Dakota grabbed Raul's wrist as stones and dirt sprayed down on him.

The scream cut off. Raul looked up at Dakota, who was holding him by the one wrist. His other arm dangled at his side.

"Quick! Give me your other hand," Dakota said.

"You killed my cousin."

"Raul, please, I can't hang on much longer. Give me both hands."

"My grandpa would want me to die before I'd accept help from the likes of you."

"Your grandpa is dead." Dakota locked eyes with the man who'd come to kill him. "Let this end here. Your cousin was a killer who had to be stopped. I'm not a killer. And neither are you."

Dakota's hand slipped on Raul's wrist.

"Let me save you. Let me save a life and call it payment for your cousin. Please, Raul. Think of the woman you want to marry. Think of God and how you want to meet Him in the next life. Take my hand and end this feud."

Raul's panic faded, along with his hate. Swallowing hard, he reached up with his other hand and took Dakota's offered one. An inch at a time, Dakota dragged the man back over the lip of the cliff. Then the two of them lay side by side, gasping for breath.

Raul rolled onto his belly and looked over the cliff. "I left those Cumberland Mountains looking for something better than a hardscrabble life. A life that shortened my pa's life and then my ma's. Grandpa Ezra had enough hate in his heart to feed him for a lifetime, but I wanted better." He gazed down at his grandfather's body sprawled a hundred feet below. Then he turned to face Dakota. "We're even. More than even because you didn't owe me a thing in the first place. Thank you."

Dakota gave a nod, then said, "Let's get off this cliff."

Exhausted, the two of them began the crawl upward.

"Are you both all right?"

The voice yanked their heads up. Dakota saw Oscar, who'd emerged from the edge of the trail well above them. Maeve stood at his side. Jake appeared next, then Kat, Seb, Brand, and the sheriff.

Sheriff Peters pulled his gun and aimed it at Raul. "The one who went over the cliff is dead. You get up here and then get your hands up, mister."

Two more men joined the others. They'd brought quite a posse to save them. Dakota was relieved that none of them had gotten shot or had to face shooting his fellow man. Only Maeve had to live with that scar on her soul.

"Do you need us to come down there and haul you up?" Jake called out.

"No, don't come down. We can make it. There's no sense in anyone else having to fight his way back up." Dakota got to his hands and knees alongside Raul, then found the grit to rise to his feet. He looked up at Maeve and saw a nasty-looking scrape across her left cheek, and her hands were bleeding from getting slashed.

"I'm sorry she got hurt," Raul said. "I'll confess my part in all this to the sheriff and take whatever's coming to me."

"I'll speak for you, Raul. You turned back to save your grandpa. You never fired your gun at Maeve or me. Let's see if we can get you home to your woman."

The two of them scrambled the rest of the way up to the trail.

Raul put his hands in the air. "I'll come along, Sheriff. I'll confess everything."

"It's a feud, Sheriff Peters," Dakota explained. "Raul here was dragged into it, and now he wants to end it."

The sheriff looked grim. "We'll sort all this out back in town. Kidnapping is a crime whether you were dragged into it or not."

Raul nodded and found his horse, held by one of the strangers.

Dakota hurried over to Maeve. "You're hurt. I'm so sorry. And I'm sorry you had to shoot a man."

Maeve, her face ashen, nodded. "I'm sorry too, but he gave me no choice."

As the two strangers and the sheriff were talking quietly with Raul, Seb said, "I know a way down there to where the body is without going over the cliff."

The sheriff gestured toward the horses. "Come and help us pick up your grandpa, Raul." Moments later, Sheriff Peters, Raul, Seb, Kat, and the two strangers rode off.

"Looks as though everything's under control," said Brand. "I'm heading back to town."

"I'll go with you," Oscar said and mounted up. "You all set off when you're ready." The two men rode away.

Dakota gathered his horse and Ezra's to make the trip back.

Jake offered Maeve a kerchief. "You're bleeding." He studied her, then Dakota. "Neither of you was shot? We sure heard a lot of gunfire."

"Nope. Now let's get back to guarding Ginny." Dakota boosted Maeve into the saddle, though she was strong and agile and didn't need much help.

Dakota mounted up, as did Jake. He watched dust kick up behind Oscar and Brand's horses as they picked up the pace in an effort to get back to town.

As the trio started the journey, riding much slower than Oscar and Brand, Maeve asked the question Dakota had been dreading.

"Who were those men, Dakota?"

27

Two men Beth didn't know burst into the jailhouse, shoving Dr. Horecroft in front of them. Dr. Snider was right behind them.

The deputy looked befuddled as one of the men took the keys off a nail in the wall, unlocked the door to the cell Rutledge was in, and pushed Horecroft inside with him.

When the jail door clanged shut and the key twisted hard in the lock, Beth was swamped with a feeling of intense satisfaction. But she was confused, too. "What did he do?"

"You found men on the jury who'd been bribed." Judge Nolte sounded profoundly satisfied.

Dr. Snider smiled a rather mean smile. Father and his cronies hadn't made friends in this town, not including the men Dr. Horecroft had bribed.

"The sheriff had us asking questions all over town. We found six men, mostly loafers at three different saloons, who had money they'd never earned and flashed it around. Two of them—the ones you noticed and talked to the sheriff about—were heard bragging about taking a twenty-dollar gold piece and not even having to sit on the jury. Another who was on the jury was sow-drunk on the boardwalk outside a saloon, and a fourth was busy buying rounds for the house."

"Dr. Horecroft spent his money very unwisely," the judge said with disgust.

"You mean that's a crime?" Ginny sounded dubious. "I suspected many times that Thaddeus had done that. He had lawsuits brought against him a few times, but he never seemed to worry about it, and he always won his cases."

"It's obstruction of justice, Mrs. Rutledge," Judge Nolte replied.

"Please, call me Ginny."

Judge Nolte gave a little tilt of her head as if she understood and approved of Ginny not wanting the name Rutledge attached to her. She went on, "Obstruction of justice can mean several things, one of which is bribing jurors to come to the decision the man bribing you wants. So yes, it's a crime all right."

One of the men stepped forward and said, "I'm Owen Riley, U.S. Marshal. Dr. Horecroft did the bribing for Mr. Rutledge's case. That makes both of them criminals. I'm going to enjoy locking them up, and not just in a jail in Cheyenne. They're going to the territorial prison."

"This is nonsense." Rutledge approached the bars, glaring at Marshal Riley. "I'll destroy you for this."

Riley looked supremely unafraid.

"You won't destroy anyone without money." Ginny stood straighter than Beth had ever seen her. "And you're never getting your hands on my parents' honestly earned money." Mama's blue eyes flashed with hope as she turned back to Marshal Riley. "I'm safe then? I'm free?"

"You're safe, Ginny." Mr. Etherton gave her a confident smile. "He won't get a life sentence, but seeing as he's an old man, five years or so will no doubt amount to the same thing. He doesn't have that many years left, and the harsh confines of prison won't be easy on him. Since he committed the bribery, Horecroft should get ten years, but we'll see what Judge Nolte says. You'll have your chance to go set those women free he's got locked up back in Chicago. And help them any way you can." Etherton walked toward the cell. "Sykes is the only one with the good sense to be afraid of what could happen to him. He may get the lightest sentence, but he'll do time nonetheless."

Sykes, sitting on a cot in the cell on the left side, set his mouth in a grim line.

The lawyer studied him. "I hope you'll go straight, but whether you do or not, without Rutledge to pay your salary, I'd say you'll be leaving Ginny alone."

Sykes didn't respond other than to slump back against the wall.

Father shouted an insult at the judge, which to Beth's mind was just plain stupid.

Horecroft settled on his cot with his nose in the air. Perhaps a few years in the territorial prison would knock the arrogance out of him.

Judge Nolte, who'd been brandishing a weapon since the men entered the jailhouse, checked her gun in a way that was so slick and polished, Beth decided it was a trick she'd have to learn herself.

"It's a decision you have to make for yourself," said the

judge, "but you should divorce Mr. Rutledge, Ginny. Such a thing is rare around here, but it can be done—especially when a husband has behaved violently toward his wife."

Mama frowned. "It's such a terrible sin, though. I made vows before God to love, honor, and cherish Thaddeus till death us do part."

"Yes, I know those vows well as I've performed a few wedding ceremonies and been married twice myself. But honestly, you don't love him, nor cherish him."

Mama visibly shuddered, then shook her head. "Good heavens, how could I?"

"You vowed to obey him as well, and you've certainly not done that for a while. Same goes for honoring him."

"Not for a long while." Mama nodded slowly, then added, "What it comes down to is . . . I've broken my vows already."

Judge Nolte didn't say anything more. Instead, she offered a kind smile, reached over, and squeezed Ginny's hand.

"Jake, will you go on ahead, catch up with Oscar and Brand? I need to talk to Maeve for a while."

Jake looked at Dakota, then at Maeve. "Is it safe for you two to ride without me?"

Dakota knew, if Raul had the right of it, that the Darnell feud against him had just ended with the death of Ezra Darnell. "Yep, I think the feud is done now."

Jake's eyes shifted to Maeve again. "I'll ride ahead enough to let you talk in private, but I'm not going far. Rutledge may still have trouble in store." With a gentle kick, he urged his horse into a trot.

Dakota and Maeve kept walking. He didn't wait for long. "Those two men were named Darnell."

Maeve's brow furrowed. "You said some men were after you. Or there was trouble following you. Something like that."

Dakota wished he could just forget the whole thing now that his troubles seemed to be over. No one had to know what all he'd been through. No one had to know about those unmarked graves back in his valley.

Then he saw her brow furrow more deeply. Nope, there was no way to avoid speaking of it.

"Ezra Darnell was the one who grabbed you and forced us to go out the back door of that fabric store. He and his family have been after me ever since I was part of the crowd that killed Ezra's grandson Vic in a shootout while he was robbing a bank."

"Part of the crowd? So was Ezra after every man who'd killed his grandson?"

Dakota shook his head. "I don't know what else that family was up to. I was in a town in Oregon on my way to find Jake. I found homesteading in Oregon didn't suit me, so I headed for Idaho and the mountains and my old friend. Vic Darnell picked the town I was in to rob a bank."

"You were there?"

"Yep, I was coming down the boardwalk when gunfire erupted inside the bank. I ducked into an alley in time to see this tall, black-eyed man drag a woman outside the bank with his arm around her neck and a gun to her head."

"Just like Ezra had me."

"The woman screamed and clawed Vic across the face. He roared, and the gun went off. She fell right in front of me. Vic didn't notice me, but he saw every man in town come running, the sheriff included. Vic leveled the gun and fired into a gathering crowd, and I, along with the sheriff, his deputy, a bleeding and staggering man who came out of the bank, and at least two men in the crowd all shot him dead. Vic collapsed beside the woman. Men out front were on the ground and bleeding. Two men in the street died. He'd killed another one inside the bank."

Dakota paused and shook his head. "Terrible thing to see. I had to stay in town and answer some questions. I suppose that's how I became the focus of a family feud. But I knew nothing about it until a second man came hunting me and tried to kill me in my meadow. He had a letter on him, written by Ezra Darnell, telling him to find me and kill me. Ezra was calling on his whole family to do the same." Dakota reined in his horse to a stop. Maeve pulled up beside him.

He shifted in the saddle to face her. "I couldn't begin any kind of life in that mountain valley so long as the Darnells were coming after me." His chin lowered, and he stared at his hands. "I've got two graves there. A testament to my surviving by my gun. That is how it's been up in those mountains for the last three years." He forced himself to look up and meet her eyes. "Raul told me that he and his grandpa Ezra, the one who you . . . that is, the one who had you—"

"You mean the one I killed."

Dakota felt nothing but regret that his actions had led to Maeve having to pull a trigger in such a way. "Yes, and I'm so sorry. Raul and Ezra are the last of the Darnells." He swung down off his horse and in two strides reached her, caught her waist, and lifted her to the ground. "Maeve, you saved me. You saved us both. You knew it was life or death. I heard you scream and turned to see you falling. Raul went after Ezra instead of me."

"I had a gun Ezra didn't know of. Beth insisted I carry it with me at all times."

Dakota felt his brow rise until his hat lifted. "Me too. She gave me an ankle holster, so I had a gun even after Raul disarmed me.

"Your courage saved me. You saved yourself. We came out of this unharmed." Dakota gently touched the raw scrapes on her face. "Mostly unharmed, thanks to your quick mind and brave heart. Thank you, Maeve, and now . . ." He gazed into her beautiful blue eyes. "What I mean to say is, my home should be safe now. A decent place where I can dare to think of the future. And I'd like to spend more time with you, see if we could have a life together. Maeve, do you . . . could you . . . ?"

She threw her arms around his neck and kissed him.

He was doing such a terrible job of asking to court her, he figured she was saving him again. Then he didn't think of much else at all. He wrapped his arms around her waist and lifted her off her feet.

It was a long time later—after he'd forgotten his question, forgotten where he was, and possibly even forgotten his own name—when the kiss finally ended.

"Yes, Dakota Harlan," she said, "I'd like to think of a future with you."

Dakota grinned. "I thought you were the prettiest thing

I'd ever seen on our way west on that wagon train. But then your pa died, and you were so hurt by what happened. And I was stubborn and foolish and . . ."

He quit talking when he saw the memory of deep grief in her expression. He pulled her back into his arms and kissed her again. Talking was only making things worse.

When this kiss ended, Maeve looked a little dazed.

Dakota decided to slip in a few more encouraging words. "I love you, Maeve O'Toole."

"I've one more year left on my homestead before I prove up on it. We could sell it to Ma and Bruce or just give it to them. Either way, I have to live on the land for another year."

Dakota knew about homesteading. "You have to live there six months out of the year. Maybe by June of next year, you'll be able to decide if we suit each other."

A smile bloomed on her face, and he knew he had a matching one. "That sounds good. It sounds good because I love you, too, Dakota Harlan." Then Maeve's smile turned into a frown. "I can't think of a way to be a judge in Idaho—it's not allowed there. And we'll be living a long way from a town. Not much need for a judge when you're alone in the mountains. But I like the judge. I admire her."

Dakota did his best to conceal a wave of relief that Maeve wasn't right now deciding to move to Wyoming and become a judge. Or a sheriff, or the governor . . . or who knew what else?

Then, because she was so close and so pretty and he was so in love, Dakota drew her close and kissed her once again.

"Hey!" Jake said. "Enough of that. Let's get to town."

Dakota pulled back and turned to see a grinning Jake, watching him kiss the living daylights out of Maeve. Heat crawled up his neck, and he knew for a fact he was blushing like a shy schoolgirl.

"Are you two thinking of getting married maybe?" Jake leaned forward, resting his forearm on the saddle horn.

"You're getting a bit ahead of us, but we are definitely thinking we want to find out if we have a future together." Maeve spoke pretty boldly for a woman who was blushing as badly as he was.

"And is your trouble with the Darnells over?" Other than Maeve, Jake was the only one Dakota had told about the family feud.

"It's over. Raul told me that he and his grandpa were the last of them, and Raul wants peace. I can finally have a life I can invite someone to share." Dakota looked down at Maeve.

She looked up at him.

He considered sending Jake back to town on his own just so Dakota could have a little more time alone with Maeve.

Jake seemed to think he was in charge. "Then let's get back to town and hold a trial, then jump on a train home."

The door to the street opened, and Beth turned to see Maeve come rushing inside. Bleeding and pale, but alive. She went straight for Ginny, threw herself into Mama's arms.

"Oh, Ginny, I shot someone." Maeve's voice broke, and she wept.

Mama held her close and murmured comforting words to her.

Dakota came next and went over to Mama to pat Maeve on the back, Jake right behind him. Then came Oscar and Brand.

Brand saw his daughter and son in the outer office. "I thought you were going to the hotel."

Michaela said, "Mrs. Rutledge wanted to wring information out of her husband in hopes of finding her kidnapped friends. I see you saved them."

"They saved themselves, but we rode back to town ahead of them to protect you. The hotel was empty, so we headed over here in time to meet up with Jake, Maeve, and Dakota."

"I think the trouble is mostly done here." Michaela had all the children corralled and seemed to be handy at it. "Can we go back to the fabric shop now?"

Jake looked at the three men in jail, then looked at Beth.

Beth said, "Mr. Etherton says all these men are likely going to jail. Father, and Dr. Horecroft especially, for bribing a jury."

"I won't spend another night in this cell." Father shook the bars as if he'd tear the cell apart. "I demand to speak to the governor."

Beth studied him for a minute, a bit alarmed by his beet-red face. Then she went back to telling Jake what had gone on while he was after Maeve and Dakota. "I'd say Mama doesn't even need to bother proving herself sane anymore. No one outside of Father and Horecroft is making such an absurd claim."

Judge Nolte shook her head. "I'd still like to have a jury

decide and make it official so long as we've already started the proceedings. That would be the orderly thing to do. Afterward we need to hold a few more trials. We can get these men locked up permanently by the end of the day." She turned to the deputy. "I'll get another jury gathered, and I'll send for the prisoners soon."

"Can we go to the hotel while you get things arranged?" Beth asked.

The judge nodded.

"So," said Beth, turning to Dakota, "tell us about the men who kidnapped you?"

Dakota sagged a bit, looking as battered as the weeping Maeve, who still clung to Mama. "It's a long story."

The judge clapped him on the shoulder. "My favorite kind."

"I'm not going to be locked up permanently." Father shook the bars violently, his face red with fury. "I'm going to see that you're fired as justice of the peace for this. I know the president of the United States."

Judge Nolte stood a bit straighter and looked genuinely interested. "You know Ulysses Grant, Mr. Rutledge? Truly? Tell me, what's he like? Have you been to the White House?"

Father reached through the bars, but no one was within grabbing distance. "You let me out of here! I want to speak to the governor."

"You know John Campbell, too? I intended to meet with him while I'm here in the capital. I can send for him if you want."

Judge Nolte showed no sign of concern about the governor interfering with her trials, including her seeing that

Father was thrown in prison. Beth thought the woman seemed as steady as the mountains. She was deeply impressed with her.

"Yes, send for him right now. I will not put up with—" Father's tirade cut off. The vivid red of his face turned darker.

Beth took a step toward him. Jake caught her arm and held her back, which Beth had to admit was wise.

Father staggered back from the bars and sat down hard on the cot right next to Dr. Horecroft.

The snobbish doctor frowned at Father for intruding on his claimed spot. Horecroft quickly rose and moved away.

Father clutched his chest. Pain cut across his expression. He went rigid, then tipped sideways and collapsed on the cot.

"Doctor, help him." Beth slipped away from Jake, who didn't hold her back this time. "He looks like he's having a heart attack."

Horecroft shook his head. "Like I said before, I'm not that kind of doctor."

The deputy fumbled for the keys. Marshal Riley strode to the jail cell and drew his gun. He aimed it at Horecroft, who, for once, didn't sniff.

"Get Rutledge out of there, Deputy," Riley said. "Is there a doctor in town?"

"There is."

"Once we get him out and the door relocked, you can run for him."

They were a few minutes getting Father dragged from the cell and stretched out on the floor and the jail door locked again. Rutledge lay there unconscious.

Beth remembered that Kat had some doctoring skills, but she wasn't there. Neither was Seb. Where were they? Where was the sheriff?

Marshal Riley crouched down beside Father and pressed one of his broad hands to Father's chest over his heart. "I think he's dead." Riley looked up at the deputy. "Go for the doctor, I reckon. But there ain't no rush anymore."

A sudden flutter behind her made Beth spin around in time to see Mama's knees give out. Before anyone could utter a shout, Oscar stepped forward and caught Mama.

Beth noticed that Maeve, who had stepped away from her when Father collapsed, now stood in the circle of Dakota's arms, her eyes still puffy and her nose red from crying. He handed her a kerchief and kissed her on the forehead.

What had happened there?

Jake ducked out of the room and came back with the sheriff's rolling chair. Brand had gone to help care for the children. Beth had probably better go out there soon, but right now she rushed to Mama's side as Oscar eased her onto a chair.

Beth found herself held back. She glanced up to see Jake had her. Their eyes met. He shook his head and gave Mama and Oscar a strange sort of look. Beth didn't understand it.

Oscar crouched in front of Mama. "Don't look at him, Ginny. No sense in seeing anything more. You've been through enough."

Mama closed her eyes. Though she spoke at barely a whisper, Beth heard every word.

"Can it really be over? Is it possible he's dead and gone? And I'm free of him at last?"

Judge Nolte said, "He's dead for a fact, Ginny. You're free, and now I only have two trials to hold this afternoon." The judge left the room, picked her son up, and said, "We need an undertaker in here. Brand, can you hunt one up? I'll watch Buck."

"Strange day. Have we even told you one of the men who kidnapped Dakota and Maeve is dead, and the sheriff has the other one?"

"I heard Maeve say she shot someone. I figured it was one of the men who took them. But I haven't heard any details."

"The sheriff is bringing the body in and his prisoner, along with Seb and Kat and the two Marshals who came out with him."

"Yes, I assumed the sheriff was busy with them."

Brand nodded. "That's what Maeve's tears are about. She killed one of 'em. I'll go find someone to knock together a pine box and dig a hole. Come to think of it, we'll need two boxes and two holes. And I'll see about a parson."

Brand left. The deputy went with him. Beth wondered if it wasn't time for all of them to clear out.

She looked down at her father's remains. It hurt to consider where the man might spend eternity, but he'd used up his time on earth chasing money and power. He'd spent none of this mortal life on faith and love. The things God called His people to do.

Oscar got Mama to her feet. He turned to the room. "I'm taking her to the hotel. Beth, you should come along.

We'll take the little ones. Maeve, you'd be a big help with that. And, Jake, you should stay and see to Mr. Rutledge. Find out when the funeral will be."

Oscar left with Mama leaning heavily on his arm.

Beth said, "He was my father in many ways. I went to him with my troubles when I was young. And now, since we set Mama free and went into hiding . . ." Her words trailed off as she looked down at him. After all these years, his face was finally calm. "Why couldn't he have been better to me, to Mama? We didn't ask for much from him. A few words of kindness would have made so much difference."

Jake drew her into his arms. Beth saw Maeve rounding up her children.

"Go on now, Maeve," said Beth. "We'll see to things here."

Brand returned with the doctor, who knelt down to examine Rutledge.

Judge Nolte said to Dr. Horecroft, "You can sit there looking down your nose at me if you like, but I'm going to make the necessary arrangements to see that you're sent to the territorial prison. After spending a few years there, maybe you'll stop thinking you're so superior to everyone else in the world."

Mr. Etherton, who was still there, left the jailhouse with the judge.

Beth heard Dr. Horecroft sniff and turned to see the man crying quietly into a white handkerchief.

It seemed the judge had finally convinced him that his future looked bleak. Beth suspected it was sinful just how much she enjoyed that thought.

28

Maeve left the children in the care of the utterly patient Michaela. She went up to her room to clean up. It had been a very long day. She moved to the pitcher of water and washbasin on the dry sink in the corner. A mirror hung on the wall above it.

Looking up, she stared at her face reflected in the mirror. Scratched up and bleeding on the right side from forehead to chin. Her hair was a nightmare, her dress dusty and torn in places where she'd slid across the rocks.

Her arm was bleeding under one of the torn spots. She felt battered everywhere. Very gently she dabbed the blood off her face, then shed her yellow calico dress. It was one of two dresses she owned, and it might be saved if she could scrub the bloodstains from it.

Right now, though, she wanted to get back down to the dining room and hear everything that had happened while she was in the clutches of the Darnells. And she wanted to see Dakota again.

That thought pulled her out of her distress. She changed into her green dress, then set the yellow calico one in the basin of water for a good soak. She combed her hair and found two bumps she hadn't noticed in her general aches and pains. After a few moments washing the blood out of the dress, she quickly hung it over a chair and hurried out of her room so fast she almost ran over Dakota. He'd been leaning against the wall outside her door, his arms crossed. He smiled when she rammed into him.

"In a hurry, pretty Maeve?"

"Dakota." His name came out like a whisper on her lips. She wanted time with him, to talk together without danger and prisoners and trials, and without babysitting.

It would have to wait.

"I was in a hurry to see you again. I can't believe how nice it is to hear you say such sweet words to me. I'm sure it's a flaw in my character to let it make me this happy."

Dakota tilted his head a bit in the tiniest of shrugs. He straightened away from the wall. "I'll try to compliment you enough that you take it as your due and don't contemplate your character when you hear sweet talk. I favor that green dress. It makes your hair look like the brightest sunrise and brings out the blue in your eyes. I'm sure sorry you're scraped up, but you're still the prettiest thing I've ever seen."

The two of them walked downstairs, Dakota's arm warm on her back. It helped her forget all the worries and ignore, for the most part, the sickening knowledge that she'd killed a man.

Maeve and Dakota entered the dining room to find it abuzz with the whole Holt-Collins clan, along with Brand Nolte and his children.

No judge was present. She was probably right now sentencing two men to be hauled away to prison.

Epilogue

AUGUST 1874

Dakota and Maeve came to Oscar and Ginny's wedding. They held it in Hidden Canyon in August, three months after Dakota and Maeve had been married.

Her ma came, too, with Bruce, now her husband. Maeve could see that the loneliness had disappeared from Ma's eyes. She'd spent time asking for her ma's forgiveness and apologizing to Bruce. Spending the winter in the same cabin with them had helped heal the strife Maeve's unhappiness had caused. And finding a love of her own helped her see things with new wisdom.

The rest of the O'Toole family came, including Donal and his new wife, Suzie, and their daughter.

They'd barely settled into the canyon when, to Maeve's delight, Kat and Seb arrived riding in a buggy.

They brought their infant son, who was cradled in Kat's arms. A stranger rode with them, yet Maeve only had eyes for her friends.

"Kat!" Maeve ran toward her, carrying a secret of her

own. She reckoned there was a little one on the way for her and Dakota. "You came all this way. It's so nice to see you."

Kat smiled. "I keep hoping they'll build tracks to Boise. That would bring us to within an hour's ride of the canyon. But so far they haven't added so much as a mile, not since the panic of seventy-three."

Dakota drew closer to Kat, Seb, and little Patrick. They'd named him after Kat's uncle who had locked her away. But he later realized his error and how spiteful he'd acted toward her, and he did his best to set things right before he died.

Seb had four new patents, but none for his invention of a battery that could be powered by the sun. But he'd built a truly ingenious mousetrap, pestered into it by Kat after a rodent infestation in their house.

Maeve was startled to see Yvette coming out of a new house, built last fall when Maeve and Dakota had visited briefly. Yvette gave them a shy smile, and then her eyes shifted to the stranger. The shock on her face had Maeve bracing herself for trouble.

The man said, "Yvette? Is it really you?"

"Remember not to touch her, Noah," Kat whispered. "Be very gentle."

The man gave Kat a little nod, then walked slowly toward Yvette.

"Noah?" Yvette stopped in her tracks, but as Noah approached her, she didn't run away.

When he was within about ten feet of her, he said, "Yvette, I've been searching for you."

Yvette had gained weight, and she was no longer pale. She looked healthy and far less delicate than last summer.

Now she was steady and calm. She wore a simple gingham dress in navy blue that looked almost regal on her.

Kat said quietly, "That's Parson Noah Wilson. He told me he spent years called to the mission field in Oregon. Yvette's marriage, the asylum, the death of her husband, Rutledge getting her out and bringing her west, her running off and hiding in this canyon—all of that happened when he was gone."

Noah heard Kat and turned to her. "I'm trying to save souls, lead them to God, but meanwhile my sister was being abused. I was in Chicago for over a year, trying to track down word of Yvette. I heard a lot about her husband, but there was no trace of her. Kat's investigators finally found me and told me what was going on. She said she was going to see Yvette and invited me to come along."

He looked straight at Yvette. "I'm here now to set things right. I'll do whatever you need, Yvette, to convince you I won't harm you."

Yvette nodded, and a tear streaked down her face. She walked into her brother Noah's arms.

He smiled with such kindness at his sister. Maeve saw he wore a parson's collar.

Beth came out of the house, her children tagging along after her. "Have you heard we're going to blast a bigger entrance into the canyon? We're done being snowed in every winter, cut off from the rest of the world for six months out of the year. We didn't think of it last winter until we were locked in, but we aren't going to let it happen again. Maeve, you and Dakota and your family are all invited for Thanksgiving dinner."

"I have news," Seb said.

"Besides the baby?" Beth looked with loving maternal eyes on Kat's little one.

"Yes. We closed the Horecroft Asylum. With Horecroft in prison, it wasn't that difficult. We found better homes for everyone there, including bringing quite a few of them to Cheyenne. We've built a good, comfortable home for those who need care, and we've set the rest free. All of the women who were locked away by cruel husbands when they were perfectly sane have proved their sanity to the satisfaction of the courts in Wyoming and are safe now.

"The territory needs more women, so they've been made to feel very welcome." Kat grinned as she bounced her daughter.

Noah came up with Yvette beside him. "If it suits Yvette, I want to stay here with her. Maybe someday, if she wants, we'll move out. But for now, Hidden Canyon could use a parson."

Joseph had come out and was talking with Bruce.

Maeve heard Bruce say, "I can't believe Oscar finally convinced Ginny to marry him."

Joseph laughed. Jake joined in, then Beth.

"What's funny about that?" Bruce asked.

"It was the other way around," answered Beth. "That is why it's so funny. Mama spent the whole winter convincing Oscar to marry her. He's had a hard time not looking at her and seeing that highborn lady of the manor he once worked for. Lucky for Mama, he also loved her. He finally said yes."

Oscar and Ginny emerged, him from the cave house, her from the cabin. Both were dressed in their very best, which was still broadcloth and calico. But when their eyes met, their smiles were richer than silk and satin.

Oscar came to be with her, and the two walked arm in arm to where the rest had gathered near the canyon entrance. Seeing the parson's collar, Oscar said, "We were going to ride to the nearest settlement for the wedding, but maybe now we don't have to."

Noah nodded. "Let's have a wedding."

Maeve felt Dakota come up behind her and slide an arm around her waist. He pulled her close so she could lean into him. She'd found love in that mountain valley with Dakota. She'd grown up enough to know her ma deserved to find love, too.

How long ago it seemed when they'd all set out on the journey west, their wagon wheels rolling over miles and miles of prairie grass.

She looked at Ginny, Kat, and Yvette and could see they'd found freedom and safety. She thought of those other women who'd been locked away, who were now free and had a chance at happiness. She could imagine her father, a man at peace and safe in the arms of God, and knew he would be happy for them all.

The journey, winding and long and hard, had begun as they chased the horizon to the west, continued as they turned toward the dawn, and finished with a showdown between Ginny and her horrible husband, between Dakota and the men who chased him, and between Maeve and her loneliness.

They'd traveled and they'd settled. They married and started families. And now, finally, they'd all followed the western light into the sunset. That light had led them all the way home.

Read on
for a *sneak peek* at

WHISPERS *of* FORTUNE

by Mary Connealy

Book 1 of
GOLDEN STATE TREASURE

Available in the spring of 2025

June 1874

A fist slamming against the door startled Beth Ellen Hart. She shrieked and dropped the china bowl she was washing, which shattered on the floor.

"Get out here! I want answers!" a man's voice shouted. He sounded furious.

Gretel came running into the room. They exchanged frightened looks.

Ellie grabbed the gun Zane kept on the top shelf of the kitchen cupboard.

The shouting and slamming went on as Ellie marched to the kitchen door, determined to drive off whoever was assaulting her house. That was her favorite bowl!

"Wait!" Gretel rushed to her side, snatched up the Winchester 73 rifle from over the back door, and stepped to the side. "Stay out of my line of fire."

Ellie nodded, then shoved back the latch on the door and jerked it open. The stranger's fist, which had been aiming at the door, missed hitting her in the nose by inches. She ducked out of the way so swiftly she fell over backward. Her gun went sailing.

A cracking sound from behind her was Gretel cocking Zane's Winchester.

The man stepped into the kitchen and reached down for Ellie.

"*Zuruckbleiben du, schmutzig schurke*," Gretel said.

He opened his mouth, probably to shout some more, then clamped his jaw shut. Gretel tended to lapse into German under stress, and that drew his attention—that and the rifle pointed at his chest. He straightened away from Ellie and stared at Gretel.

Ellie scrambled to her feet, ran for the gun she'd dropped, and aimed it again at the man, who stood there looking addled. She was well away from Gretel, so they had him at the point of a triangle.

Ellie had no idea what Gretel had said but could guess and added her own warning. "Get off my land."

The man was not overly tall, five-foot-nine or so, with dark curly hair under an odd, round hat with a narrow brim. He wore a dusty suit of clothes that looked to be many years old. Clean-shaven with blue eyes that shot lightning at her.

He saw the guns and didn't attack if that was his plan.

"Where are my brothers?" He was still mad, snapping at them, face taut and fists clenched. But he stayed put. "I'm not leaving here without them."

That was when Josh stepped up behind the man. "Do I need to send for the sheriff?"

It was a bluff. The sheriff would be unable to get to their ranch for about an hour, and that was if they sent a man for Dorada Rio, the closest town to their northern California ranch, on a galloping horse, found the sheriff immediately, and rode straight back at full speed. And Ellie wasn't about to hold this man at gunpoint for that long.

"Talk, mister," Ellie said. "What do you mean barging into my house like this?"

"He punched Ellie, Josh. Knocked her to the floor." Gretel's hands trembled on the heavy rifle.

Josh shoved the man forward. "Sit down."

He took the gun from Gretel and pointed the barrel toward the floor. "You punched my sister?"

"I don't want to sit down. And no, I did *not* punch your sister. I was knocking on the door. She pulled it open and was in the way. I—"

"You're not going to tell me you hit my sister right in the face with your fist, are you?" Josh said it as if he were the very voice of doom.

"I did not hit her—I would *never* hit a woman. She ducked and stumbled back and fell." The man's blue eyes shifted to Ellie. "Tell him I didn't hit you."

Ellie had a very sweet moment letting him sweat as he looked between her and her tall, blond Viking of a brother. She had the same Nordic coloring as him but was built with finer lines, thank heaven. But truth was truth. She didn't need to add reasons to think ill of the man. He was awful enough.

"He was pounding on the door when I opened it." She looked at Josh and caught a spark of humor in his eyes. "His fist came right at me with no intent to punch me. I ducked and fell just like he said. He never touched me."

"Give me my brothers now, and I'll be glad to get off your stinking land. We're leaving California and heading home to New York."

They all turned back to the disheveled, antagonistic man.

Ellie had some notion of what he might mean, yet it galled her to cooperate. "What are your brothers' names? And don't think we're going to let some stranger come riding in here and leave with our boys."

"*Our* boys?" The man's eyes narrowed. "They're *my* boys. My brothers' names are Thayne and Lochlan Mac—"

"MacKenzie?" Ellie's heart sped up. She rested a hand on her heart. "Those boys are your brothers?"

"They're here then?" His breath whooshed out, and he bent forward as if he might collapse. "I'm Brody MacKenzie. You took my brothers off the streets of San Francisco. I'm here to take them back with me."

Ellie lowered her gun and stared at Mr. Brody MacKenzie. "I'm Beth Ellen Hart. I go by Ellie. This is my brother, Josh, and the woman who aimed that rifle at you is Gretel Steinmeyer."

"We have over two dozen children here at our school," Josh said, setting the rifle back on the pegs over the door. "Every one of them orphans. If those boys are your brothers, then why were they living on the streets?"

"And hungry," Ellie added, hands propped on her hips. "Wearing nothing but rags."

"Cold. Soaked through from the winter rain," Josh went on.

"Uneducated." Ellie glared at the man.

"Unwanted." Josh crossed his arms tight over his chest.

"Unloved, even by their brother," Ellie said. "That is, if you *are* their brother."

"I am their brother. They ran off—I've been searching for them."

She could see as much. The man wasn't a spitting image,

but similar enough, especially similar to Thayne, even down to the Scottish brogue in the way he talked. "If you weren't taking care of them before, how are we to believe you'll begin taking care of them now?"

Brody's shoulders sagged, and he sank into a chair at the kitchen table. He rubbed his hands over his face. "They're alive and well? Were they bad off when you found them?" Then his temper flared. "What are you doing with them, them and all the children you sweep up off the streets as if you think they're trash? Are you forcing them to work on your ranch? If they've signed anything, indentured papers and the like, I'll fight you in court. They're too young to sign—"

"Stop talking before you make a bigger fool of yourself than you already have." Josh stepped to the door and said to Ellie, "Let's take him out to see these boys we're forcing into labor." He jabbed a finger out the door. "But you're not riding off with them until you convince us they'll be safe with you this time. Because they sure as certain weren't safe with you before when they slipped by your notice and managed the journey alone all the way to California from New York. Lead the way, Ellie."

Ellie stepped up to look closer at Brody MacKenzie. She saw it in his eyes, a shine that could've been tears. Relief that he'd found them? He seemed to care about his brothers. At least right now he did. But Josh had the right of it, and she hardened her heart against feeling any sympathy for Brody. He was going to have to convince her before she let those two troublemaking scamps out of her sight.

His brothers. It had to be them. He hoped and prayed and kept the tears from falling through sheer grit.

Brody followed the woman. Ellie Hart. She had on a pretty yellow calico dress that almost matched the yellow of her hair. He'd hardly looked around when he came riding in wild with fear, which he covered with anger.

"You know, this ranch is notorious in San Francisco for snatching up children and hauling them away, never to be heard from again."

The woman, Ellie, glanced back over her shoulder, then looked on past him. "We're notorious, Josh."

A faint chuckle sounded from behind Brody. "I can't wait to tell Zane he's known as a kidnapper and child-enslaver. That oughta make him mad."

"Michelle will calm him down, I expect."

Both of them laughed.

Brody listened to the back and forth at the same time he rounded the house, a nice-sized ranch house, and gazed past the huge barn to see sheds and more houses and a big whitewashed building two stories high. Every structure was well built. The houses had gardens out front with fences encircling modest yards. A prosperous ranch that almost looked like some of the small towns he'd visited.

Horses grazed in a corral. Chickens pecked at the ground behind a wire fence. He smelled hogs but didn't see them, but they could be behind any one of a dozen outbuildings. And spread out over miles of rolling grassland, he saw red cows with white faces, grazing and fat and contented.

But it was the big building that drew him.

Ellie must have noticed, though she seemed to be walking fast, her attention averted.

He, of course, was focused on the house and not paying the pretty blond woman with the sassy attitude any mind.

"Your brothers are most likely in class. Though they've been known to sneak off and not return until mealtime." This time she looked at him with a single arched brow.

"It's them all right. Those two are hard to keep ahead of. I shoulda known better than to go off to college. They were too much for Ma, and heaven knows Pa was no help."

That earned him a sharp look, but she didn't say why. Probably blamed him for abandoning them. Fair enough. He blamed himself.

Ellie reached the door and swung it open to complete silence.

It was a school. He could smell it. Chalk dust and books and, well, he couldn't say what else exactly. He just knew a school when he smelled one. They stepped into a wide hall lined with several doors in a row straight across from him and two sets of stairs leading to the left and the right.

"The upper floor has bedrooms. Several children in each room and bunk beds. We call it a dormitory. The boys on the right, the girls on the left. The upstairs is divided so there's no access between the two sides without coming down here. Most rooms are for three or four, but your brothers stay in a room where it's just the two of them. That's because we aren't full."

His brothers had always shared a room more fit for a closet, and when Brody was home, he slept in there with them. The two of them in a room big enough for four would be the finest place they'd ever stayed.

Ellie continued, "The children are in special individualized classes this time of day." She pointed to the door farthest to the right. "Morning is four grades divided up by age, the afternoon targeted to each child's skills. Thayne has shown an unusual gift for math and science. He focuses on that in his afternoon classes, with a few related subjects like physics and calculus."

Thayne, his impish sixteen-year-old brother, had a talent for arithmetic? How had they gotten him to sit still long enough to find that out?

"And Lochlan is fascinated by geography. He's always studying maps and asking questions about the world at large."

Now, that sounded like Brody's fourteen-year-old brother. He was searching for MacKenzie's Treasure. He probably loved geography because reading a map might lead him to a gold mine, though it never had for their pa.

"We keep the rooms quiet, Brody." Ellie spoke softly as she reached for the doorknob to the right. "I'll go get your brothers and bring them out. My older sister, Annie, is their teacher for this session, which this late in the day will be special skills. Be very quiet. Annie believes that teaching the children to direct their own studies, work independently, and most of all control themselves are the main goals of a teacher."

She opened the door. Though Brody kept quiet, he was standing right there and saw Lochlan in plain view right in front of him.

Lochlan saw him. His eyes went wide. He leapt to his feet, screamed, and jumped a full foot off the floor. "Brody!

Thayne, come quick—Brody's here!" He turned to the room and shouted, "My brother is here!"

Brody took one second to see the severely annoyed face of the teacher and winced, but only for a second because his brothers came charging at him, and he found himself overcome with happiness and relief.

His brothers' boots thundered across the floor. There was an eruption of talking and excited laughter from the schoolroom. Then they hit Brody so hard he'd've fallen if he hadn't staggered into Josh. Josh kept him from going down under the onslaught.

And then Brody held them. His brothers. Alive and well. "I found you! Thayne, Lochlan . . . thank God, thank God."

His brothers, now nearly full grown, were all right. And now Brody had another chance to do things right. Be a good big brother. Show these two he loved them and wanted to take care of them.

Mary Connealy writes romantic comedies about cowboys. She's the author of the Brothers in Arms, Brides of Hope Mountain, High Sierra Sweethearts, Kincaid Brides, Trouble in Texas, Wild at Heart, and Cimarron Legacy series, as well as several other acclaimed series. Mary has been nominated for a Christy Award, was a finalist for a RITA Award, and is a two-time winner of the Carol Award. She lives in eastern Nebraska with her very own romantic cowboy hero. They have four grown daughters—Joslyn, married to Matt; Wendy; Shelly, married to Aaron; and Katy, married to Max—and seven precious grandchildren. Learn more about Mary and her books at

MaryConnealy.com
facebook.com/maryconnealy
petticoatsandpistols.com

Sign Up for Mary's Newsletter

Keep up to date with Mary's latest news on book releases and events by signing up for her email list at the link below.

MaryConnealy.com

FOLLOW MARY ON SOCIAL MEDIA

Mary Connealy

@MaryConnealy

@MaryConnealy

More from Mary Connealy

Beth Rutledge and her mother's one chance to escape Beth's tyrannical father is a wagon train heading west. Wagon train scout Jake Holt senses the secretive Beth is running from something and finds a new hope for his future in protecting her. Can they risk trusting each other with their lives—and their hearts—with danger threatening their every step?

Chasing the Horizon
A WESTERN LIGHT #1

After living in hiding for six months, Kat Wadsworth and Sebastian Jones are desperate to start a new life in the west—and marrying each other may be the only way to freedom. But will the dangers from their pasts tear apart their hopes for a better future and a chance at love?

Toward the Dawn
A WESTERN LIGHT #2